INSTANT PRAIRIE FAMILY

This Large Print Book carries the
Seal of Approval of N.A.V.H.

INSTANT PRAIRIE FAMILY

BONNIE NAVARRO

THORNDIKE PRESS
A part of Gale, Cengage Learning

Detroit • New York • San Francisco • New Haven, Conn • Waterville, Maine • London

GALE
CENGAGE Learning®

LIBRARY OF CONGRESS CATALOGING-IN-PUBLICATION DATA

Navarro, Bonnie.
    Instant Prairie Family / by Bonnie Navarro. — Large Print edition.
        pages cm. — (Thorndike Press Large Print Gentle Romance)
    ISBN-13: 978-1-4104-6092-9 (hardcover)
    ISBN-10: 1-4104-6092-4 (hardcover)
    1. Families—Fiction. 2. Large type books. I. Title.
PS3614.A929I57 2013
813'.6—dc23   2013016051

Published in 2013 by arrangement with Harlequin Books S.A.

Printed in the United States of America
1 2 3 4 5 6 7 17 16 15 14 13

"For I know the plans I have for you,"
declares the Lord, "plans to prosper you
and not to harm you, plans to give you
hope and a future. Then you will call on
me and come and pray to me and I will
listen to you."

— *Jeremiah* 29:11, 12

My deepest thanks are due to my Savior and Lord. May He receive all the glory for any thing I might ever accomplish.

I would be remiss if I didn't give thanks and honorable mention to:

Joanne, I blame you for empowering me to believe that I could write a story someone else would actually want to read. You said someday you'd see me in print. Thanks for believing in me even when I wasn't so convinced.

Betty, Dad, Martha and Terry. You all took your time to read and suggest corrections on different manuscripts. I learned something from each one of you.

Cesar, Liz, CJ, Gaby and David — thank you for letting Mom work on her book even when you wanted dinner/to talk/clean clothes. . . . I love you guys!

There are so many more who have helped me on my journey to write — to each of you, thank you and God bless.

CHAPTER ONE

Harlan County, Nebraska, 1881

Will scooped up six-year-old Tommy and called to Willy over his shoulder, "It's time to go, son. The wagon is hitched and we need to leave so that we can get to the river before nightfall." Will had left detailed instructions with Jake, his nephew, about the care of the livestock and what Jake should be doing in the next three days. Now everything was ready for them to leave — everything except his oldest son. Willy had dragged his feet all morning, and Will was quickly losing his patience with his name-sake.

"Are we going to go get the new Auntie Shelia?" Tommy asked, his little face full of excitement. His eyes were the same color as Caroline's had been — an expressive hazel that changed hues with her mood. Did the boy actually remember Auntie Shelia? No, that was impossible. Tommy was only three when Auntie Shelia had come to stay with them after her niece Caroline's death. She stayed six months before she declared the West "too dangerous and uncivilized for anyone to hope to raise a respectable family."

"No, Tommy, not another aunt. She's our new housekeeper," Will corrected gently, trying to find the right words to explain. "Miss Stewart is coming to do the cooking and cleaning and help you and your brother with your studies. She will be like a grandmother to you but isn't related to you. She'll be our housekeeper. Do you understand?"

Will glanced out of the window impatiently, aware of the sun rising high in the horizon. It must be close to nine and they had a full day's ride to get to the river before dark. From the river it was only a little more than a two-hour ride and they would be in Twin Oaks with time to get cleaned up well before the train arrived tomorrow at noon.

Miss Stewart was due in on that train and he needed to be there. It wouldn't do to have his new housekeeper step off into the small prairie town and not have the family there to extend their welcome.

Will hadn't been all that set on the idea of bringing in a housekeeper when his mother had suggested it, but after several letters back and forth, he'd become convinced Miss Stewart was the perfect woman for the job. She was only one of a few dozen women who had replied to the ad his mother had placed in the *Christian Ladies' Journal* who seemed to want the job for the right reasons. Most of the others were only thinly veiled attempts to trap a husband. Miss Stewart wrote that she was ready to move on from her sister's home where she had lived for years, and that she wanted to settle in with a family who loved the Lord and where she could put her education and her gifts of cooking and cleaning to use.

Instead of answering his father, the boy yelled to his brother, leaving Will nearly deaf, "Hurry, we're going to go get our new house."

"Not *house*, Tommy," Willy snickered, finally sauntering down the stairs. At age nine he felt he knew all there was to know about life and delighted in informing his little brother. "Our new *housekeeper*. She'll probably take one look at this mess and make Pa take her right back to the train station." He sounded almost hopeful. Willy was right about one thing — their house wasn't likely to make a good impression. He and the boys would have to do their best to make up for that.

"Hey, that's enough. Now both of you head out to the wagon," Will ordered, setting Tommy back on the ground and glancing around his kitchen. The place had become messier as time went on. He had a bad habit of burning the oatmeal, and two skillets sat soaking in the sink were reminders of his lack in the culinary arts. One more thing Will had included in his instructions to Jake — make the place somewhat presentable before they arrived with the new housekeeper.

Will imagined a woman his mother's age. From what he had read in her letters, her character seemed to be above reproach, and that was his main interest — that, and how well she cooked. Hopefully Miss Stewart could teach his boys some table manners, as well.

Finally, Will and the boys were in the wagon, moving along toward the river. The sky seemed so big and far above the earth and stretched out in all directions without any hindrance. The prairie plants, just having started to grow again after the winter, danced at knee level and waved on the breeze that kept the sun from completely baking both man and beast. Will was grateful for his hat. There were no trees to offer shade on the large expanse of prairie until they came closer to the river.

As he drove, he took in the breathtaking scenery. His thoughts turned to how majestic God was, having formed all this with just a word. Will didn't need to be in church to be awestruck by God. Creation was enough to hold him spellbound and speechless. The boys asked questions and he took advantage of those opportunities to show them God's handiwork.

After a full day's drive and a good night's sleep by the river, Will headed into town, glad to be almost at his destination. He couldn't help but be impressed by the way the small town of Twin Oaks had grown from just five houses in the middle of nothing a few years ago to a small but bustling village. New settlers seemed to be arriving all the time. People were still taking advantage of the Homestead Act that President Lincoln had signed back in 1862. The same law Will and Mathew had taken advantage of ten years ago. Will found a spot in the shade of the train depot and tethered the horses to the hitching post.

Their first stop once they were in town was the barber. He wanted to impress Miss Stewart — not scare her off. The boys had not had a haircut in more than a year. He hadn't been very vigilant about combing out the snarls, either. Once everyone looked civilized again, the barber offered them each a piece of hard candy from a jar on his countertop.

Main Street was crowded — plenty of people waiting for goods and travelers off the incoming train. Back out on the street, he headed the boys toward the mercantile. Glancing at his pocket watch, he assured himself there was still time to pick up supplies before he needed to meet the train. Afterward, he could take the new housekeeper and his boys to lunch at the one and only hotel in Twin Oaks.

Standing in the doorway of the store brought back memories of his father's store back in Philadelphia with all its sights and sounds. His throat tightened and he was surprised as a wave of nostalgia caught him unexpectedly. He took in the sight of wares stacked on wooden shelving and in barrels on the floor. Would his boys ever see his father's store?

Pushing aside his sudden homesickness, he set to work, choosing supplies. Warning Tommy and Willy not to touch anything, he let them wander around to look at the toys and gadgets on display. Meanwhile, he bought some coffee, sugar and a few other cooking items women used to buy at his

14

father's store. He didn't even know how to use most of them but figured maybe Miss Stewart would. He hadn't savored home-made baking since Mathew's wife, Mary-Ann, had died. It would be a treat just to have someone who knew their way around a kitchen again. He would ask the new housekeeper if she had ever made raisin bread or bread pudding. . . .

He picked up the small crate of raisins and made his final selections. At the counter, he greeted Josh, the owner.

"Good to see you again," Josh said, tallying up the purchases on a piece of paper and then entering the figure in his ledger. "I haven't seen you since you brought in your wheat last fall."

"Yeah. I like to stock up when I get out. It's more than a day's trip out and I wouldn't risk it in the winter," Will rejoined. He wasn't really in the mood to chat, but he didn't want to seem rude, either. "Town seems to be growing."

"It is. We're getting more people every year. Are you going to be staying in town overnight or are you headed back?"

"We'll be headed back." Will was used to keeping his life to himself, but Tommy had other ideas.

"We gotta take our auntie House back to

our farm," the little tyke explained in his mixed-up way. The shopkeeper blinked at Tommy and scratched his head, but Tommy continued on without a break. "She's gonna be a grandma to me and keep the house nice. She's even gonna teach us stuff like how to be gent'men. She's gonna be really nice — not like our other auntie, who was mean and yelled all the time. . . ."

"Tommy." Will was surprised at the last statement. Tommy couldn't possibly remember his great-aunt. He must have been parroting something he heard from his older brother, or his cousin. But, no, it wasn't likely Jake had said anything — the teenager wasn't the type to tell tales. If anything, Will wished he was more in the habit of speaking up for himself. Willy, like his brother, had no such problem.

What did Willy remember of his great-aunt? Will had been too busy trying to keep the farm afloat to pay much attention to how the woman treated the children. He was going to have to do a better job this time. He wanted his boys educated but not at the cost of their being mistreated.

Once again, doubts assailed him — was he doing the right thing by letting a total stranger into his home? Maybe he and Jake could handle the boys on their own. But he'd given Miss Stewart his word, and she had packed up her whole life to come out to Nebraska. He had to at least give her a chance. Maybe he could let her stay for a few weeks while he watched how the boys reacted to her. Meanwhile, he'd pray about sending her back or having her stay. She might decide Nebraska wasn't right for her after all. She'd hardly be the first to feel that way. In the meantime, there was no sense in borrowing trouble.

After all, he had been praying for this since last spring. God directed Miss Stewart to answer his ad and she would be arriving within the hour. Obviously God's hand moved in this and had sent her here. Tommy and Willy needed a woman's influence in their upbringing.

With that thought in mind, he prayed for wisdom and headed the boys out of the mercantile and off to the train station. The sound of the locomotive whispered on the wind as it came closer to town. Its whistle announced its approach before it even came into view. In just a few minutes, Miss Stewart would step off the train, and Will would see how right he'd been to bring her to Nebraska.

Within a few minutes, Abigail Stewart

17

would be arriving in the town that was to be her new home.

The prairie looked so different from the rolling hills of Ohio that had been her only home for all of her twenty-six years. Nebraska felt as if someone had taken a huge rolling pin and flattened everything, leaving only waving grasses and flowers. Even the trees were missing. But the colors were vibrant as Abby watched the world pass by, and she couldn't help hoping that they symbolized a bright, happy new life she'd have with the widowed Mrs. Hopkins and her children, free from Abby's domineering sister and her brother-in-law's inappropriate attentions.

How would she be able to recognize Mrs. Hopkins? She had never asked for a description before. She'd just assumed that she would be able to see something in the woman's eyes that would match the gentle spirit and spunk Abby inferred from her letters. Now she wished she'd asked for more details.

Abby glanced around the stuffy passenger compartment at the other passengers traveling with her these last few days. The loud Erving family spread throughout the car. Watching them, Abby couldn't help wondering what her own nieces, Megan and Hanna, were going to do now without Abby there to encourage them. They were beautiful girls, almost on the brink of womanhood. Would suitors begin to call on them soon? What sort of lives would they end up leading? And the rest? How would Harold get his studies done with Peter always bothering him? Would little Katie even remember Auntie Abby? The girls had promised to keep in touch, and Abby knew she would cherish their letters and the news they would share. She only hoped she'd have lots of good tidings to share by return post about her new home and the family she hoped would accept her as one of their own.

As the conductor opened the door to the car and called out, "Twin Oaks, Nebraska. Next stop," Abby stuck her knitting into her satchel. She checked under her seat, pulled her satchel strap up over her shoulder and hugged it close. It held her letters, coin purse and knitting. Her heart sped up as she saw the town come into view. It was small and somewhat rough, as Mrs. Hopkins had warned her, but it looked fresh and exciting to Abby as she hoped that maybe she would find a place to belong to here.

As the train bounced and lurched to a stop, Abby tried to stand and found herself tossed against the conductor. Mr. Galvan had proved to be kind, making the trip as comfortable as possible for everyone. He regaled them with stories about other trips and the fascinating people he'd met over the past three years working for the railroad. The stories were a little marred by the man's terrible memory for names, but were very entertaining all the same.

"Careful," he chuckled, "you don't want to get banged up right before you meet Mrs. Hooper."

"Mrs. Hopkins," Abby corrected softly, "and thank you for all your help."

"It's been a pleasure to assist you on your trip. If you ever need anything, you can always leave word with the train station. Maybe I'll look you up in a few months . . . see how you're faring with Mrs. Hoskills."

"Mrs. Hopkins," Abby corrected for a second time.

"Twin Oaks!" Mr. Galvan's voice boomed, cutting off their conversation. He moved past her and stepped to the door of the car so that he could assist the passengers while they disembarked.

Abby clutched the seat in front of her, waiting until the last lurch of the train, and then followed the rest of the passengers to the door. She wasn't sure if it was the jerky motion of the locomotive or — more likely

— the nerves of meeting Mrs. Hopkins and embarking on this new adventure that had her stomach twisting. What a first impression that would make — to get sick just as she stepped off the train.

Taking in a slow, deep breath, she prayed silently that God would protect her and lead her to the right place. The smoky air from the train did little to settle her stomach, but her nerves calmed slightly as she closed her eyes and imagined God watching her step onto the wooden platform. It didn't manage to go quite as smoothly as she'd imagined. Between the noises, the smoke and the bright sun, she tripped, lurching forward.

A strong and calloused hand reached out and caught her upper arm and kept her from falling. She blinked, finding herself face-to-face with a stern frown chiseled into a bronzed face, piercing blue eyes focused on hers. His face was shadowed by his straw hat, as if shrouded in mystery.

"Careful, miss." His voice were low and gentle, surprisingly cultured for a man in ripped overalls, a faded black vest and a threadbare cotton shirt. He held a child in his other arm. The boy clung to his shoulders as the man stepped back and released Abby. Strangely, she felt drawn toward him.

He made her feel safe.

"Thank —" Her words were cut off by the shrill of the train's whistle and the belching of smoke that followed. The man looked past her, obviously searching to find someone else. It shouldn't have bothered her to so quickly lose his attention, but he had seemed nice . . . sincere.

Now was not the time to consider her confusing feelings. She needed to look for Mrs. Hopkins. Maybe the woman would be waiting with a wagon over by the station so they could get Abby's luggage off the train and head home. Abby made her way through the throngs of people to the end where men were unloading the freight. Seeing her three chests set to the side, she sighed with relief. She turned to study the faces of the people rushing around her.

Suddenly she felt very small and alone. What would happen if she couldn't find Mrs. Hopkins? The thought had never even occurred to her until she stood watching the other passengers meeting with their families or heading off to the livery to procure transportation. Soon she was completely alone. Minutes passed, but there wasn't a woman nearby who could have been Mrs. Hopkins.

She took a seat on one of the benches and

prayed, hoping Mrs. Hopkins would arrive before she concocted a backup plan. The sun shone bright and the air stifled her very breath. It was hotter here than it ever got back at home in May. Her stomach churned, reminding her that the last thing she had had to eat was a greasy sandwich of scrambled eggs and some unidentifiable meat she'd barely swallowed down at daybreak at a tiny train stop.

Where could Mrs. Hopkins be? Did something happen to keep her from coming? Abby tried to pray, but the thoughts all got jumbled up in her head.

Will waited while a large family with a passel of kids piled off the train. A few men and a pretty, young lady who needed some assistance disembarking followed. Maybe Miss Stewart was having trouble gathering her things or had difficulty with the jerky motion of the train's stop. Did she need aid to exit the train? Will hoped he hadn't hired someone who was too feeble to be able to carry out basic chores.

"Excuse me, sir. Could you tell me if there are any more passengers getting off at Twin Oaks?" he asked the conductor.

"No, sir. Everyone's disembarked," the man answered. "Is there someone you're looking for?"

"Our auntie House," Tommy replied before Will could get a word in edgewise.

"He means our new housekeeper." Willy offered the information before Will could intervene.

"Yeah, her. She's old like our other mean auntie, but she'll be nice 'cuz Pa's gonna pay her to be nice and teach us lots a'stuff like how to be gent'men." Tommy picked up the story, hanging off his father's neck precariously to peek into the train.

"I'll bet she saw the prairie and got off the train back in . . . What state is that where the prairie starts?" Willy questioned midsentence.

Taking control of the conversation before the boys told all of the family secrets, Will eyed the conductor again. "Are you sure Miss Stewart wasn't onboard? She should have been in her fifties. She was coming to fill a position of housekeeper and tutor for my children. She would have been coming from Ohio."

"Nope. The only woman traveling alone was Miss Stevens." The conductor's gaze followed the girl who had just tripped off the train, and he pointed toward her. "That's her. She was going to be a housekeeper, all right — but for a widow woman . . ." He looked deep in thought as if he was trying to remember something. "Mrs. Hopple or Hope."

"That young lady?" Will clarified.

"Yes, sir." The conductor looked Will over from head to toe through narrowed eyes. "You had better behave around that young lady. She's very special," he warned in spite of his obvious disadvantage in height and build. Will looked down on the smaller man and wondered wryly just exactly what the man thought he would be able to do if the situation arose.

There was no reason to upset him, though. "I don't doubt it," Will said in a pacifying tone. "I have no intentions of bothering anyone. I just came to look for my new housekeeper. Are you sure she wasn't on the train?"

"No, sir, I've been on the train since we headed out of Illinois three days ago. There was no other woman that came alone except for Miss Standish. I hope everything is all right with your new housekeeper. Maybe she will be on next week's train."

Will felt the stirring of annoyance, then something akin to anger. If Miss Stewart wasn't on the train, she had just made off with five dollars' worth of his hard-earned cash. He had sent her a ticket and asked her to let him know if there were any obstacles that would keep her from arriving on this train. There was plenty of time for her to have sent a letter or a wire. He knew that she hadn't because he'd checked both at the post office and at the mercantile for any messages before coming to the train depot.

"Thank you for your time." He barely remembered to be civil as embarrassment and frustration warred within him. What kind of fool must the conductor think he was?

"Let's go get something to eat." Will forced a pleasant tone even though he was simmering inside.

"But shouldn't we wait for Auntie House?" Tommy questioned innocently.

"She didn't come. She's just like all the rest of the women. They won't live out here in the wilderness and let the Injuns scalp them. She won't come to live out here. Even our own mother didn't want to stay with us here." Willy shouted the last part and darted off, not paying attention to the wagons or horses on the dirt street.

"Willy! Wait, son! You can't go running —"

He caught up to Willy two blocks away. The boy was hunched over, hiding in an alleyway with his face in his hands. Just before Will reached him, he let out a sob.

"Willy." Will set Tommy down and pulled Willy into his arms, holding him tight. "I don't know why Miss Stewart didn't arrive when we expected her, but it's all going to work out. Maybe she wasn't the one God wanted taking care of you and Tommy. Or maybe she is, and she'll come on the next train."

Even as Will said the words, he realized he was too far behind with the farm chores to make the trip again in a week. He would have to leave some kind of message at the train station just in case. And if there was a next time, he certainly would not be bringing the boys with to have their expectations dashed to the ground.

"No one wants to live out here. Auntie Shelia said it and so did Ma. It's a savage land with savages running around with no clothes on, killing people. I'm glad she didn't come. She would have been mean just like Auntie Shelia. Women are just trouble. I'm glad we don't have any at the house." The boy straightened his shoulders and pulled away from his father.

Will wasn't sure exactly what he should do. Willy's speech just showed him how much he had failed his boys. His own

27

mother was wonderful . . . It was a crying shame the boys hadn't had a chance yet to know a woman like her — kind, generous and loving. But how could he possibly convince his sons of that if the only women they had lived with were women who had made life miserable at home? Was it time to think of sending the boys back to Philadelphia to be raised where they could get an education and where his mother could instill some appreciation for women into them?

"I know it's hard to believe, but there are some women who are good and gentle. Like your grandma and my sisters, your aunts and then there's Mrs. Scotts. You like her. . . ." The boys *did* like Mrs. Scotts, and the other women who attended their small church. But with the busy lives these farmers' wives led, there wasn't much time for visiting with neighbors. They only saw them for a little while at church the one Sunday a month they had services. And that short amount of time wasn't enough to really know anyone. Even Caroline had been pleasant enough to their neighbors for a few short hours at church each month. It was when they were home that her mood had changed.

He stood and took Tommy's hand in his

right and Willy's in his left. "What d'ya say we go get something to eat now? We need to head back in an hour or so if we're going to get to the river before nightfall. Maybe we can bag that stag we saw last night."

Tommy happily started chattering about their trip back and what animal he wanted to hunt as they headed back down the main street to the hotel. Willy swiped at his face with his hands and then his nose with his sleeve before Will could produce a handkerchief.

"Where's your kerchief?" he asked.

"I forgot, Pa." Willy blew his nose soundly.

"I ain't got no kerchief, Pa," Tommy reminded him. "You were gonna give me one and then you forgot."

"Sorry, son. We'll get you a few at the house." At least he hoped that there were still some hankies somewhere in the house.

A few minutes later, Will and the boys sat at a table in the dining area of the hotel, perusing the menu. "Pa, what are you going to eat?" Tommy's questions never stopped. Without letting his father answer him, he launched into his own opinion of the food, what he wanted, and ended with another question. "Why don't you cook like this, Pa?"

"Well, son," Will hedged. "I guess some

things I just haven't learned yet."

"Maybe our auntie House . . . I mean our Miss Auntie could do it better," Tommy reassured him.

"Don't you understand anything!" Willy yelled at his brother. "She's not coming!"

"But I want her to," Tommy whined. "I want someone to cook better than Pa and fix my clothes so we could go to the meeting with nice clothes like Jill."

"Boys!" Will exclaimed, glaring at his offspring. He gave a short lecture on the right way to behave in public. Even as he was speaking, he remembered his father saying something very similar when he was young. When both boys calmed down, he nodded approval.

The waitress came and took their order, smiling and teasing the boys before she left. Comfortably plump, the woman looked to be about Will's mother's age. "Maybe we can ask her if she wants to be our auntie . . . How do you call it again?" Tommy quizzed his brother when the waitress left.

Before Will could stop the conversation, Tommy turned his attention to the door. Standing up in his chair, he grinned, pointing and then waving at someone who had entered. "There she is, Pa. That lady that you caught at the train. Maybe she'll be our —"

"Tomas, sit down and put your arm down!" Will was about to pick both boys up and take them to the wagon. It was downright embarrassing that he had come all this way for nothing, and now the boys were making a ruckus here.

"But she's here, Pa. She looks really nice," Tommy whispered this time, dropping back into his seat but still staring at someone behind Will.

"I'm sorry, miss," he could hear the waitress answering the woman. "We don't have any jobs here. There are hardly any customers except on the days the train comes through. Why don't you come in and have a bite to eat and maybe by then the lady you're waiting for will come by?"

Since his back was to the two women, Will wasn't able to see what happened next, but the expression on Tommy's face brightened. Before he could stop his son, the boy shot off his chair toward the stranger.

"Come sit with us, lady. You look nice. We need someone to teach us how to eat nice and not like a bunch of wild hogs."

Will turned in his chair and caught the surprised look on the woman's face. She quickly disguised it with a smile. "Well, hello to you, too, little man." She crouched down and looked into Tommy's eyes while she spoke.

Will was taken by her soft, sincere voice. She sounded as though she actually enjoyed talking to the little boy. Will opened his mouth to call Tommy back to the table, but the words died before reaching his lips when he saw the rapture on his son's face.

"I'm not a little man, I'm just a boy. My brother says I haf'ta be more'n eleven to be a man. He's gonna be a man soon 'cuz he's already nine," Tommy informed her, holding out eight fingers until she helped him lift one more.

"That's nine." She smiled, ruffling his hair.

"I just got my hair —"

"Tomas." Will didn't know what to do with his son. He seemed bound and determined to get the whole town laughing at his antics. "Leave the lady in peace and come back to the table."

"But, Pa, she don't have nobody to sit with and we could learn how to be gent'men if she were at the table," Tommy argued, taking hold of the woman's hand.

"Tomas, you need to heed your father, dear." Her melodic voice soothed some of Will's embarrassment, and her eyes sparkled with delight. She straightened back up and led Tommy to the table without withdrawing her hand from his.

Reluctantly, Tommy sat down and let her go, but as she turned to leave, she suddenly turned back to look closer at Will. "Oh, my! You're the one who —"

"Yeah," Tommy answered for his father, "he caught you at the train. You were gonna fall on your face."

"Yes, I was. I don't think I had a chance to thank you, sir."

"Don't mention it. I'm glad you didn't get hurt," Will mumbled uncomfortably. It had been years since he was in polite company.

"Can she eat with us, Pa? Please." Tommy pushed the issue.

"She probably wants some peace and quiet after her train ride, Tommy."

"Yeah, you talk too much," Willy whispered to his brother. Tommy's face fell and he bit his lower lip.

"I'd love to eat with you, young man. You're the most handsome gentleman who's ever invited me to sup with him. I'd be honored, but your pa might want to have you boys all to himself."

"It would be our pleasure to have your presence at our table," Will responded, belatedly standing in the presence of the lady as his mother had taught him. "Please, have a seat, if you'd like." Even as he stepped around to hold out the chair between Tommy and Willy and opposite his, he wondered what he was thinking. The young woman had just given him the perfect out and instead of taking it, he asked her to join them and endure his sons' antics. Maybe it was just the idea of talking to another adult or maybe it was the worried look she was trying hard to hide from the boys.

"Thank you again," she murmured. The waitress set a menu in front of her and soon returned with a glass of water for everyone.

"Well, my young friend." She smiled down at Tommy. "I don't believe we've been properly introduced. My name —"

"I'm Tommy," he interrupted, "and I'm six years old." He held out his hands and this time he had managed to get six digits to stand in the air.

"It's a pleasure to meet you, Master Tommy." She grinned and shook his hand as if he were a grown man.

"And you would be . . . ?" She turned her attention on Willy.

Will did all he could not to stare at the young lady. Her eyes were a mix of green and blue and she smiled genuinely at his son. Her blond hair had been pulled back into some sort of braids and then wrapped into a bun. With the jostling about of the train and the wind, little spirals had escaped, bouncing close to her diminutive ears.

She couldn't be more than eighteen. What person had sent her out on the train by herself? Didn't they know that the prairie was full of single men? Many hadn't had an opportunity to socialize with a lovely lady for months or even years. Where was her father or brother? What was she to do now that no one had shown up to the station? And who was so irresponsible to have a young lady like her come halfway across the continent and then not meet her train?

"He's my big brother. He always tells me what to do. He's sweet on Jill. So, what are you going to eat? Pa likes the chicken 'cuz we mostly eat venison and rabbit on the farm. I'm gett'n' the same thing 'cuz it's got potatoes in it. I think I like potatoes."

"That's very nice, Tommy, but you didn't tell me you brother's name."

"I told ya you talk too much," Willy muttered.

"I do not!" Tommy answered his brother with a glare.

"Do, too!"

"Do not!"

"Do, too!"

"Boys!" Barely keeping his voice low, Will intervened and frowned when he saw the young lady biting her lower lip. Was she trying not to laugh at the boys or trying not to show her discomfort? He had had almost all the humiliation that he could take for one day. "Behave yourselves."

His warning was understood and both boys lowered their eyes. "Forgive us, miss. We don't get to town very often and it seems we've left what few manners we have back home."

"Don't think another thing about it, sir. My nieces and nephews were always saying things without thinking them through first. I find your boys refreshing." She smiled reassuringly at both boys.

"Well, I should try to start the introductions again," Will stated, wondering why her smile made his stomach flutter just a bit. It must have been the hunger for his supper sending ripples though his middle. "I'm Will Hopkins and this is Willy." He pointed to his older son.

"It's a pleasure —" The young lady had turned to Willy, extending her hand to shake his, when she froze and turned stunned eyes back to Will. Willy stared at her strangely, his hand in the air.

"I . . . What did you say your surname was?" she asked in a choked voice.

"Hopkins, but around here we usually are very . . ." Her face had gone deathly white and she looked as if she was going to faint.

She looked too stunned for words, barely gathering herself together enough to speak. "I . . . Where is Mrs. Hopkins? Where is Francis?" she stuttered.

He hadn't heard anyone call him that in years — in fact, other than his mother, no one called him that at all. He could feel himself flush, and tried to talk over it. "I'm, um . . . My father was . . . I'm Francis, Francis William Hopkins. I go by Will most of the time."

"But you're not a widow!"

A widow? Why would anyone think he was —

"I thought . . . My mother's best friend was Frannie, Francis . . . and if you . . . if you're . . . Why didn't you tell me who you were at the station? You just walked past me and left me there!" The confusion on her pretty face gave way to obvious anger.

"How'd you know my given name? What are you talking about?" Will asked, curious and accusing at the same time.

"Your ad."

"What ad?"

"The ad that you placed in the ladies' Christian monthly pamphlet," she explained. "I subscribe to it and in April of last year, there was an ad . . ." She pulled her satchel up onto her lap and started sorting through her things. Finally she pulled out a paper and handed it to him.

He only read the first few lines before he glanced back up to study the young woman again. It was the ad his mother had created to find him a housekeeper. The ad Miss Stewart had answered. But that meant . . . No, it couldn't be. This girl didn't look a day over twenty, and the letter he'd received had clearly stated that his new employee was in her fifties. The woman in front of him, who looked as if she might give in to tears at any moment, *couldn't* be Abigail Stewart.

"What's wrong, miss?" Tommy asked her, having come to stand next to her, his small hand on hers.

Will watched as some of the anger and frustration melted out of her expression as she looked down at his son. "I'm not quite sure of that myself, honey," she answered, pressing his hand with hers. "It's been a long trip and I have had a very taxing day. I was looking forward to meeting my new employer and her . . . *his* family. But this

hasn't gone at all like I thought it would."
She looked up from Tommy to glare at Will.
"Especially the part where I was left alone
on the train platform while your father
walked away."

"You're . . . you're Miss Stewart?" Will
said incredulously.

She straightened her back and tilted her
chin up to look him straight in the eye. "Yes,
I'm Abigail Stewart."

Any answer Will might have given was
interrupted by Tommy's response. Throw-
ing his arms around the woman's waist, he
squeezed tight while yelling out, "You're
our auntie House!"

CHAPTER TWO

"Housekeeper, not Auntie anything," Willy hissed at his brother.

Abby didn't know how to respond to that, so she addressed their father. "I came all the way from Ohio just to be part of Mrs. Francis Hopkins's household. Now what am I going to do?" she asked out loud, not expecting an answer from him.

"But you're not old!" Willy burst out. Abby tried to focus on the boy, but her head felt clouded.

"That's right. You wrote you were fifty-eight." Will eyed her suspiciously.

"I did no such thing. I'm twenty-six, as I told you in my letter." How could he say something so strange? She had been a little uncomfortable when Mrs. . . . er . . . Mr. Hopkins had asked her age, knowing that the posting had specifically requested a "mature" Christian woman, but she decided to be honest, deciding that if her honesty somehow lost her the opportunity to work for the family, it was because God was closing that door. When there had been no further mention of her age in the letters, she had assumed her new employer had decided that it wasn't important.

"Here, I'll show you." Mr. Hopkins reached into his worn denim shirt pocket and pulled out a pile of letters that even from a distance Abby recognized. Her heart sank. There was no doubt about it. She had been corresponding with *Mr.,* not *Mrs.* Hopkins.

He shuffled the papers and then scanned one, holding it out to her, his strong, calloused finger pointing to a paragraph. As she took it, she noticed that the page was watermarked and that the ink had run. Even Abby had to admit that the number she had written out did look like a fifty-eight.

"I'm sorry. It must have gotten wet. I *did* write that I'm twenty-six. I never intended to be dishonest or misleading."

"I believe you," he replied gruffly. "But I'm afraid that doesn't resolve the problem. I'm sorry if there was a miscommunication, Miss Stewart, but I was specifically looking for a, um . . ." He looked uncomfortable as he searched for the right wording. "A more mature woman. Someone closer to the age

41

of my mother."

"Well, I'm not the age of your mother, but I can cook, clean and teach as well as anyone twice my age." Suddenly, staying here and keeping the job was important to her. If Mr. Hopkins withdrew his offer, where else could she go? She couldn't go back to Ohio. Emma and Palmer would never welcome her back, and if she went anywhere close by, they would make life impossible for her and anyone who was daring enough to help her. No. She had to find a way to stay out here in Nebraska. And since jobs for women in the area seemed to be scarce, her best chance was to convince Mr. Hopkins that she could be his housekeeper after all.

"I don't doubt your capacity, miss. It's just that on the farm it's just me, the boys and my nephew, Jake. It wouldn't be proper or right for us to have you out there with us, a single woman of your age. I'll take care of paying your passage back to Ohio and then you can be with your sister again." His words were meant to be reassuring but elicited the opposite effect.

"I can't go back," she whispered to herself. This was worse than not being picked up at the station. Before, she had wondered if something had interfered with Mrs. Hopkins's arrival, but now she knew she had been judged unwanted again.

"Why not? Did something happen to your sister?"

"My brother-in-law . . ." She almost spilled out everything but then remembered the boys listening. Straightening her back, she lifted her chin. "I can't. I'll have to look for work around here."

"I doubt there will be very much in the way of work for a decent woman." He studied her for a moment more and then shook his head. "Why did you even apply to come out on the frontier at your age? You should be looking to settle down and marry. Have a bunch of kids of your own."

He had no idea how she'd longed for that — a husband and children, a home of her own. But there had been no chance of that. No man in Ohio had any interest in a girl who wore her sister's old castoffs and was too busy minding her nieces and nephews and looking after the housekeeping to go to any social events. This was the only way for her to leave her sister's house — to find a job somewhere else. What would she do if that chance was taken away?

"I'm sure that once you get back to Ohio, some young man will be real glad to see that you've come back where you belong.

43

And no doubt your family will be glad to have you home, too."

"I wish it were that simple," she answered. "I have lived with my sister and brother-in-law since my parents died when I was thirteen. My brother-in-law is very powerful . . . I can't go back now that I left against their wishes."

"So you disobeyed your sister and brother-in-law to come out here?"

"Yes. I came because . . ." She glanced at the boys and bit her lip. "I had to get away from Palmer — my brother-in-law. I didn't feel quite . . . safe living with him anymore," she finally finished, hoping he would understand what she had left unsaid. "But my sister, Emma, felt that I had a responsibility to stay and continue to take care of the house and the children. The day your last letter came to the house, Emma found it and I had to snatch it from her or I would never even have gotten the money or ticket. I ran all the way to my pastor's house, and he and his wife helped me get away. I even have a letter from Pastor Gibbons for you . . . or at least it was to be given to Mrs. Hopkins."

She reached down and once again sifted through the different letters until she found what she was looking for and handed it over to Mr. Hopkins. As she watched him unfold it, she felt dizzy. What if he still decided to send her back? What was she going to do?

"Have you made your choice?" The poor waitress was back, pad of paper in hand.

"Um . . ."

"Why don't you try the chicken like me?" Tommy prompted.

"Or she could try the steak that I'm gonna get," Willy suggested.

"I don't know," she answered honestly. She didn't really feel like eating anything and was afraid that food wouldn't stay in her churning stomach even if she could swallow past the huge lump of fear wedged in the middle of her throat. She took a sip of her water and willed it to stay down. "I guess I'm not really that hungry right now. It does all sound so good, but —"

"Don't worry about the money," Mr. Hopkins interrupted with a deep frown on his face, his eyes not even lifting for the first page of the letter. "I'll cover it. It's my fault, after all, that you've come all this way for nothing."

Suddenly Abby knew that she had to get outside and breathe some fresh air. Her stomach threatened revolt. Even with the letter from Pastor Gibbons in his hand, the man was going to refuse to hire her.

Without explaining anything to anyone, she bolted from the room, out the door and around the side of the building. She was almost to the back of the clapboard restaurant when she couldn't keep her stomach from emptying any longer. For the first time in her life, she wished she had died with her parents. What was to become of her? She was truly alone in this world — and in this strange and unfamiliar town. Back home, the sky had been high and the hills had surrounded her, but she had not known the immenseness of God's creation until she sat hour after hour and watched prairie grass wave to an endless clear sky. She was a small speck on a wide-open prairie and only God cared she even existed. No wonder King David had asked, What was man that God was mindful of him? She was as insignificant as a stalk of the prairie grass.

"Oh, God, What am I going to do now?" she cried. The sobs that racked her body were almost as painful as the retching. She leaned her forearms against the clapboard wall and hung her head between her elbows. She didn't even feel the coarseness of the building scratching her arms. Closing her eyes she prayed for a home. Somewhere to go where she could rest — where she could feel safe. She had traveled more than a thousand miles thinking she found a new home only to find it was the biggest mistake of her life.

Will sat staring at the spot the girl . . . Miss Stewart, had just vacated. He almost hoped that this was just a bad dream and he'd wake up any minute now to find that he was still camping down by the river on his way into Twin Oaks to pick up his new house-keeper. But Tommy's little hand pushing on his shoulder, trying to get him to pay attention to yet another barrage of questions, made him aware this was all too real. The new housekeeper was a young, beautiful girl who looked as if a stiff wind could carry her off. She wouldn't last a week on the frontier.

"Pa, where'd she go?" Tommy asked, his confusion making Will regret even more having started all this craziness. Surely he and Jake could handle the boys on their own just as they had done in the past. Maybe he would not plant in the western field he had cleared last month. He would still make a profit, though not as much as he had hoped. Still, that sounded better than adding more chaos and anxiety to his boys' lives.

"Pa!" Tommy's hand pounded harder and Will finally focused on his small son.

"I don't know where she went. Maybe she

needed to get a breath of air." What did he know about women anymore? He'd been a failure at being a husband, and it had been more than ten years since he had seen his own mother or sisters.

"Um, sir?" The waitress was back again. This time she had two plates full of mashed potatoes, gravy, corn, chicken and broccoli. The third had a large steak and a baked potato with the same side vegetables. "I have your meals."

She set a plate in front of each of them and then leaned a little closer to him. "Is the young lady all right? Will she be joining you again?"

Will groaned and closed his eyes. That was the question, wasn't it? Would she be joining them on their trip back to the farm, or would he send her back to Ohio? The sliver of the letter he had been able to read stated the pastor's approval. According to the pastor, Miss Stewart was an upstanding Christian girl, well respected by the other members of the church where she had attended since she had been little. The pastor indicated that he had known her parents and wanted to make sure she was arriving to a Christian home where she would be protected and respected. It had confirmed what Will surmised about her from her letters.

The only problem was her age — how could he bring a young woman to live with them? True, they wouldn't be completely alone, thanks to Jake and the boys, but it still didn't seem proper. Yet it hardly seemed proper to abandon a young woman in a strange town, either.

"Oh . . . all right!" He gave in to his guilty conscience. He needed to go search her out and see what solution he could offer. It was getting later in the day and he still needed to be back to the river by nightfall. "Can you keep an eye on my boys for a minute?" he asked the waitress, wondering what he could possibly do to make this situation better for everyone.

"We'll be just fine here, right, boys? I remember when mine were this size." The waitress smiled at Tommy and Willy and then nodded to Will.

Maybe he could ask Mrs. Scotts to let Miss Stewart stay on their homestead. The Scotts were his closest neighbors, and Mrs. Scotts had always struck him as a kind woman. He played with that idea as he left the building and blinked in the afternoon sun. Once his eyes adjusted, he turned and followed the forlorn sound of someone sobbing. When he found her, she was leaning against the building, crying so hard she looked on the verge of collapse. She was the picture of distress and disillusionment. Knowing he had created this big mess, causing her so much misery, struck him like a sucker punch to his stomach.

He had prayed and sought God's guidance each step of the process that had brought her here. Mother had started everything when she suggested he advertize for a housekeeper last spring. Being that it was her idea, he'd asked his mother to write his ad and get it placed in a good Christian publication. Miss Stewart's copy was the first he had seen of the original ad. He never even dreamed she had used his given name — Francis, the name he had grown to hate as a boy growing up. Miss Stewart was not the first person to think it a woman's name. How could it have gone so terribly wrong? Now the poor girl was in a strange place with no one to count on and nowhere to go.

God, I need a little help here, he prayed as he approached, wondering what he could possibly say.

"Um, Miss Stewart?"

She jerked around so quickly that she almost fell. Her pallid face looked as if she had powdered it with flour. Even her lips looked gray. Her red nose and red-rimmed eyes contrasted her lack of color.

She spun away from him just as quickly and her stomach heaved again, although she brought nothing up. A sob escaped her throat and ripped his heart in half. He stepped closer. Supporting her elbows with his hands, he felt her body shaking.

He felt an unaccustomed surge of protectiveness. He wanted to help this girl, shield and protect her from any source of pain. But right now *he* was the cause of her distress. What could he say or do to make that right?

Abby had thought the day couldn't get any worse when she fled the restaurant, but apparently she was wrong. Now he was here watching her toss up her accounts. How embarrassing.

"I'm sorry, Miss Stewart. I wasn't expecting you to be . . . I had thought . . . I've made a mess of this."

His hands still supported her elbows and he sounded truly contrite, but what could she say? It was all right? That it was understandable after he had brought her all this way into the middle of nowhere that he was going to abandon her and leave her with

51

nothing?

The nightmare didn't seem to be ready to end. Silence stretched out and neither one knew how to break the uncomfortable tension. At least her stomach had settled to resemble a simple storm instead of a full-blown sea squall.

"Listen, I admit this is a mess." He stated the obvious. If Abby hadn't been so tense, she might have seen a bit of humor in that. Right now she didn't have the energy to be amused.

"Really!" She speared him with a pointed look.

"I'm . . . Why don't we go back and sit down? Maybe if you eat something . . ."

"It'll come right back up," she mumbled before he even finished his idea. "All I want is to go home . . . to have a place to go and lie down, a place that's safe, where I belong."

The last word caught in her throat. A place to belong and to be loved — it was what she had been searching for a long time. Her fight drained out of her as quickly as her ire had ignited. What was she doing, telling this man her heart's desire?

"Um . . . I was thinking. I've got neighbors a few miles away who might be willing to let you stay with them while you work for us. At least until we can come up with another solution." He paused and then asked abruptly, "Do you know how to ride a horse?"

Abby swallowed hard. He was offering her an option. Granted it wasn't much of an option since it depended on this other family agreeing, but it was a better option than nothing. Clearly he wasn't planning for her to stay permanently since he'd hardly want her imposing on his neighbors for very long, but at least she would have a place to stay for a few days. She nodded, afraid to say anything.

"We've got an extra horse that you could take each day. . . ." He was already planning, but Abby couldn't suppress a shudder. Did he expect her to ride the prairie for a few miles on her own each morning and night? Would it be safe? "We'll work something out, at least until harvest. The winter months we spend closer to the house and I can see to the boys. In the meantime, I'll write to my mother. . . ."

He continued to talk, but she was having a hard time concentrating.

"Well?" he asked, obviously waiting for her to respond.

"Thank you," she whispered. She almost sank to the ground in exhaustion. The entire

53

trip was now taking its toll. From the moment she had received his letter and realized she was finally free of her sister and brother-in-law, she had slept very little, first packing and then traveling by coach and finally by train for the last week. A woman alone, she only dared to catch catnaps and felt so vulnerable. She had assumed that once she had arrived, everything would be calm and she would be shown her room and be able to rest — not sit for almost an hour in a strange town with no one looking for her and then discover that her job itself might fall through.

"I think you need to get in, out of the sun, and rest. Shall we?" Without waiting for her to answer, he slipped an arm around her waist and half walked, half carried her to the front of the building.

"Mr. Hopkins, I can do this on my own," Abby declared as firmly as she could in her shaky voice. She couldn't afford to leave him with the impression that she wouldn't be able to take care of herself, much less do her work. She swiped at the tears on her face and groaned inwardly. Her face must be a sight, all red and puffy.

"All right," he acknowledged, releasing her waist and tucking her arm around his like a perfect gentleman, turning them both toward the front door.

Abby firmly tapped down the hope that things were going to work out. It would be doubly devastating for her to start feeling as if she fit in and then have to pack up and leave. But the way Mr. Hopkins opened the door for her, led her back to the table and pulled out her chair, she felt certain she would be safe with this gentleman farmer.

The boys had both been eating their food, but when they saw their father lead Abby back inside, their eyes lit up and Tommy started his barrage of questions. "Is she okay? Will she come home with us? Are you gonna ask for your food now? Is she still sick? Do you want to try some of mine?"

"Tommy, she's not gonna come to our house 'cuz Pa made her cry," Willy hissed at his brother.

"Well, boys. We've talked and Miss Stewart is going to come with us for a while. I'll see if the Scotts can let her stay with them until we can make some other arrangements."

Abby nodded her head, but even that slight motion sent everything spinning. She just wanted to lie down somewhere quiet and sleep. The waitress came back with a teapot. Before Abby realized what she was doing, the waitress had poured a cup and then sweetened it with a sugar cube that she had plucked from the sugar bowl in the center of the table. The boys' eyes grew large when they saw what treat was concealed in the bowl.

"This might help settle your stomach, miss." The matronly lady spoke softly, placing the cup and saucer in front of Abby. "Why don't you try a few sips at a time? It's chamomile — it always helps me feel better when I've had a rough day." She smiled and patted her shoulder, reminding Abby of Mrs. Gibbons, the reverend's wife from back home. Abby wished that she could let the older woman coddle her a bit more. She managed to keep the tea down and drank yet another cup before the boys became too restless.

She hoped it would be enough to give her strength for the trials that lay ahead.

What had he gotten himself into? Will wondered to himself for the hundredth time as he drove the wagon back toward the homestead. They'd stop tonight at the river. He and the boys could camp out under the stars and Miss Stewart could sleep in the wagon. Getting home and dropping her off at the Scotts' house on the way would be the easy part.

The Miss Stewart he'd imagined had been a sturdy, solid woman who knew her own mind when she said she was unafraid of the challenges of prairie life. This beautiful, delicate girl was another matter altogether. For now she seemed determined to give the job a try, but how long would that last? How long would he have — weeks, maybe a month or two — before she realized that Nebraska was a place where no young woman could ever want to be?

There was no convincing her of that now, of course. She'd have to see it for herself. Until then, perhaps Miss Stewart could help Willy to be more sociable. Maybe she could train Tommy not to say just anything that came to mind — or maybe not. He hoped she could feed them something more substantial than what he normally managed to burn or leave half-raw. Maybe she could get some meat on their bones and make his house feel more like a home . . . Or maybe he'd just invited trouble to make itself comfortable at his dinner table.

Not that she would be that much trouble. She seemed well educated and her letters bespoke of a nice girl, but to have a beautiful, single, unattached woman out in the middle of the prairie full of single men, all looking to settle down and start families in a place few women would venture . . . He might just have opened the door to a whole lot more than a housekeeper. Since he employed her, he would be responsible for her safety and reputation, and he'd also have to ensure that she didn't make any decisions she'd later regret. She seemed so set on not returning to Ohio that she might fall into marriage with one of the local men. He'd do everything he could to make sure *that* didn't happen. She needed to be free to leave the prairie whenever she chose — the choice that Caroline had never had.

Out of the corner of his eye, he watched her shift around to look over the landscape. He studied her profile. What must she be thinking? Was she asking herself what she had just gotten herself into, as well? The wind had pulled tendrils of hair out from her pins and he was sure that if she hadn't been so tired from her travels, she would have been trying to control the mass of corn silk better.

Stealing a glance at her sitting at his side on the wagon bench, he pondered how to explain their route. "Listen," he started, trying to broach the subject, then cleared his throat and tried again. "Our homestead is not very close to Twin Oaks. In fact, it's more than another six hours' ride from here, so we'll be stopping at the river to spend the night."

He turned his eyes back to the road, feeling her stiffen next to him. Her words still echoed in his head, the way she had said that she wanted to "Go home . . . To have a place to go and lie down." He would have let her stay at the hotel tonight and headed out at first light, but that would have meant he wouldn't get her to the Scotts' until late in the night and then it would be too late to get home. Jake would be on his own for five days. It was too much to ask the boy.

"I can sleep with the boys out under the sky and you can have the wagon all to yourself. I know it's not the hotel or anything fancy, but by tomorrow night, you'll be bedding down at the Scotts' house. Mrs. Scotts will take real good care of you and make sure you get the rest you need after this long trip."

The line of saplings and small trees at the edge of the river came into view. "See those trees?" He pointed to the horizon.

"Hmm."

"That's the river. We'll be there in just a few more minutes."

Once they had arrived at the river, he helped her down from the seat and held her upright until her legs stopped shaking and supported her weight. Acting the consummate gentleman, he didn't even look angry. Abby couldn't say if it was the fear of what her future held or the long ride that had her shaking so bad.

"Why don't you walk around here by the wagon for a minute and get your land legs back? The boys and I will go and check that there's nothing around to bother you and then you can freshen up down by the river." His words were soft and she felt protected. Maybe her first impressions had been correct. He made her feel safe.

Within a few minutes, Tommy ran back to her. "We made lots of noise so no critters would come out and scare you, Auntie House." She followed hesitantly, finding Mr. Hopkins and Willy in a small clearing with a sandy bank sloping into the river.

"We'll go and set up camp now, Miss Stewart. You should be perfectly safe here. We'll stay out of sight, but all you have to do is give a yell and we'll come running," the man reassured her as soon as she came into the clearing. As they left, she heard Tommy whine about having to wait for a swim, but she was glad they were gone for a minute. The water looked so cool and refreshing.

When Abby ventured back to camp afterward, she found a small tent erected and a fire started. The boys sat on both sides of Mr. Hopkins and were watching as he cooked some sort of meat.

"Hi, Auntie House," Tommy called out, hopping up and running toward her. "Do you feel better now?"

"Yes, thank you, Tommy. But can I ask you a favor?" she questioned, squatting down to be at eye level with the boy. His chest puffed out a little and he nodded solemnly. "Can you call me Auntie Abby?" Even as she asked, she glanced at Mr. Hopkins and cringed inwardly, wondering if it would be all right with him. "My nieces and nephews call me Auntie Abby and I'd feel better if you called me that instead of Auntie House."

"Sure. You're going to be a much better auntie than our old one. She was mean."

"Well, I'll do the best I can." She tried to cover her surprise as smoothly as she could.

"Now, Tommy, we need to talk nicely about Auntie Shelia. Remember what I told you?" Mr. Hopkins's voice brought her head up quickly.

Tommy stood and thought for a minute and then his eyes lit up. "Always say please and thank you?"

"Well, yes, that, too. But I meant about talking about other people," Mr. Hopkins hinted.

"He means that 'if you can't say nothin' nice, don't say nothin' at all,' " Willy piped up.

"My mother used to say the same thing. I think that's good advice," Abby encouraged. "So, what are you men cooking over there? It sure smells good."

Abby went closer to the fire and watched Mr. Hopkins struggle to flip the meat in the fry pan without getting too close to the fire. "What can I help with?" she offered. If they had been in a kitchen she would have set a table or taken over the cooking. She felt completely out of her element out on the prairie with three strangers.

"Careful of the flames, miss." Mr. Hopkins's voice shook her from her musing. "We don't want your skirt to catch on fire."

"I . . ." She blushed. She should know better. "Thank you."

"Pa's making venison steaks. He got the lady to give him some bread. Now we can eat like kings."

Tommy's little hand found hers and he tugged her to follow him. "Look over here. The deer and the raccoons and even the foxes and coyotes come to drink at the river at the time the sun goes to bed, so we figure we're gonna bag us a great big one," he boasted, his chest puffed out and his eyes bright with excitement.

"I'm sure you are a fine hunter," she praised. "I'll bet your brother and your daddy both taught you well."

"More like Pa's gonna teach us. I haven't never hunted 'fore. But maybe Pa'll let Willy shoot."

"No, Willy's not going to shoot tonight." Mr. Hopkins's voice was deep and smooth, causing a chill to run up her back. She had almost forgotten the man was there while she had been enjoying her enlightening chat with his son.

"But, Pa," Tommy whined, "you said yesterday that tonight we could bag a big one. Maybe the one with the big horns."

"Those aren't horns, silly. Those are antlers," Willy corrected his little brother. Then he pleaded his case. "But, Pa, you said we could use the venison."

"Well, I've changed my mind." Mr. Hopkins's answer left no room for argument.

"But, why, Pa? Why'd ya change your mind?" Tommy pressed the issue.

"Because I did. We'll go hunting once we're back at the house." Somehow, Abby suspected he had changed his mind because of her presence.

"It's time to eat," Mr. Hopkins announced, ending the conversation.

He slid the last of the meat onto a tin plate. Glancing around, he groaned, handed the plate to Willy with instructions to hold it for a minute and then went around the wagon. He came back a moment later, carrying a barrel for water. He set it far enough back from the fire so that there was ample room and then indicated she could have a seat.

"I'm sorry I didn't think to bring a chair or even a stool."

Once she was seated, he handed her a tin plate, slipped a piece of meat on it and set two dinner rolls on top. The boys were settled with similar plates where they sat on the dirt with their legs crossed in front of them.

"Father God," Mr. Hopkins began to pray, "we thank You for Your provisions and Your traveling mercies on this trip. I ask You to bless the food to our bodies and keep us safe on our journey home. Thank You for keeping Miss Stewart safe and for giving her the willingness to work for this simple farmer and his sons. Please lead us to make wise decisions and trust You every day. Amen."

The word *home* stuck in Abby's head as she ate. How she wished that she was going home. She had until the harvest to convince Mr. Hopkins that she was a hard worker and should be kept on. Only God held the solutions to her problems in His hand, and He hadn't let her know what they were yet.

"Hello, Herbert," Will called to the older of the Scotts brothers as he stepped down from the wagon. Mr. and Mrs. Scotts had attended church alone for so long that Will had forgotten the couple's two grown sons still lived with their parents. Rumor had it, the Scotts brothers thought that riding into Twin Oaks and drinking on Saturday nights was a much better way of spending their free time than worshiping in the Lord's house on Sunday mornings.

"Howdy, Will." Herbert approached from the shadows of the barn where he had been working. His eyes strayed too long on Miss Stewart before he looked at Will. "And hello, pretty lady. Don't think I've seen the likes of you around here. You —"

"Are your ma and pa around?" Will asked, interrupting Herbert and standing between the man and the wagon. Will was starting to reconsider the idea of leaving a young lady, any young lady, on a farm with the likes of

Herbert or Elvin. Why hadn't he thought of them before? A desire to mount back up and head off to his own claim without waiting for an answer almost won over his sense of courtesy, but now that he had come, they needed to at least greet the elder Scotts.

"Naw. Pa's out in the fields, and Ma went off to see to Jankowski's woman. Her time was close and her husband didn't want to see to all their kids and the birthing. Don't see why the woman needs so much help. What with all the little squallers she's already borne, a body'd think she could handle it herself by now."

Will cringed at the coarse way Herbert spoke about such a delicate subject. A glance at Miss Stewart confirmed her surprise. Now he wished he hadn't even attempted to bring her here. She needed a safe, comfortable place to stay — like his mother's home. Miss Stewart had implied that her brother-in-law had been less than respecting to her person, and now Herbert didn't bother to conceal the way he looked too long at Miss Stewart's womanly attributes.

Will had a sudden desire to make her feel safe. Where had that thought come from? Yes, his mother had taught him to be a gentleman, but the powerful need to protect

Miss Stewart from Herbert took him by surprise. If the man kept looking at Will's new housekeeper like that, he might just have to teach the younger man a lesson or two about respect.

There was no way he would leave Miss Stewart here. They would have to make some other arrangement. Maybe he could use the barn or fix up the soddy to sleep in so that she could stay in the house. Climbing back into the wagon, he called over his shoulder, "Then I'd best be on my way. You let your ma and pa know we came to visit."

"But, Will, you're not being very neighborly. You didn't even tell me your sister's name," Herbert called after him, coming to stand on Miss Stewart's side of the wagon.

"She's Auntie Abby and she's gonna be our new house . . . house . . . What is it again?" Tommy whispered to his brother even as Will clicked his tongue to the horses.

"Housekeeper!" Willy answered his brother. "You don't remember nuttin'."

"Hey, I just can't —"

Will turned the wagon around, knowing he was being less than friendly with his nearest neighbor, but he couldn't stay any longer without losing control of his temper. Miss Stewart was a lovely, respectable woman who deserved to be treated like a lady. Soon enough she'd be headed back East, where she belonged. In the meantime, as her employer, Will knew it was up to him to protect her and make sure she was safe.

"I'm real sorry, Miss Stewart. I didn't know Mrs. Scotts had gone to stay with the Jankowskis." He didn't dare look at the small woman next to him. It was just about two in the afternoon and they still had another hour to go before they made it to the house. What was he going to do for her?

"It's all right. You couldn't have known. I'm sure we can come up with something. Maybe I can sleep out in the barn if there's no place for me in the house."

"It's not a question of a place for you," Will tried to explain. After all, he had thought ahead and planned for a house-keeper. "You can sleep on the first floor in the parlor. It's been converted into a bed-room." He didn't elaborate that the conver-sion had been for Auntie Sheila and had never been rearranged once she left.

"It's just that it might not be . . . It might ruin your reputation to be living on the homestead with two men and two boys and no woman to chaperone." Even as he forced the words out, he felt his face flame. "Not that there would be any reason. We'll . . . Jake and I will behave as gentlemen at all

68

times and you can sleep in the parlor or up in the upstairs if you want. We'll sleep out in the barn," he offered.

"I don't want to put you out of your own home — but we'll do whatever you say is best." She didn't look at him but kept her face toward the waving grasses stretching out in all directions.

Relieved that he could at least offer some protection from gossips, Will stole a glance at Miss Ab . . . Miss Stewart, he reminded himself. He supposed it was all right for the boys to refer to her as Auntie Abby, but he would still be reserved and careful around her. He didn't want to be any more familiar with a pretty, young woman than he needed to be. That's what had gotten him into trouble when he was barely able to shave.

CHAPTER THREE

Abby jounced on the wagon seat and took in the view as they drove up to the farmhouse. The house walls were of stout weather-beaten, whitewashed planks settled on a foundation of stones and boulders. Mr. Hopkins hadn't stopped at the front entrance for obvious reasons since the weeds grew knee-high right up to the house. Instead, he pulled around into the barnyard where the dirt was hard and flat, giving testimony to constant traffic. The barn was made of the same planks as the house minus the paint.

Something akin to excitement ran through Abby when she saw a small back porch running the length of the house with a bench swing in one corner. She could imagine swinging out there on cool evenings after her housework was done, just as her mother used to when Abby was small. On closer inspection, Abby's excitement dimmed. She doubted anyone had swung on the swing for a few seasons given the amount of dust and spiderwebs that clung to it. What must the house look like?

One more jerk and the wagon came to a halt. "We're here, miss. I can't promise that it's very welcoming but . . ."

Abby looked at Mr. Hopkins and found his expression endearing. He'd mentioned on the trip that he had built the house with his brother and that they had taken the better part of a year to get the main parts done. He said something about having to care for Caroline and the boys, and how that had slowed him down. Now he looked embarrassed as if it wouldn't measure up to what she expected. Mr. Hopkins's humble clapboard home represented an opportunity to prove she was an able housekeeper and educator. While it might never truly become *her* home, she could make it a comfortable one for his family.

"Is everything all right?" His voice called her back to the present. Glancing down from her perch still atop the wagon bench, she found him looking up at her expectantly. His hands were extended to help her climb down from the wagon and she mentally chastised herself for not paying more attention.

"Oh. Yes, Mr. Hopkins. I was just admiring your home." Just a hint of a smile touched the corners of his lips, but the pride that shone in his eyes reminded her of Tommy when she praised him.

Mr. Hopkins's hands were firm and strong as he lifted her at the waist and set her on her feet. "Thank you, miss." He stood a little straighter and surveyed it himself. "She looks a little rough now." He glanced at the house and shook his head. "I guess it must not look like much, but it's dry and warm when it's cold and wet outside. We make do."

"I'm sure it's just fine," Abby reassured him, seeing a glimpse of an insecure little boy behind the tough exterior of her employer.

"If you want to just go on inside," he said, turning toward the back of the wagon, "I'll get your trunk and other boxes in short order."

"Come on. I wanna show you my room." Tommy took her hand and started to pull her up the stairs.

"Let's go take a look," she agreed, and let herself be led into the kitchen. She blinked as she stood at the threshold and waited for her eyes to adjust to the light. Something smelled as if it had died and was rotting in the middle of the room. It was enough to make her hold her breath. When she finally released the pent-up air, she tried to keep from thinking about what could be making such a stench. As her eyes adjusted, she could take in more of her surroundings. She held back a groan. What could she expect from four men who had been on their own for a number of years?

The floor was the same rough planks as the walls but caked with dirt from the barnyard. The large table stood in the very middle of the large kitchen, its entire surface dirty with lumps of something stuck to its once-smooth surface. Three different-size pots took up part of the wooden counter; each stank of rot and had something decaying inside it. A filthy stove sat in the corner, its pipe connected to a hole just above the grimy window.

It was nice to see that at least there were two glass windows in the kitchen even if they didn't have screens. She would have enough natural light on most days (once she washed the windows) so that she wouldn't even need a lantern or candles. The hand pump connected to the sink looked modern and meant she wouldn't have to lug water from somewhere outside every morning to start the day. But in spite of those conveniences, she clearly had her work cut out for her.

"C'mon." Tommy had run ahead but was now back, tugging on her hand again.

"Ahem." A deep voice from behind startled her, chasing her away from the door.

Mr. Hopkins stood with her hope chest on his shoulder as if it were a bag of feathers. "I'll take this into the room on the first floor and then you can decide where you want to stay. I . . ." His nose curled as he stepped farther into the room. "Jake!" he exclaimed, frowning as he took in the pots on the counter. "I asked that boy . . ." he muttered under his breath.

"I'll get the kitchen straightened out in no time, sir."

"It's not right for you to have to start working today. I'm sure you just want to rest after your long trip." His face looked bright red and his eyes didn't meet hers. Abby found his embarrassment charming.

"I'll be fine. I'll just need to freshen up a bit and then I could pull something together for supper."

"Are you going to cook like they do at the hotel?" Tommy piped up, still tugging her hand. Willy hovered at the doorway, trying to act nonchalant.

"Well, I don't know if it'll be just like the

restaurant, but it will be enough to fill you up. My nieces and nephews like my chicken and dumplings. We could also make fried venison steaks when you go get a big one with your pa. But today I think I'm just going to have to see what's in the pantry and make something simple. Tomorrow we can make a menu. You can show me how many letters and words you already know," she offered.

"What's a menu?" Tommy turned to his bigger brother, but Willy just shrugged.

"A menu is the list of the foods for you to choose from. At the restaurant, the lady gave one to you to look at so you could decide what you wanted to order. Here at the house we will make a list for the week ahead of what we are going to make each day so you can get really hungry the days that we make your favorites. It helps to know what we want to cook so that we can make sure all the ingredients are available."

"What's 'gredients?"

"*Ingredients* are the things we need to make that food, like flour and butter and eggs. . . . Now, how about if we go help your pa put my stuff in my room and then we can chat?" Abby offered, following the man who had disappeared into the second doorway on the hallway from the kitchen. Once out of the kitchen, she discovered it wasn't a hallway but a large living room with a comfortable-looking davenport and a rocking chair facing the center of the room. The center wall was a massive fireplace with an ample hearth. The door Mr. Hopkins entered shared the wall with the fireplace. That room would be nice and warm come the winter — if she was still working for the family then.

The bedroom itself was sparsely furnished, with a large bed sagging in the center. The only other piece of furniture was a forlorn nightstand. Everything had a layer of dust, and the spiderwebs in the corner looked like spun cotton.

"Where would you like your chest?" Mr. Hopkins stood in the middle of the room, looking surprised to see the condition of the place. "Um, I hadn't been in here. . . ."

"I think it would be best if you left it out in the living room for a few minutes until I can tidy up just a bit," Abby suggested tactfully.

"Are you gonna sleep on the couch?" Tommy asked.

"No." Abby shook her head and smiled at the small boy, ruffling his hair. "I'll be sleeping in here, but I think it would be better to air out the room and sweep up a little.

Don't you agree?"

Tommy nodded energetically. Willy hung back at the door, not venturing into the room but watching everyone else.

"Could you do me a favor?" Abby asked Willy, knowing Tommy would probably follow. "Would you go find me the broom and dustpan?" As soon as Tommy and Willy had raced off, she tried the window, but it wouldn't budge.

"I'll go get your other things, miss. Unless there's something else that you would like me to do first?" Mr. Hopkins offered. His hands resting on opposite sides of the door frame reminded her just how big Mr. Hopkins was. He looked capable of building a house on his own.

"Could you give me a hand with the window?"

Mr. Hopkins crossed the room in five large steps. The room shrank with each step. He towered above her as he stood next to her. He pushed a lock on the top of the lower frame and then grunted as he tried to free the window. It took two tries, but suddenly there was a rush of fresh air sending dust dancing across the room.

"Thank you, sir," she choked out, just before sneezing from the dust.

"No problem. I'll go open the kitchen

windows, too. Might as well get it aired out in here. I'll have to put screens on as soon as I can so you'll be comfortable in here in the summer, assuming . . ." Before he found the words to finish his thoughts, he stalked out of the room.

The boys raced in, fighting about who was going to give her the broom. "Thank you, gentlemen." She acknowledged both of them, causing Tommy to have a fit of giggles. "Now I need you to go out in the living room until I'm ready for you in here. I'm going to get some of this dust out." She tied a handkerchief around her face, covering her nose and mouth, making both boys giggle. Too much in a hurry to change, she told herself that the clothes that she had traveled in needed a good washing anyway, so a little more dust wouldn't hurt.

In a few minutes, she swept up the dirt and dumped it unceremoniously out the open window. She took the bedspread and sheets off the bed, even though there wouldn't be time to get them washed and dried before nightfall. She opted to get as much of the musty smell out as possible. She hung the bedding on the lines extending from the side of the house to a stand twenty paces away. Beating the dusty linens helped to relieve the tensions that had built up over the last few weeks and gave the boys something vigorous to do.

Rinsing off at the outside well, she returned to the kitchen, happy to find that the three pots had vanished. A good breeze flowed through from the two windows and the doorway to the living area. Someone left a fire started in the stove, but she opened the door and checked it anyway. She put water to boil in the only big cauldron she could find in the pantry. She couldn't start dinner until she got some of the grime out of the kitchen. Broom in hand, she made quick work of sweeping the bulk of the dirt off the floor.

Two hours later, she had the table and counter spotless, the supplies Mr. Hopkins brought from town put away in the pantry and dinner finished. There hadn't been time to make bread, but she was glad to see there were all the ingredients she would need tomorrow. For tonight, a simple fare of biscuits and fried meat would be all she could offer. Mr. Hopkins had promised a visit to the smokehouse tomorrow so she could take inventory.

The windows let more than just the breeze in. A bee and a few flies all got a good whack from her wooden spoon for their efforts to visit her kitchen, but the boys' laughter and shouting rode inside on the breeze, too. The latter far outweighed the first. She smiled, listening to them play with their hoops as they ran around the barnyard with sticks in their hands, competing to see who could last the longest before the hoops would wobble and fall.

Finally, the spotless table set with clean dishes, she stretched her arms to the sides and then over her head. She had always worked hard at Emma's house, but today, she did more in a few hours than what she usually would do in a whole day. Traveling left her stiff and out of sorts, and last night's sleep had been fitful. Even with the reassurance that Mr. Hopkins and the boys were sleeping in the tent a few paces from the wagon, Abby had startled awake to every small sound. As tired as she felt now, though, she was sure she wouldn't have any trouble sleeping tonight.

"Gentlemen, it's time for supper," she called, descending the back stairs.

Tommy dropped his stick in the dust and let the hoop roll off as he sprinted to her. "Can we come in now? Pa said we needed to let you sleep, but it sure smells like you were cooking. Can you come see my room now?"

She grimaced at the last question. What

would she find upstairs if the downstairs was so dirty? She wasn't sure she could take any more surprises like that tonight. At least the mess gave her hope that if she could do her best job, she would show Mr. Hopkins how much he needed her. It wasn't just a question of taking care of the mess. From the state of the pots and pans, she'd gotten the idea that Mr. Hopkins wasn't a very good cook, either. He was strong and tall but lean. The boys were on the skinny side, too, but with a few weeks of her meals, she was sure that she could have them filling out very nicely.

"Do you want to let your pa and cousin know it's time to eat?"

Without letting go of her hand, Tommy stopped, looked over his shoulder and let out a holler that almost left her deaf. "Auntie House says it's time to eat."

Turning again toward the house, he started to tug again, but she stood her ground. "Is there something else that you need to do before you head on in?" she prompted.

"Nope. I told 'em," Tommy stated matter-of-factly.

"I was thinking about your toys. Do you always leave them in the middle of the yard?"

"Huh?" Tommy glanced around, confused, until he spotted Willy carrying in the other hoop and stick. "Oh. Wait here for me, Abby," he called over his shoulder as he let go of her hand and charged off to collect his forgotten toys.

"Auntie Abby," a deep voice corrected from the open doors of the barn. Mr. Hopkins had been observing from the shadows. Would he be angry for her familiarity with the boys? Would he approve of her work or was there something she had done that upset him? If only she didn't feel like she was on trial.

"Auntie Abby," Tommy repeated.

"Supper's ready," she announced, regretting it immediately since Tommy's voice had probably been heard into the next county.

"So I heard." His voice held dry humor. Could he actually be amused by Tommy's antics?

From across the barnyard, Abby thought the corners of his lips twitched, and she wondered what his smile would look like. Although Mr. Hopkins seemed very reserved with her, the boys didn't fear him. In fact, more than once she watched them climb all over him like playful little pups. From the wagon she had almost been sure she heard him laughing with the boys as they had settled down to sleep by the riverside the night before.

Abby's brother-in-law, Palmer, had never interacted with his children like that. Trying to remember her own father, she felt sadness at the faded memories. Closing her eyes for a brief second, she remembered his scratchy chin nuzzling her at bedtime, after he had read her a story and listened to her prayers. Had they wrestled as well and she just couldn't remember or was it a game reserved for boys only? Her nephews loved to wrestle each other and she delighted in tickling them. How would they be doing now?

Tommy ran back to her and started his now familiar tugging on her arm. "Let's go!"

"Okay." She smiled again and let him pull her along.

"Tomas Daniel!" It was a command, not a shout, but it brought Tommy up short and got her attention, as well. "You should never *pull* a lady. You need to learn to walk at *her* pace," Mr. Hopkins instructed his son, having almost caught up to them with his long strides. He let the others enter first, holding the door open when they reached the porch.

Another young man stood there, too. He was thin and tall, with the same sandy-brown hair and light blue eyes as Mr.

Hopkins, and he stood waiting on the porch while she and the boys washed their hands in the sink. Abby wondered where the other man had been as she hurried around to make sure that the table was ready. The boys scampered to their places at the table and climbed up, Tommy kneeling on his chair so he could reach.

"Miss Stewart." Mr. Hopkins turned to the younger man next to him. "I'd like to introduce you to my nephew, Jake Hopkins."

The poor boy's face was beet-red. He looked everywhere but at her. He nodded and mumbled something that she couldn't quite understand.

"It's nice to finally meet you, Master Hopkins. I hope you didn't have too much work to do while your uncle collected me from the train."

"Um, no, ma'am, I mean miss." His voice cracked between words and then he dropped the soap his uncle had just handed him. Although Abby had not thought it possible, his face turned even redder.

"She's Auntie Abby," Tommy corrected, leaving both Abby and Jake with an uncomfortable situation. It was obvious that he was a teen and could not as easily call her auntie, especially since he was living with his uncle.

Mr. Hopkins settled the matter. "Around here we usually use just first names for the boys, so you can address him as Jake. No need for master or mister." He didn't offer for her to call him by his first name, which was just as well. She wasn't sure she wanted to be on a first-name basis with her employer, either.

After a pause, she decided to change the subject. "I hope you're all hungry. I made enough to feed an army."

After everyone was seated, Mr. Hopkins asked for God's blessing on the food and the hands that prepared it. He also asked for wisdom and grace for the adjustments to come. Abby enjoyed the boys' constant chatter as they filled their cousin in on all the things that they saw on their trip into town. It was becoming evident that it was not a common event.

Before she thought it was possible, all the plates were empty once again. "You cook really good. Gooder than Pa. He always burns everything," Tommy announced.

"It was really good," Willy confirmed. He had not yet directed any comments to her. Now that he had, she felt as if she had won a prize.

"The boys are right. You did a fine job with supper, Miss Stewart. Thank you,

85

especially seeing as how you must be completely tuckered out." Mr. Hopkins's gaze confirmed that he was not just being polite but he meant every word. "Is there anything else you'll need tonight?"

"I still have to make up the bed and clean up here, but I think I'm all set, sir. Thank you." She rose to start clearing the table, and everyone scrambled to help. She had left water heating on the stove so she could make washing dishes a quick job once everyone had cleared out. To her surprise, Mr. Hopkins rolled up his sleeves, poured part of the hot water into a basin in the sink and started to shave off a few slices of soap. Soon he had the dishes in the sudsy water.

"Pa, can we show her our room now?" Tommy pleaded.

"That's up to Miss Stewart. She might just want to get some rest," he answered with his strong forearms submerged in the water.

"Not just yet," she answered Mr. Hopkins, then turned to the boys. "Why don't you help me get the blankets off the line outside before it gets too dark and then you can show me your room? I think you said something about blocks your pa made for you. I'd like to see those tonight even if we don't have time to play. Tomorrow we'll

86

have time to explore and see just how much you can teach me about your house."

"I'm not a teacher," Tommy giggled. "That's your job."

"But you know lots about where the clothes are, where the tub is for washing the clothes and what your favorite foods are. You can teach me all those things while I teach you how to read. I even brought some books so I can read you some stories when we get settled."

"Could you read us one tonight? Please?" Tommy cajoled.

After offering to take over the dishes again and being assured everything was under control, she turned to the boys. "How 'bout you help me with my bedding first? Then we'll see what time it is. Maybe your pa wants you to be in bed soon."

She sought a confirming look from her employer but found him silently staring at her. "How 'bout we talk in just a minute, once you're done getting the bedding?" he suggested, and turned back to the dishes before she could answer.

Her new room smelled fresher now. She stood back and inspected her work . . . Well, the work she did after the boys "helped" her to make her bed. One more thing she would need to add to her list of lessons for them. Mr. Hopkins had come into the room with a bed key and tightened the ropes under the mattress so it no longer sagged. She closed the window most of the way, leaving only a crack open so the air could continue to circulate without the bugs eating her alive.

"Excuse me, Miss Stewart. Did you want me to put your chest and boxes in your room now or leave them here?" Mr. Hopkins stood right outside her door, awaiting her answer. He took up the majority of the doorway with his broad shoulders and muscled forearms perched on each side of the door frame.

"If you could bring them in here, that would be very nice. Thank you. You could put them right there." She pointed to the corner under the window and moved so he could get past her even as the boys climbed onto the bed.

"Boys, it's time to go get ready for bed." His statement was met with groans, but neither boy argued as they left the room. He looked up to see her watching and grinned as if he knew a secret.

"Now," he whispered, "Tommy will be back in five seconds to ask if you can read —"

"Pa, can Auntie House read to us?" Tommy shuffled back into the room right on time.

Abby fought not to laugh out loud as Mr. Hopkins gave her a knowing glance and a wink above Tommy's head.

"I was about to talk to her about that, but if you don't get ready for bed, there won't be time for anything other than prayers." His voice was as stern as ever and didn't give away the humor Abby read in his eyes.

"But she could come for prayers, couldn't she?" Tommy persisted.

"Tomas Daniel," Mr. Hopkins said in a deep, low voice.

"Yes, Pa. I'm going but, please." The boy was close to whining.

"Go get ready for bed." The command left no room for argument.

Tommy left the room, walking like a man sentenced to face the firing squad. Abby watched him walk away and then turned to find Mr. Hopkins watching her with a guarded expression, the lighthearted humor forgotten.

"You don't have to go upstairs and help with bedtime, Miss Stewart. You've done more than I expected today. Is there anything you need?"

Disappointment sliced through her. Why

should it matter if she helped the boys into bed or not? But it did. She wanted to hear the prayers and kiss their foreheads just as she had done with her nieces and nephews for the last fourteen years.

"I would love to read them a story if it's all right with you." She bit her lower lip, trying to find a nice way to imply that he might not want her involved in such a private family time. "I don't know your routine with the boys. What they do at bedtime or what you will expect me to do in the days to come."

"Well, it will take some time to get used to having a woman around here again," he stated cryptically.

"I imagine. I was wondering . . . I don't want to ask anything that's none of my business, but just how long has it been since a woman lived here?"

A shadow passed over his face for a minute and she held her breath, afraid she had just offended her employer on her first day there.

"It's been two years since my wife's aunt left." His vague answer left her with more questions instead of answers. Did the boys still miss their great-aunt? How much time would she have to work here before the end of the harvest? Should she hold them at arm's length so that when she left, they wouldn't miss her too much? Would it even be possible to hold them at arm's length? After only two days, Tommy already tugged on her heartstrings and somber, grouchy Willy seemed to dare her to love him.

Minutes later she was sitting between the two boys on the side of Tommy's bed, reading to them. By the time she had finished the story, not only had Tommy climbed up on her lap, but Willy had slid over to look over her shoulder at the pictures. Story done, they took turns petitioning God with their heartfelt prayers for the cows, the horses, family they had never met, for their pa and their cousin, and they included her, as well. She said a few prayers of her own. Her thoughts traveled from her sister's family to the Gibbonses and then all the people she had met on her trip. She asked for God's blessing on this new family that she felt privileged to know.

When she gave a kiss good-night to Tommy, he insisted that his big brother needed kisses, too. She willingly complied and grinned when Willy groaned but turned his face toward her instead of away from her. As she stood, Mr. Hopkins cleared his throat. His eyes had a glassy look to them and she wondered if that was a good sign or not.

CHAPTER FOUR

The horses had settled in for the night as if it were the most common thing in the world for Will and Jake to be sleeping up in the hay loft. It was reminiscent of his boyhood visiting his grandparents' farm, when he and his cousins would get to sleep with one of the uncles up in the loft. It reminded him again of all the things his boys were missing out here. Back East, two of his sisters were already married and were starting families of their own. When would his boys meet their cousins?

But his parents understood why he had to stay. Why he had to make this work. It was not just his dream. It had been Mathew's dream first. Up here, in the loft he had built with Mathew, it felt as if his brother were still here on the farm. Will missed him with a deep sadness even after all these years. Sleeping up here with Jake, a replica of Mathew at age sixteen, brought back a flood of memories.

Mathew was five years older than Will. He'd always dreamed of going West to claim a large homestead. When Mathew married MaryAnn, they'd planned to move West just as soon as they saved enough to buy a homestead. Will worked at his father's store hoping to earn enough money to outfit his own wagon and tag along for the adventure of a lifetime. At nineteen, he still couldn't own land, but he could help Mathew settle. Two years later, he could claim the land nearby once he was of age. Everything had worked according to plan — except his marrying Caroline.

At first, Caroline came to Will's father's store to buy little things like penny candy or ribbons for her flaxen hair, but as time passed, Will noticed she often came and spent time there without buying anything. He invited her to a church social in the fall and they got along well. Somehow, without realizing it, he managed to take her to each of the socials and even walked her home from the store a time or two. Most people assumed they were courting and Will didn't do anything to discourage the idea. She was pretty enough and popular. He should have paid more attention when she started bringing sweets she had baked herself. But he hadn't seen the harm. Everyone knew he'd be leaving soon with Mathew and Mary-Ann. Yet he couldn't help noticing that every time he mentioned homesteading, Caroline would change the subject or tell of all the perils she had read in the newspapers and dime-store novels.

By February, he and Matt began the process of outfitting their rigs and laying aside the supplies. His head was so full of adventure he didn't pay too much attention to what was going on around him.

Just four weeks before they were to leave, Caroline came crying to the house late one night, making a big scene about his leaving her. He offered to drive her back to her home in his father's buggy, planning to explain to her on the way that they had no future together. Memories of that night still flooded his head. If only he had taken one of his sisters along.

"I'm sorry, Caroline," he tried to console her, holding the reins loosely, guiding the horses to her drive. "I never said anything about us being anything other than friends. I guess you just came to the wrong conclusions. I don't think you would be happy with me. You like your pretty clothes and your nice parties and that's all good and fine, but I'm traveling out to the frontier. There are no shops for pretty clothes out there. There are no parties to go to on Christmas Eve."

"But," she gasped, tears streaming down her cheeks, her nose red and runny, "you took me to all the socials. I told my friends that surely you would ask me to be your wife. I started on my dress and asked Julie to be my bridesmaid. You could wait for a few more months. Let Mathew and MaryAnn go this year and then we could meet them there next year. . . ."

"No, I'm not getting married now! I'm just nineteen. I want to live life without being tethered to a wife and a family. I'm sorry you started to make plans, but I never said . . ." He stopped the buggy but sat still, wanting to finish their conversation in the semiprivacy of her yard, blanketed in shadows.

"You're leaving me!" Her cry was shrill and carried across the quiet night.

"I'm going with Mathew and MaryAnn. I've been dreaming about it for years now. You knew my plans."

"But I thought you loved me. I thought we'd get married in the spring!"

"Caroline, I'm sorry. I don't mean to hurt you, but I don't —" Before he could continue, she threw herself in his arms, kissing him soundly on the mouth. The force of her movement almost toppled them off the buggy seat and he reached out, catching her shoulders with his hands to keep them both from falling. Before he could set her away from himself, he heard the creak of the front door opening. Caroline's father stepped out and glared at him.

"Caroline, what is the meaning of this!" Mr. Kellogg roared.

"Oh, Papa!" she exclaimed, spinning around with a smile on her face. "I've got such wonderful news. Will just asked me to marry him and of course I accepted. I suppose we shouldn't have been celebrating quite like this, but I was just so happy to finally hear him admit how much he loves me."

Will remembered feeling numb. Completely numb from head to toe — as if someone had dunked him in ice water. What had he just heard? Had Caroline gone completely mad? Hadn't she heard a word he had said? He was starting out on the adventure of a lifetime in just a few weeks and he had no plans of taking her along.

"Well, boy, now that you've sampled the goods, I expect you to make my daughter an honest woman." Mr. Kellogg clenched his fists at his side and stared Will down as if daring him to refuse Caroline. Swallowing hard, he nodded. Realizing too late Mr. Kellogg would take it as an affirmation of all Caroline had said.

"I expected you to come and talk with me first, like a respectable man would, boy, but I guess there's not much I can do about it now. How do you plan on supporting my daughter?"

"Pa, he's got a job with his father at their store. You have nothing to worry about," Caroline answered, taking Will's hand in her own and squeezing as if they were the happiest of couples.

"Then I expect you to come here tomorrow night and have dinner with us, young man. I have a few more questions to ask you, but it's late and it won't do to ruin Caroline's reputation by causing a scandal out here. Come along, Caroline, it's time to go inside." Mr. Kellogg assisted his daughter down from the buggy, eyeing Will with a stern look the entire time.

Will finally found his voice. "Yes, sir. I'll see you tomorrow evening." He waited in stunned silence until their door closed behind them and then somehow made his way back to his own home in a fog. What had just happened? How was he going to get out of it? One thing he was certain of. He had planned and dreamed of homesteading in Nebraska, and no one, not even Mr. Kellogg or conniving Caroline, was going to keep him from traveling with his brother. If Caroline insisted on the farce of a marriage with him, it would be on his terms.

The next night, his worst fears were confirmed. Caroline and her mother had already started to make preparations for the wedding. In the days that followed, Will felt trapped in a whirlwind of activities, each one pulling him closer to his doom.

Three days before they were to leave for Nebraska, he and Caroline were married in a small ceremony with his family, her family and a few close friends on hand. At first, he resented Caroline's high-handed way of trapping him into a marriage, but he tried to get along with her. For the first month of travel, she also tried to humor him. Soon all facade fell away as the trip became more demanding. How Mathew and MaryAnn put up with his black moods and Caroline's simpering and sniping sometimes astounded him. Just as he had assumed, Caroline whined about the lack of stores, creature comforts or even basic necessities out on the trail.

Now he looked back and wondered if there had been some other way to avoid hurting each other. She never adapted to the prairie. He never gave in to her demands to move back. At some point, he stopped trying to make her happy. At first, he tried to be a good husband, providing for her needs, helping with the children, but she always found something to complain about.

He didn't regret his boys, however. They were the only good thing that came out of his rushed marriage. They were his inspiration to make the farm a success. Someday they would inherit all that his hands had labored to build. With God's blessings, he wanted to leave them a legacy — something they could in turn pass down to their children. Jake would also be part of the inheritance. His father and mother's dreams had brought them out West to begin with. Will vowed to leave Jake the legacy that Mathew once dreamed of giving his son.

Sighing, he decided to turn the night, his efforts and the coming days over to the Lord. He just wished God would let him know what to do about Miss Stewart.

Just the night before, he'd known that the men in the area would be interested in his housekeeper, and now he was even more certain. She was pretty and soft-spoken, and if dinner had been any indication, she could cook. Both boys were already quite taken with her, and poor Jake hadn't been able to string two coherent words together at the table. Out here, the lack of eligible women meant that even women long in the tooth or dull-witted were courted by many eligible bachelors. Miss Stewart would cause a stampede. Exactly what Will wanted to avoid, for the sake of his own peace of mind, and Miss Stewart's well-being.

He regretted having stopped at the Scotts' homestead earlier in the day, too. Since this coming Sunday was only the second of the month, they still had two more weeks before there'd be another service, and news would spread. Hopefully by then, he would have some idea as to what to do for Miss Stewart. After all, her pastor had written a letter putting her care and well-being in his hands. He would see to her safety and provisions — and it wouldn't be too hard to do if the fringe benefits were meals like the one they had had earlier. But he wouldn't let himself get too attached. Once she realized what life on the prairie really meant, Miss Stewart wouldn't be staying long — he was certain of that.

The first twinges of pink and orange were streaking the sky to the east when Abby groaned, stretched and struggled out of bed. She had slept well for the first night since leaving Emma's house. Seeing the sun pushing up into the sky, she quickly dressed and brushed her hair.

Today she would take inventory of the house. She needed to scrub every single floor, wall and ceiling before she would be satisfied, but she also needed to see about clothing for the boys, do the washing, clean out the pantry . . . The list went on and on and Mr. Hopkins never did really tell her if he planned for her to stay or if he was set on taking her back into town next week. He had said she could stay until the harvest, but that was when he'd thought she'd be staying with the Scotts. Did the deal still hold true? She shook off her fears. There was no point in wondering about it. Until he told her otherwise, she was still employed as a housekeeper. Her first job was to determine what the most pressing need was and concentrate on it.

Lighting the fire in the stove was actually easier than on Emma's stove. She put water on to boil and then started to look through the pantry. The milk from last night had been kept in a jar and placed in the root cellar under the stairs, so she went down and found it. She wondered if there were fresh eggs.

Heading back upstairs, she heard the kitchen door squeak and paused for a second. Surely it must be Mr. Hopkins, but there was no other noise, as if someone was sneaking in. Fear for the boys' safety sent her rushing back up the stairs, a milk jug clenched in her fist as her weapon.

"Miss Stewart?" The whispering voice was deep and sent her heart into her throat as she reached the kitchen.

"Mr. Hopkins?" she squeaked out, as if anyone else would know she was here, much less come into the kitchen unannounced at this time of the day.

He stood at the doorway into the main house but spun around as she answered. His grin confirmed he realized how silly her question was. It also confirmed her suspicion that he was a handsome man when he smiled. "Good morning, Miss Stewart. Did you rest well?"

"Yes, sir. Did you?" she asked as she set the milk on the counter, commanding her heart to stop beating so loudly. She was afraid the noise would wake the boys.

"I rested very well, thank you." His tone was light and friendly. "Is there something you need?"

"I didn't know if I needed to gather the eggs. Do you need me to go and milk the cows first thing in the morning? Do the boys get up on their own or do you wake them at a particular time?"

He looked at her strangely. "Miss Stewart, do you know how to milk a cow?"

"No, sir. But I learn quickly," she assured him, afraid he would think about taking her back to the train station.

"Well, it's just as well. I'll do the milking if that's all right with you. My cows are my girls and they are very stingy with anyone else. As for the hens, I'll take you out to the henhouse and show you around in a little bit. This morning, however, I brought the eggs and milk." To prove the statement, he backtracked out the door, bent down and reemerged with a pail of milk and a basket of eggs.

"Thank you. Is there something special you would like to eat this morning?" Abby asked, hoping to get off on the right foot.

"Anything other than burnt oatmeal would be ambrosia."

"Ambrosia! I had thought that we'd try for something simple like pancakes and bacon. I'm not sure that I can come up with ambrosia," she teased, knowing that if the pots from the day before were a hint to the breakfasts that were the normal fare at the kitchen table, her mother's light, fluffy pancake recipe would be well received.

The boys and Jake were drawn like flies to

the kitchen as soon as she started frying bacon. By the time they washed and dressed, she had a stack of pancakes she figured would hold them for the time being. Instead of eating with the rest, she stood at the stove and continued to flip pancakes, keeping a steady flow coming until everyone had eaten their fill. Jake and the boys made quite a few comments about burnt oatmeal and other cooking failures. Mr. Hopkins took the ribbing in stride and didn't seem at all put out with the boys or his nephew. The easy teasing was refreshing after all the tense meals at her brother-in-law's table.

As soon as the boys and Jake headed out to the barn, the kitchen became silent. The dirty dishes were stacked once again in the sink, but this time Mr. Hopkins remained seated, sipping his coffee as he watched her take the griddle off the stove. "You haven't eaten anything yet," he commented, bringing her attention away from the dishwater.

"Um . . ." A plate sat on the back of the stove for her as soon as she finished the dishes.

"Have a seat. Eat while they're still warm. Then you can wash everything at once. They were very good, by the way. Ambrosia." He smiled, standing to pull out a chair for her.

"Thank you." She acknowledged his compliment but still felt a little shy as she set her plate on the table, sprinkled sugar over the pile and then returned to the stove for her own cup of coffee. "Would you like some more?" She waved the coffeepot toward him. At his nod, she filled his cup back up before taking her seat again. He returned to his own and sat watching her eat. After a minute he shifted.

"Right after breakfast we usually take the boys with us to the barn and have them sorta help with chores. They're not big enough to handle a shovel and muck out the stalls, so we have them curry the horses while Jake and I do the heavy work. It keeps them occupied and within sight. Now with you here, we can start leaving them in the house, but it means you'll have them underfoot in here. Or would you rather we make them do their chores while you do whatever you need to do in the morning?"

"I'd never presume to tell you what to do, Mr. Hopkins. I am more than willing to care for them the entire day and find ways to get my work done with them 'underfoot' as you say. I also know they need to learn lessons you can teach them in the barn and in the fields. Things I have no knowledge about. I'll leave the decisions to you. Just let me know what you decide."

"Fine," he agreed with a nod of his head. "Then we'll plan on them coming out to help with barn chores right after breakfast. Then they can come back in and you can give them something to work on, whatever works well with your plans. Since you're new to the farm, I'd like to tell you what the boys can and can't do." He paused, waiting for her to acknowledge him, but she had a mouthful of pancake so all she could do was nod. His eyes twinkled and she wondered fleetingly if he had done that on purpose to fluster her.

"They are not allowed to play in the barn or barnyard without an adult with them at *all* times. Little boys tend to move quickly and could spook a cow or horse. An animal's natural reaction would be to kick and that could easily kill a man, let alone a boy. The boys are also not allowed to venture down by the creek or out to the fields on their own. They love to fish and when it gets too hot, we even take them swimming but —" he glanced at her over the coffee cup as he paused to take a sip, his cheeks turning slightly pink "— I don't expect you to have to take them into the water."

The idea of watching the boys fish had a certain appeal as long as they could bait their own hooks. She had never learned to swim, nor did she plan on learning. She would leave the swimming lessons to Mr. Hopkins.

"That sounds reasonable," she said.

"It's not only the animals themselves that pose a threat to the boys. The equipment in the barn is also heavy and some have sharp edges like the saws and the axes. They are not to touch my tools unless *I* am with them. If you need wood chopped or something fixed, please let me know, and I'll get things shipshape."

Again she nodded, the last bite of pancake melting in her mouth. She looked down, chagrined that she had eaten it all. She didn't remember tasting it. Her lukewarm coffee washed the rest of the pancake down and she found Mr. Hopkins's eyes studying her once again.

He had a way of doing that. It made her feel as if he was trying to see into her soul. As if he could really see if she was being truthful or just accommodating. Honestly, she would find it hard to deny him reasonable requests. She was starting to believe again that she had been right to think that God had brought her here. When she'd learned that her Mrs. Hopkins was a *Mr.* Hopkins, she'd started to doubt, to question. But now certainty filled her again. Maybe because the boys pulled on her heartstrings.

It was not that Mr. Hopkins neglected his boys. On the contrary, it was clear that he tried so hard to do everything and he genuinely loved them, but he had no help. Things like table manners, housekeeping and book learning had been forgotten in the attempt to keep the farm running. She wanted to help the boys, teach them what she could and fill them with love and all the mothering they had missed out on these last few years. But what if she were only here for a few weeks or months? Would her presence be missed when she left? Would it be better to keep a distance from the beginning?

No, she couldn't do that. If it was not in God's plan for her to stay, then she'd resign herself to the change later. For now she knew that this was where she belonged, and she'd make the most of it for as long as she could.

"Do you have any questions, Miss Stewart?" he quizzed.

"Well, is there something you want me to work on today? I mean, there are a lot of tasks needing attention." She paused, trying to find a delicate way to say things. "But I was wondering if you have one thing that stands out as more urgent."

"No, ma'am. As you can see, we have been very remiss in our chores around the house, so there is more work to do than I think you'll be able to do in three years." A slight blush colored his ears. "It didn't get this way overni ht, and with the boys always underfoot, you may not have as much time as you are used to for tidying up and such. Whatever it is you decide to do, take your time. Just see to it that you don't wear yourself completely out. And if you need anything, you just let us know. It would be nice to have a noon meal right about mid-day and the dinner ready close to six in the evening. Other than that . . . you women seem to know better than I do what's what."

"I do have another question. Do the boys know where to find the washtub and the soap? Do they know where to find the dirty clothes? Where do you put the clothes that you need mended?"

This time a full-blown smile filled his face, transforming him into a handsome man, looking years younger than he had looked at the train station two days before. "Miss Stewart, that sure sounded like three questions to me." He chuckled good-naturedly and before she could come up with some sort of response, he continued. "Now, this is a farm where no woman has dared invade in more than two years. If it still stays together on its own, we wear it. Once it falls apart, we discard it. I've never learned to thread one of those itsy-bitsy needles, much less pull one through some shirt that's just gonna get mistreated again."

"I see your point. You may find that I try and change some of those habits in the days to come. Please let me know if I overstep my bounds." Abby kept from smiling, but she was sure the glint in Mr. Hopkins's eyes matched her own. Glancing around the room, still dirty and gritty everywhere but the sink and countertop where she had cleaned yesterday, she wondered if she had bitten off more than she would be able to chew. The only way to find out was one bite at a time, starting with the breakfast dishes.

"I'll be sure to do that, ma'am."

"Huh?" She turned back to him from her perusal of the room, already mentally planning what she would do first.

"I'll be sure to let you know if you overstep your bounds." He smiled at her, and her heart skipped a beat. "And, yes, the boys know where the soap is kept. The washtub is hanging in the pantry and another in the barn if you need it. Are you planning to wash clothes today?" he questioned softly.

"If it's all right with you, sir," she answered just as softly.

"That'd be fine. I'll just go and start the fire in the yard for you, then. I'll also get the water hauled out there."

"Thank you." Thinking their conversation was done, she stood and she noticed he stood as well, whether to get to work or out of respect, she wasn't sure.

"Um."

His hesitance brought her attention back to him from the dishes she had started to place in the dishwater.

"Breakfast was very good. Thank you."

"My pleasure. I love seeing the boys enjoy their food," she confessed, not mentioning that watching the men devour the food had left her just as satisfied.

"Well, it is nice to have someone who knows what they're doing in the kitchen for once." He chuckled as he left the room. Only after the door shut behind him did Abby dare to look back over her shoulder. Through the window she watched his strong, tall form quickly cross the distance and then disappear into the barn.

CHAPTER FIVE

"Okay, boys, it's about time to go and check on the laundry," Abby called out to the boys playing in the front room.

She had washed all the clothes yesterday and then worked on washing the kitchen cabinets. Today she had tackled the bedding. The sheets and covers from all four beds upstairs were hanging on the lines in the yard and she had swept the rooms out, including the cobwebs from the corners and the ceilings. Her arms ached, but she was happy with the way things were staring to look — a little more civilized. Given another few weeks, she would have the place clean.

She stepped out of the kitchen and caught Tommy with a hand up under his shirt, scratching again. She had washed that shirt yesterday. Had chiggers or fleas gotten into the wash while it dried yesterday? Her own clothes felt fine. "Come on, boys. Come help me get the sheets for your beds."

They left the city of blocks they were constructing on the floor without complaint but without much enthusiasm, either. As Willy passed her, he scratched his belly, too. Tonight she would insist on a bath for both boys.

Outside, she inspected the bedding and, not finding anything crawling around on it, she carefully took each item down, folded it and placed it in the basket she had found in the pantry. The boys had been subdued the majority of the morning. She wondered if they were already tired of spending their days indoors with her instead of out, playing and working with their father and cousin. It was a depressing thought. She had hoped to become fast friends with them, but chances of that were slim if they were already missing life before her arrival.

With the possibility of little critters on their bodies, Abby opted to leave them playing with their blocks while she wrestled the bedding back on the feather-stuffed mattresses. Making Mr. Hopkins's bed, she let her eyes wander, learning about her employer. Mr. Hopkins had a number of books in his room, stacked on his small nightstand next to the large bed. He had taken his pillow out with him to the barn but had left the rest behind. His clothes had been hung on their pegs on the wall, and his two other pairs of trousers were folded and stacked on the side table under a window. The other piece of furniture in the room was an elaborate dressing table Abby assumed to have been the late Mrs. Hopkins's. Although her things were hidden inside the drawers and a layer of dust sat heavily on everything, it was as if her presence was still in the room.

Did Mr. Hopkins feel the connection to his late wife here, in the room they had shared? Did he miss her terribly? Many men, once they were widowed, didn't wait very long at all to remarry just to have help with the house chores and the children. Society seemed to understand and accept that many second marriages were marriages of need and convenience instead of marriages based on love and friendships, especially on the prairie. Yet Mr. Hopkins hinted he wanted a housekeeper who was older to avoid ideas of marriage. Had his love for his wife been so all-consuming that even a few years after her death, the idea of sharing his life with another woman was unthinkable?

Mr. Hopkins was kind and gentle with just the right sense of humor thrown in. He didn't seem to be a romantic, but what did Abby know about such things? She had never been courted.

A glimpse in the mirror above Mrs. Hopkins's dressing table revealed a disheveled girl who had thin blond hair that never conformed to the knots she fashioned at the nape of her neck and went every which way with the slightest breeze. Her face was slightly flushed with the heat of the late spring sun and the heavy work she had been doing. No wonder no one ever took notice of her.

She hurried to finish straightening out the quilt. It felt as if she were trespassing in a forbidden area. She glanced around once more to make sure everything was in place and then left, closing the door behind her.

Once she was done upstairs, she returned to the living room and found the boys lying on the floor, slowly pushing the blocks around with little interest, both scratching different appendages. For the first time, she noticed that Tommy's cheeks were unnaturally pink and Willy had a glassy look about his eyes.

"Tommy, are you feeling all right?" she asked, anxiously watching his eyes and noting the same glassy look.

"I'm itchy. Som'pin bit me," he complained, and Abby held her breath as she signaled him to come to her.

"Let me see." She sank down on the davenport and reached out for the smaller boy's shirt. He lifted it and she stared, wide-eyed, at the welts all over his torso. "Do you have these anywhere else?"

"Uh-huh, my back is itchy but I can't see it," Tommy whined.

"Let me take a look." She gently turned him. Taking his shirt completely off, she studied the rash marking his back. "You'll be getting this all over in a little while. Willy, do you have these, too?"

"Yeah. They itch!" He was close to tears and Abby groaned, wondering what kinds of medicine and herbs were at her disposal.

When she had been fourteen, she and her nieces and nephews all shared the chicken pox. While it was not any fun, she remembered the doctor telling her it wasn't as dangerous as the smallpox. As long as they kept the fever down and the boys comfortable, they should be all right.

"Well, boys, it looks like you have the chicken pox. We're gonna have to set you in the washtub with some oatmeal so you won't itch so much. I want you to come out to the yard with me and we'll see if we can't help you feel a little better."

"This is silly," Tommy told Abby a little while later as he and his brother sat in the washtub in the shade of the only tree in the barnyard. Willy had been very self-conscious about bathing out in the middle of the yard in broad daylight, but once Abby promised not to look while he stripped down and got in, he quickly complied.

She dragged a stool out from the kitchen and set to mending shirts while the boys splashed each other. She let them play until they looked cool. She helped Tommy out and got him dried off and into his underwear and a large, holey shirt that had obviously once been his father's. Someone had lopped off the sleeves at the elbows so that it would accommodate the boy's shorter arms. Willy insisted on getting himself dressed and demanded she leave him alone. Knowing he was tired, itchy and running a fever, she didn't argue.

Since the front room was cooler than the upstairs, she had them lie down on towels on the floor and she read to them until they were both asleep. While they slept, she checked on dinner and continued to clean the kitchen. She briefly entertained the idea of running out to the far fields to let the men know about the boys, but it wouldn't make any difference in how fast Tommy and Willy got better. In the end she figured it would only worry Mr. Hopkins while he should be concentrating on the fields.

When the boys woke, they were as uncomfortable as they had been earlier and she prayed for patience for the next few days. She settled them to play with the blocks again in the cool of the front room and made frequent trips back to the kitchen. Each time she peeked out to see if the men had returned to the barn. Her heart skipped a beat and then sped up too fast when they finally returned. Would Mr. Hopkins be angry she hadn't told him at once?

"Boys, I'm going to tell your father about the chicken pox. Stay in here and play nicely. I'll be right back." She hurried out to the barn.

"Um, good afternoon, Mr. Hopkins," she called out, making both men spin around from taking the harnesses off the horses. "Jake."

"Good afternoon, Miss Stewart." Mr. Hopkins studied her carefully, his eyes then darting to the house and around the yard. "Is everything all right?" The concern in his voice matched his gaze.

"Um . . . yes. I was able to do the washing and dinner's on the stove, but . . ." She bit her lip. How should she tell him? What if he decided to take them to the doctor and leave her at the train station on the way? She hadn't even been in the house for a full three days!

"Is there something you need, Miss Stewart?" Mr. Hopkins's gaze froze her in place. He knew something was afoot.

"I just wanted to tell you that the boys have chicken pox. They started itching just after lunch and now they're covered in the rash. I gave them a bath in oatmeal and lukewarm water and then they took a nap, but I wanted you to know. I can handle this, sir. I took care of my nieces and nephews when we all got the chicken pox a few years ago. It wasn't pleasant, but it's not too dangerous as long as we can control the fevers and keep them from scratching."

"Are you sure it's chicken pox, Miss Stewart?" Mr. Hopkins quizzed her as he all but dragged her by her upper arm toward the house. His grasp was firm but not painful. "Jake, see to the horses. I'll be out in a bit," he called over his shoulder as an afterthought.

"Yes, sir. I remember it well from when I had it myself. And then two years ago, Katie and Peter had it and I took care of them, as well. Since I had already had it, I couldn't get it again and I . . . Well, Emma was not interested in trying to keep her children comfortable." Abby bit her top lip to stop from rambling.

"Auntie Abby, I want some more water," a small, cranky voice called out to her as they crossed the kitchen.

"Okay, darling, I'll get you some in just a minute," Abby answered the child, watching Mr. Hopkins to see what his reaction was.

"Pa, Pa!" both boys chorused. They climbed to their feet with less energy than normal, but they still embraced him as he bent down and put himself at their eye level.

"Hey, boys, I heard we have some turkey pox around here," he teased, but the look in his eyes belied his lighthearted banter.

"Auntie Abby said it was chicken pox," Willy corrected. "Right?" he confirmed with a confused glace at Abby.

"Yes, I'm just teasing," Mr. Hopkins re-assured the boy. Nodding he turned and studied Abby. "Do they need a doctor? The nearest one is a day's ride past Twin Oaks."

"No, as long as we keep them cool and comfortable, they should be fine." Abby infused her voice with confidence. She had nursed the others through this. Maybe this was the opportunity she needed to prove she was indispensable here. "Have you and Jake had it?"

"Yes, ma'am." He stood and once again towered over her. "I had it when I was a little younger than Tommy is now. Jake had it the fall before . . . before his parents died. I'll go see about those chores now. Is there anything else you need?" he asked, his attention on his boys.

"Do you have willow bark or something else to keep fevers down?"

"Yes, ma'am, although I don't know how to use the stuff. I bought some just in case when we were in town last fall. There was a bad flu here last year. I wanted to be sure I had some on hand."

"If you would show me where I can find it?"

"Yes, ma'am." Mr. Hopkins gave Tommy's shoulder a squeeze and ruffled Willy's hair. "I'm going with Miss Stewart and then out to the barn to milk old Bess and the other girls. You mind Miss Stewart, now."

Later that night, after the men had bathed the boys once more, Abby stood next to the bed and tucked the boys in their beds. She had listened from the rocking chair near the window as Mr. Hopkins read three stories before their prayer time. Dispensing hugs and kisses to the miserable boys, she had headed downstairs to go to her room when she heard the boys calling out for their father. Since he'd already gone out to the barn, she went up and found herself once again seated on the rocking chair. This time she settled it between their twin beds. She read to them and sang songs she had learned as a small girl from her mother.

When they both were finally asleep, she brought a pillow and the quilt from her own bed and settled on the floor between them so she would be able to hear them whenever they woke. As it turned out, they woke frequently. She didn't sleep more than an hour at a time. By the time the sun was peeking over the horizon, her eyes felt gritty but she forced herself to start breakfast for the men.

The next few days were long and miserable for the boys and Abby. She tried to humor them with stories and singing. More than a few times, she spent hours just holding them on her lap in the rocking chair. Even Willy called for her the minute he woke up. She would bathe them three or four times a day and would always be ready with another glass of water and some bread or cookies. Meals had been simple soups so she could leave them simmering while she spent time with the boys.

"I'm sorry, Mr. Hopkins. I made rabbit stew with potatoes again. I wish I had more time. . . . I'll have a better meal for us tomorrow," Abby blurted out as soon as Mr. Hopkins had finished saying the blessing on Wednesday night. "I haven't had a chance yet to mop the floors or dust upstairs. I'll get to it as soon as —"

He raised his eyebrows and looked steadily at her as if she were a stranger from another planet. "This is the best rabbit stew that has ever been served at this table and your bread fills in all the rest of the space in our empty bellies. You've been taking care of two sick boys. I don't know how you got to making dinner at all. Don't worry about the housework. It'll still be there in a week from now." He chuckled and returned his gaze to his plate.

That night the boys fell asleep earlier, so she took advantage of the quiet house and scrubbed the kitchen floor until it returned to its original color. Her back protested by the end. If felt as if a hundred splinters still stuck in her hands and knees, but the kitchen was finally clean enough to satisfy her just as Tommy called from upstairs again.

Will wondered what was going on inside the house as he milked the cows. There was no smoke rising from the chimney. In the week since Miss Stewart had arrived, she managed to be up and ready by the time he brought in fresh milk each day. They had all started to get used to the little touches she brought to the house. Although the boys had the chicken pox, they still were eating more than they had before. She had yet to burn anything. Even Jake commented about how nice it was to have two socks without holes and a shirt that had all its buttons.

His wonder changed to worry when he walked into the kitchen, ready to receive the cup of coffee she always had ready by then, only to find the stove still cool and no sign of his housekeeper. Had something happened to her or the boys during the night? Surely if there was something wrong with the boys, she would have alerted him.

Pacing in the kitchen didn't get him any answer, so he quietly headed out to her room, debating if he should knock or just wait in the front room, but the problem was already resolved when he reached her door. It was open. Her bed looked as if it had not been touched and there was no sign of her in any of the other first-floor rooms or in the root cellar.

For a moment, rational thought fled, and he was left with nothing but the deep, aching fear that told him she had left. *She's just like Caroline and Auntie Shelia.* His thoughts ran away, making his stomach churn with anger. *She ran off already.* It was what he had expected, but it still made him furious. At her, for leaving them in the lurch, and at himself for believing — even just for a few days — that he might actually have found a woman he could rely on.

But before the anger had a chance to build, common sense reasserted itself. She couldn't have run off. Where would she have gone in the middle of the prairie? She knew no one out here. The closest neighbors were an hour's ride away by horse, and all the horses were still in the barn.

Rushing up to the boys' room, he held his breath and listened carefully, hoping against his better judgment to hear her soft murmuring with one of his sons, but there was only silence. Similar lumps on each of the twin beds confirmed that both boys were sound asleep and fine. Disappointment knifed him in the gut.

Where could she be? He checked his own room, Jake's and even Matt and MaryAnn's. Neither he nor Jake had ever cleaned out that room. Returning back to check on his boys, he stood at the doorway, wondering where she could have gone off to. Turning to retrace his steps, he halted abruptly and turned around, rubbing his eyes. Two small, shapely bare feet were sticking out past the end of Willy's bed. Drawing closer, he couldn't believe his eyes; she was asleep on a pallet on the floor between the twin beds. Why?

He wanted to shout for joy and yell at her for her foolishness in the same breath. How could she be sleeping on the floor? What was wrong with her bed? She could have used his bed or Jake's if she hadn't wanted to be on the first floor. Was she secretly scared of sleeping in the house without another adult? If she had just said something, he would have tried to find yet another solution.

He knelt down beside her and gently shook her shoulder. "Miss Stewart? What are you doing sleeping on the floor?"

It took her a minute to wake up. "Are the boys okay?" Her voice was gravelly. She rubbed her eyes and blinked at him. Something caught in his throat and he turned away for a moment. Even in her sleepy state she was obviously aware of where she was. Ignoring him, she sat up and checked one sleeping form and then the other.

Will studied the face of the young woman. Why hadn't he noticed yesterday how tired she was? Was she getting sick herself? When she had mentioned something about not getting anything done with the boys sick, he brushed it off as something to be expected with them underfoot all the time. After all, he had plowed and planted his fields in half the time of last year and covered three times more acreage with the boys in the house. If God granted him the sunshine, rain and heat necessary, his wheat crop would be three times as large as last year's.

But as he watched her try and force herself awake with those telling dark circles under her eyes, he realized he hadn't been paying attention to his home. The boys had been sick and all he had done to help was oversee their bath after dinner and then help Abby . . . Miss Stewart get them into bed. Tommy insisted Auntie Abby be there when they said their prayers. Why hadn't he noticed her fatigue?

"How much sleep did you get last night?" he asked, remembering the clean floor in the kitchen. Had she stayed up and scrubbed the floor on top of everything else?

"I don't know. They slept better last night. I think the worst is probably over." She glanced outside, and color drained from her face. She wrapped her arms around her middle and he remembered the same gesture when she was sick in the alleyway back in Twin Oaks the first day. Her eyes filled with fear.

"Are you all right?"

"I'm sorry I overslept. I need to get downstairs and start breakfast. If you'll just give me a moment —"

"No. You need a few more hours of sleep." He reached out his large hand, placing it on her thin shoulder, and stopped her from standing. "Go sleep in your own bed for a few hours."

Instead of looking pleased, she looked crushed. "I'm sorry. I'll get breakfast going and then there's all the —"

"There's nothing wrong with needing more sleep," he said, more gruffly than he intended to. What drove her? She was almost falling over from weariness and yet she was apologizing for not having breakfast ready.

As he watched, her eyes filled with tears and she turned her face into her hands and sniffed. She stood and fled the room. He watched her leave. "What did I say this time?" he asked himself out loud.

Minutes later, he slunk back down the stairs, careful not to make too much noise so Miss Stewart could sleep. Except he could have made as much noise as he wanted because standing in the kitchen, her feet still bare, was Abby, trying to fill the coffeepot with water from the pump. Tears streaking her face, she wiped them away quickly with the back of her hand as she turned her shoulder to him.

"Why aren't you resting?" he asked, frustration darkening his words.

"I need to make breakfast. You can't go out and plant on an empty stomach."

"I'm not planting today. You need a rest. I didn't realize how much work the boys had been, being sick and all. I'll get breakfast ready. Don't worry about it."

She looked so fragile and small, trying to wake from her exhausted slumber just a few minutes before, and now barefoot and crying in the kitchen.

He had seen enough tears from Caroline to last a lifetime, but they had never made him as uncomfortable as Miss Stewart's tears. Maybe that was due to his suspicion that Caroline's tears had been a display to manipulate many a situation in her favor. Miss Stewart's were obviously sincere, and the result of exhaustion. In fact, she had worked very hard since the first day she stepped across the threshold and hadn't murmured a single complaint.

To take care of her basic needs would only be the Christian thing to do, especially since she had worked herself to exhaustion caring for his family. It was easy to see why the boys were taken with her. He had seen her when she read to them at night, cuddling Tommy on her lap and wrapping an arm around Willy's shoulders. She had won them over with her kind words and affection. It was only right that they take care of her as if she were part of the family, too — even if it were only for the summer.

That excuse seemed to fit. He clung to it and squared his shoulders, ready to do battle with the feisty, crying lady. She was going to get some sleep, even if he had to force her to.

She hadn't responded to what he had said, just kept going through the motions of putting breakfast together. She set the water on the stove. Picking up the bread from yesterday, she started to slice it.

"Why don't you sit down and I'll cut it up for you?" He stood right beside her and reached out for the knife. She released it with a weariness resembling surrender.

"I'm sorry. I was going to do this. I usually have more energy than this. I know you need to get out to the fields and I don't want to slow your progress down. I wanted to —"

"I've done more this week than I did in three last year. You've already more than earned your keep." Suddenly it made sense, the way she was wearing herself down, refusing to stop working — she was worried he would send her back East without a referral because she had not been able to keep up with her chores. "You could'a told me they weren't letting you get any rest. I would have come in from the fields earlier so you could have taken a nap, or I could have had them sleep out in the barn with me."

"That's just what I want!" she almost shouted back, clearly frazzled. "I come here to take care of your boys and your home and end up forcing everyone else to sleep out in the barn. I could sleep out in the barn, Mr. Hopkins. Then everyone else could have their own rooms back."

Abby stood looking out the window, her fingers clutching fistfuls of skirt at her thighs. Her tears had stopped but were threatening to spill over the long blond eyelashes framing her expressive eyes.

Standing close, studying her profile, he saw the light glint off the specks of blue and green in her eyes, changing from green to blue and back again with every word she spoke.

"That's not going to happen here, miss. You won't be sleeping out in the barn when there's a perfectly good house here that'd be more comfortable and safer. Now, why don't you just go to bed and get some sleep!" He was too exasperated by the girl to keep his voice down.

She didn't look at him but spun away and fled to her room. He could hear her muffled sobs a few minutes later when he went as far as the hallway to check on her. He couldn't bring himself to knock on the door. Ma had once said that a woman just needed a good cry every once in a while. He hoped that was all she needed.

When Tommy appeared in the kitchen a while later, Will motioned his son to be quiet. He was amazed Tommy didn't question him until he was seated at the table.

"Pa, where is Auntie Abby? She wasn't in my room when I woke up. I like it when she's there 'cuz she gives me kisses on my head and then helps me get my shirt all buttoned up right."

Inspecting Tommy's shirt, Will realized that Abby's help had been missed. "Here, son, let me help you." He rebuttoned his son quickly as he explained, "Auntie Abby was really tired today because of all the hard work she's been doing around here for us. I told her to go get some sleep so she could play with you boys later. We're gonna be real quiet this morning so she can rest, okay?"

"Yeah, we can be real quiet like we have to be when she's rocking me and Willy is asleep." Tommy's sweet voice added to Will's guilt. His boys had been up in the nights, miserable and grumpy, and he hadn't been there for them. At least Abby had been.

"Pa, we gonna wait for Auntie Abby to make us breakfast?"

"No, I've got it all fixed already," Will answered, ignoring his son's groan.

"But, Pa, I like the way Auntie Abby makes breakfast. She doesn't make it start on fire."

"Hey, that was only once. I was doing better lately. I fried some eggs and put them on bread with butter." Lifting the platter from the back of the stove, he set it on the table and sat down in his spot.

"I like butter. Why didn't we have it before?"

"Because no one took time to churn the butter. We were always too busy with —"

"Pa, can we make Auntie Abby my new ma?" Tommy's question stopped Will's lungs midbreath. Neither boy had ever mentioned having another mother.

"No. She came to be the housekeeper, and

she's not here to stay. She's going to go back," he stated as calmly as he could still gasping for breath. He should have thought about how attached the boys would get to her. After all, she was the first woman who had ever shown them any real affection.

"But I don't want her to go back. I want her to stay here with me, forever and ever. She says 'I love you' and kisses us when she puts us to bed. I want her to do that all the time. I want —"

"There are lots of things that we want in life, Tommy. Most of them we never get," Will retorted sharply.

"But she's really pretty and she sews really good, too. She made a shirt for Willy and is almost done with mine. She said she's gonna have something for us men to wear by the time we go to meetin'."

"Tommy, she's a really nice lady, but she's only here for a short time so that she can take care of you and Willy and teach you some book learning this summer. She deserves to go find some nice place to live in a town somewhere not in the middle of the prairie. Then she can get married and have kids of her own."

"You could marry her, Pa. Jenny said her Ma was telling Mrs. Scotts it was high time you got us boys a new ma. I think Auntie

Abby is a good one. She even smells good. Jenny said if you married a new ma, she wouldn't be my ma but my stepmother, and she said that stepmothers beat on their stepchildren. But I don't think Auntie Abby would. Only if I were really bad."

"Well, I have no plan on getting you a new ma," Will stated with enough volume that Tommy sat staring at him for a minute in silence.

Jake chose that moment to come in through the back door, looking around for the new housekeeper. When Will explained that she was resting and that no one was to disturb her, Jake's smile fell and the boy slumped into a chair and waited for his breakfast with a glum expression. Willy finally came down and they all managed to eat the sparse breakfast Will put on the table. Even with the boys still itchy, they all went out to the barn to finish chores.

By dinnertime, Abby made a full meal and had bathed the boys again. She smiled at everyone around the table and thanked them for letting her rest all morning. They all seemed to agree if it meant she was going to go to so much trouble with dinner, including raisin tarts for dessert, they would be willing to let her sleep in more often.

Will had sent the boys up to ready for bed

when he turned and noticed Abby's grimace as she stuck her hands in the dishwater. "Did you burn your hands?" he asked, curious more than worried.

"No, I'm fine," she denied through gritted teeth, a fine line of perspiration dotting her forehead and upper lip.

"Let me see." He stepped closer and almost said a few choice words. Each hand looked like a pincushion with ten splinters or more, and her palms had blisters the size of peas. "What happened?" he demanded, clasping her wrists between the thumb and forefinger of each of his hands to keep them in view.

"Nothing. I'll be fine," she denied again, tugging her arms back without success.

"If it were nothing, you wouldn't have blisters and splinters. Did this happen last night?"

She stood still, not even speaking. He was intently looking at her hands when he noticed her trembling. He looked up to find her eyes on the floor, but her fear was almost palpable. He led her to a chair and pulled it out.

"Have a seat. I'm going to pull these splinters out before they get infected. Why didn't you say something earlier?"

Even as he asked, he gently pushed her

into the seat. He really didn't expect her to answer. He had benefited from all her hard work and yet he hadn't paid attention to her; just one more reminder why he failed in his marriage. Not that he was looking for another marriage — with Abby or anyone else — but that didn't change his responsibility to her as someone in his care. He was not going to let her get close to him, but he should at least let her know she was safe.

Living on the frontier, he always carried a sharp knife sheathed on his belt. Holding it to the flame in the oven for a moment, he wiped it on a clean cloth and sat down in the chair facing Abby.

"Put your hand out like this." He indicated how he wanted her hand over the clean cloth on the table, and then he started to use the tip of his knife to tease the splinters out. He could tell that she wasn't happy with the arrangement, but she didn't make a noise. Brave woman.

"I remember the first time I tried to help my pa with the boxes in the back of the store." He wasn't sure why he started to ramble, but she relaxed slightly, so he continued. "I must have been about Tommy's age. Pa told me to leave them alone, but I wanted to help. I tried to take them apart with my bare hands and got more splinters than I thought possible, but I broke up each and every box. Too bad my pa planned to use the boxes for produce out front." He shook his head self-deprecatingly and chuckled. "After he pulled the splinters out with his pocketknife, he gave me my first pair of work gloves and then we remade the crates."

Will glanced up from his work and noticed that she looked less frightened. In fact, she was smiling a little. "What?" he asked, a little more gruffly than he had intended. Having shared his childhood memories with her made him feel just slightly vulnerable.

"Nothing." She tensed.

"You were thinking something that made you smile. What was it?" he probed, this time keeping his voice soft and his eyes on her hand.

"I was just wondering if you were more like Willy or Tommy when you were a boy." Her voice was so soft he strained to hear it. When he glanced up again, her gaze turned away.

"I think my parents would say that I was as ornery as Willy and as impulsive as Tommy. I know they were always at wits' end to try and do something with me." He grinned at the thought and went back to prying tiny pieces of wood out of her palm.

"This might hurt a little," he warned before he used the tip to slit her skin open just a bit more and then nab the splinter. Her sharp inhale confirmed the sting, but she didn't flinch.

"That was the last one on this hand," he announced, not yet letting go of her wrist. It was soft and small inside his palm and he was reminded how slender she was. It had been a long time since he'd held a woman's hand in his. Before he could dwell on those thoughts, he let her right hand go and set to work on the left.

"So, you have an older sister and . . . ?" He left the sentence hanging as he forced another sliver out.

"It was just the two of us. She was married by the time our father died of the fever and then, a few weeks later, our mother . . ." The catch in her breath softened his heart a little.

"How old her were you then?"

"Twelve, turning thirteen. Emma and Palmer took me in. It was their obligation and they never let me forget it. *I* was an obligation." She bit her bottom lip and he wondered what it must have felt like to grow up not being wanted. "So I did as much as I could not to be a bother. I helped with the children. They are really darling."

At the mention of her nieces and nephews, she smiled until he pulled another sliver out and she winced. "At first they had a house-keeper, but after Palmer offended her, she left and they had me do the majority of the work. I didn't mind. It gave me a purpose and I could see to the children, but Emma was never satisfied with what I did."

"I'm sorry your sister didn't appreciate your work. I certainly do. You've made this place much more like a home than it was before. I don't think I've looked forward to breakfast since MaryAnn died. My brother's wife was a good cook. I miss her — and him."

"I'm sorry. How long ago did they die?" Her compassion brought his focus from her hands to her eyes. He hadn't meant to say that out loud. Only Colin, his pastor and close friend, and Jake knew how hard Matt's death had been for him.

"It's been almost seven years. They headed to town in a sled a few weeks before Christmas to buy gifts and something happened to spook the horses, I guess. They ended up flipping into the river. By the time I went to find them, there was nothing we could do." Will cleared his throat, pushing aside the memories of the mangled sleigh and his brother and sister-in-law still trapped under it in the cold, rushing water.

"I'm sorry." Her voice made the memories recede into the past were they belonged. He cleared his throat once more and returned his focus to her hand that still lay limp in his. He knew she was watching his face, but he didn't dare look up and see pity in her eyes. He had seen enough pity in the eyes of the neighbors at the funerals. "It must get lonely out here with all the responsibilities of the farm now on your shoulders."

Her understanding soothed like a balm. A comfortable silence filled the room. Finally every splinter was out.

"You'll need to wash these and then I think I have some salve in the barn that'll help with the sting. I'll go get it."

"Thank you." She stood and he pumped the water so that she could let it run over her hands.

When he returned, she had almost finished the dishes and he forced himself to breathe deeply and take firm command of his temper before he spoke. Why did she insist on doing things that could hurt her?

"You shouldn't be washing those dirty dishes with your hands all cut up like that. I'll finish up." He was proud he'd kept his voice low.

"I . . ." She looked as if she was about to

explain but dropped her shoulders and turned back to the sink.

"Wash them off and we'll get them all bound up for tonight."

Not waiting for her to answer, he started to pump the water again and let her gingerly wash her hands under the cold spray. Holding out a clean towel, he wrapped her hands in the cloth and patted them dry. He used the salve on the cuts and blisters, some of which had opened while she was washing dishes, and then wrapped her hands in strips of clean cloth.

"Thank you," she whispered, without looking up. "I'm sorry to have troubled you. Is there something else I can do for you tonight?"

"No, you were no trouble. I want you to get some rest and take care of those hands. It won't do for one of those cuts to get infected." He wondered if she thought he saw her as an obligation, as well.

Nothing could be further from the truth. She was worth her slight weight in gold. The house was cleaner than it had ever been since he'd built it. The boys were getting better now and he would never have had any idea how to nurse them through the chicken pox. But he wasn't foolish enough to think that she would stay for too much longer. Sooner or later she would be demanding he pay her way back to civilization. He didn't dare dwell on why that thought bothered him tonight. Must be that he'd been missing another adult to talk with.

She shifted on the chair she was sitting on and he realized it was getting late. His cows didn't like him making them wait come morning, so he'd best be getting off to bed, especially since he was starting to feel a friendship stirring between him and his housekeeper. He'd have to be careful not to get too attached.

But maybe a friendship, knowing she was only going to be there for a short time, wasn't such a bad idea. She needed someone to talk with, as well. Maybe he could make a habit of talking with her after dinner in the evenings — just to see how things were going with the boys and their studies — that type of thing.

"I'm gonna head on out now, unless there's something else you need," he offered, reluctantly standing when she shook her head. "Good night."

"Good night," Abby said softly as he strode out into the night. He shut the door behind him and made sure it was secure.

CHAPTER SIX

Sunday dawned bright and breezy. Abby quickly made breakfast and left a chicken baking with lots of onions, carrots and potatoes floating in the water that half filled the pot. Cooking was so easy now that she had the kitchen set up precisely the way she wanted it. It felt as if she had lived there all her life even though the calendar indicated only three weeks had passed. After breakfast, she made the boys put on their new shirts. They looked very handsome in their dark blue matching shirts and she regretted not having found time to make pants for them yet. Mr. Hopkins and Jake had also cleaned up nicely. They both sported white shirts under gray vests she had mended, washed, starched and ironed.

Abby had managed to coax Jake into letting her cut his hair the night before, and he looked dashing. Cutting Jake's hair had reminded her of the times she had done the

144

same for her nephews. She wondered how they were doing and when, if ever, she would get to hear news from them.

The men all sat in the wagon, waiting for her as she stepped out of the kitchen door. Mr. Hopkins drove right up to the steps and disembarked long enough to pick her up by the waist and set her on the wagon seat. They headed to the meeting house before she had time to worry about how she looked herself.

Having chosen to wear her favorite dress of light pink with plum roses printed on the fabric, she hoped the other women at the church would overlook the fact the fabric was slightly worn in places. She prayed her bonnet would hold her curls in place in spite of the teasing prairie breeze. The last thing she wanted to do was to embarrass Mr. Hopkins by arriving at the Sunday meeting with her hair in disarray and her dress less than acceptable.

The boys kept a constant chatter going, telling her about all the children — all five of them — that would likely be there. The children closest to Tommy's age were sisters who lived on the other side of the Scotts' homestead.

"Why couldn't God give us some boy neighbors? All we got around here are a bunch of girls! Uck!"

"Hey, mister, I'm a girl, too," Abby teased.

"Yeah, but you're a nice girl. Not like them. They think that catching frogs and diggin' for worms is gross," he reasoned with her. Abby felt humbled by his admiration even as she shuddered at the idea of actually handling frogs. Mr. Hopkins grinned at her as if he could read her thoughts. In the last week, they had grown comfortable with each other. Abby felt as if she had a good friend in her employer.

Willy told her about the other children who lived farther away. Jake hesitantly filled her in on details when the boys' explanations were confusing. By the time she saw the small chapel in the distance, she was sure she would recognized each of the thirty or so members of the area who frequented the church.

As soon as the wagon stopped, they were surrounded by people. The boys scrambled down the back of the wagon and ran off before Mr. Hopkins could loop the reins around the brake and hop down. He turned and helped her down in a movement as natural as breathing. Mrs. Scotts was the first to introduce herself and expressed her disappointment at arriving at home to the report of having missed her newest neighbor's visit.

Before Mr. Hopkins could introduce her to everyone who gathered, someone started to clang the bell. As one, the group turned and swarmed in through the doors. Before long, they all found seats in the twelve rows of long wooden pews of the quaint church. Abby found herself pulled along with the flow, all the way down to the third pew, and seated between the two boys with Mr. Hopkins on one side and Jake on the other. The tall, young circuit preacher greeted everyone at the door.

"It's a pleasure to finally meet you, Miss Stewart." The preacher gently pressed her hand with both of his as she entered the doorway on Mr. Hopkins's arm. "Will's shared all of your letters and I'm sure he and the boys are enjoying your cooking since anything has to be better than his."

"Except, of course, yours." Mr. Hopkins surprised Abby by being so informal with the young preacher, but the others around them just laughed.

"I confess, Miss Stewart, that my cooking is not much to write home about." Pastor MacKinnon's green eyes danced with merriment and Abby felt at ease. He couldn't be any older than she was, but he made her feel at home.

Abby enjoyed the service. Pastor MacKinnon possessed a gift for making connections to the Bible and everyday life. Surely God had placed her where she was for a purpose. Just like Ruth, the foreigner in an unknown land, God would use her to minister to others. She already saw some of her work paying off just seeing the boys looking so civilized in their dress shirts — until Willy used the back of his sleeve to wipe his nose. She consoled herself with the thought that she had just begun.

When the service finished, Abby was surrounded by the women of the area, and Mrs. Scotts began introducing everyone. Some of the women were openly friendly, while others seemed to hold back a little. All the apprehension she had felt when they had headed out that morning seemed silly now. Her new neighbors seemed to be completely taken with her dress. In fact, her dress was by far the fanciest and newest of all the women's.

Since the area was populated by more single men than families, there were only eleven women over the age of thirteen and all of them were married.

"Now, Miss Stewart, you must try and join us for our monthly quilting bee. We all meet here the last Friday of each month,"

Mrs. Ryerson suggested. Abby longed to participate and be part of the women's group but what would Mr. Hopkins think about the idea? Would he let her come on her own for a few hours as long as she got all her cooking and cleaning out of the way before she left the farm? Would he let her take the boys? Would he teach her how to drive the wagon?

Just as she was pondering the idea, she noticed that Herbert Scotts had arrived with his brother and was speaking with the preacher toward the front of the church in hushed tones. About to turn back to what the women were saying, she noticed the younger of the brothers gesture toward her, his eyes straying to areas of her body that made her cheeks flame. The women around her seemed to notice the men's presence, and Mrs. Scotts looked surprised to see her sons. Remembering how uncomfortable she had been under the stare of the man on their brief encounter at the Scotts' home the first day Mr. Hopkins had brought her from Twin Oaks, she forced herself to pay attention to what Mrs. Phelps said as she tried to calm her racing heart. The tingling sensation that crept up her neck and left her ice-cold didn't go away. Why was the preacher talking with them about her?

When she glanced back, Pastor MacKinnon had left the Scotts in one corner and retreated with Mr. Hopkins to the other side of the room, where they talked with their heads bent together. Abby couldn't see the look on the pastor's face, but Mr. Hopkins turned shades of red she'd never seen. His anger was almost palpable. What must have been said? He sent the Scotts boys a look that would have cowed lesser men, but they just smirked back at him and then turned their unashamed gazes back on her.

Abby chanced another glance at Mr. Hopkins and Pastor MacKinnon, only to see that they were headed her way. Mr. Hopkins looked like a thundercloud about to burst.

"Excuse me, ladies," Pastor MacKinnon's greeted them all in a congenial voice. He smiled at everyone. "I would like to speak with our newest neighbor for a few minutes alone, if that's all right with you all. Could I ask you to take your visiting outdoors and enjoy the beautiful fresh air and slight breeze God gave us this fine day?" As the woman all gathered their reticules and began to leave, he asked Mrs. Phelps, Mrs. Scotts and Mrs. Ryerson to wait outside because he wanted to discuss something with them, as well.

He extended his right hand out to Abby and once she had placed her own hand in his, he clasped it. "Would you allow me to pray for you and your future?" he asked, waiting for her nod.

"Father God, You know the plans You have for our newest member to this congregation. Plans You promise will build her up and not destroy her. I pray You guide her and be with her as we discuss Your will in her life. Grant us wisdom, understanding and peace. In Your name, I pray, Amen."

The pastor dropped her hand but continued to stand close. Strangely, Abby was more aware of Mr. Hopkins's presence, standing stiffly next to the pastor, only a step away, anger rolling off him in waves like the ripples of water in a river.

"Thank you, Pastor MacKinnon," she murmured. It was reassuring he had asked for wisdom, but she wondered what he was talking about. Surely they had had new people join the community before. Why had his prayer seemed so cryptic and serious? What had happened to the light jesting before the service? Why was Mr. Hopkins still looking like a bull about to charge, his nostrils still flaring?

"It's truly a pleasure to meet you, Miss Stewart. Although it seems that your arrival here has been a series of surprises. I hope we can work some of them out now."

She sent a questioning look at Mr. Hopkins. It was a brief contact, but she saw his look soften slightly and wondered again what was going on. Her mind whirled as she tried to remember anything she could have done that would have provoked his anger, but she came up empty.

"I have known Will since I started preaching in the community about, what, seven years ago, right, Will?" Mr. Hopkins acknowledged him with a nod but didn't comment.

"Will is a man who always looks to God for guidance. One who tries to do the right thing no matter the cost to him." The pastor's words seemed strange and pointed.

"In fact, when he shared the idea of hiring a housekeeper, I encouraged him to follow God's lead. I even carried a few letters back and forth from Twin Oaks. Will tells me there's been some confusion because you are not the grandmotherly woman he expected. He said you expected to find a widow woman, not a young widower at the train stop. Both of those errors may have been completely innocent, but they have caused a bit of a problem. I know God has a purpose in all of this and I suspect I know what that purpose is."

Abby wondered about God's purposes, too. It was such a relief that she had found a safe home with a family who loved God and made her feel useful and appreciated. But the temporary nature of the situation still worried her. She spent a lot of time in prayer about her future.

"However, there is a small complication," Pastor MacKinnon continued with a glance at the young men still smirking in the front of the chapel. "Herbert and Elvin Scotts have come and presented their concerns." He took a breath, as if wondering how to word his thoughts. "They came to inform the congregation that your reputation is at risk because you've been living on a farm with no chaperone and two men. Now —"

"You know I'd do nothing to harm Miss Stewart's reputation," Mr. Hopkins said with a glower.

"I know you fear God and would never intentionally compromise Miss Stewart, but owing to circumstances, I am afraid not everyone in the community will see it that way. The Scotts have come and said that either one of them would be willing to marry Miss Stewart so she can save face and have a secure future."

Abby gasped and felt as if the world were

spinning. What had the preacher said? The Scotts had offered to marry her to protect her from Mr. Hopkins? Mr. Hopkins had been a perfect gentleman the entire time, treating her respectfully and sleeping out in the barn. The glances and outright stares the two brothers didn't bother to hide were scandalous. How could they think she would ever agree to marry either one of them? They would be no better than Palmer. The thought made her shudder.

"Miss Stewart, I imagine this must be a shock to you but we need to discuss your options. Are you all right or do you need to sit down a minute?" The pastor's words sounded tinny and far away, but their meaning finally penetrated her foggy mind.

She wet her lips, cleared her voice, testing to see if it was going to fail her, as well. "I would like to sit for a minute," she agreed, unsure if her legs were still under her. She felt numb all over.

Warm, solid arms came to support her right arm and around her waist. Surprised, Abby felt Mr. Hopkins infuse a sense of peace through his gentle grip as he aided her to the nearest pew. Both men hovered near her as she sat, closing her eyes, praying this was just a bad dream. She had finally started to feel safe and at home in Nebraska and now this. . . .

"Miss Stewart. Can you answer a few questions for me?" Pastor MacKinnon asked in a gentle voice, his concern evident in his tone. She couldn't speak past the boulder lodged in her throat, so she nodded.

"Has Will done anything untold or inappropriate to you?"

"No!" The accusation was so ridiculous she lost no time in answering. "He's been a complete gentleman. He and Jake sleep in the barn every night. They have been very kind."

"Good." The young preacher grinned at Will. "I didn't want to have to beat him up. It's been a long time since I've gotten into a fistfight and I'm not completely sure I could take him, but I'd try."

The pastor was trying to make a difficult time a little lighter. She appreciated his efforts, but she doubted Mr. Hopkins did. His expression didn't change.

"The only reason the Scotts knew she was here was that I thought she would be able to stay with Mrs. Scotts," he said, his tone making it clear he blamed himself for this problem. "Now I'm glad I didn't leave her there. I doubt she would have been safe."

Mr. Hopkins glared at the young men.

They reminded Abby of vultures waiting for a wounded animal to die before swooping and picking it apart.

"Unfortunately, I suspect you're right. I doubt the Scotts boys would have been as respectful. But they are determined that something be done to 'restore Miss Stewart to her place of respect in our society' and they feel the only way to do that would be to have someone marry her. Since it is widely known you don't want to marry again, Will, they are offering to let her choose between them for the one to take the *responsibility* from you and provide for her."

"Since when have they cared about anyone's respect?" Mr. Hopkins roared.

"Since she came wrapped in such a nice package with nobody to defend her." The pastor looked pointedly at Mr. Hopkins again.

"I was the one who got her all mixed up in this mess — I'll be responsible for my actions. But I did not, in any way, compromise Miss Stewart."

"I know that. But it's not enough just convincing me. If she doesn't marry today, they are threatening to ask the church to vote to excommunicate you both from among us. I don't think they will get enough to vote in their favor, but it will still be humiliating for all of us and leave a shadow of doubt in some people's minds."

"And her having to marry today won't leave the same doubts?" Even with Mr. Hopkins's voice pitched low, his fury was still evident.

"I can't say there won't be those who will see her as having been forced to marry and think the worst, but many will be more open-minded. They'll probably assume that marriage was always your intention, and that this Sunday was your first opportunity. Most of the people around here know you, Will, and they'll take your word that nothing happened between you two."

"So, what are you suggesting?" Will looked pointedly at the pastor, but Abby groaned as she put the pieces together.

"That you marry Miss Stewart today," Pastor MacKinnon answered in a matter-of-fact tone.

"You want *me* to marry *her*? Today!" Mr. Hopkins tried to keep his voice low, but Abby was sure that he could have been heard in the next state.

By the time she had applied to work for the Hopkins, she had already given up on marriage. No man had ever come courting. She never believed she was overly beautiful or graceful, but when she was younger she had harbored dreams that someday she would find a man who would love her for the woman she was . . . maybe not a priceless jewel but a woman who could care for him and his home and make his life comfortable and fulfilled. After seeing all her friends, even some of the more homely ones, marry and start families, she resigned herself to the fact that she was not marriage material. She repelled eligible men. Certainly Mr. Hopkins had no interest in marrying her. She remembered little things he had said since she had arrived. That he hadn't wanted to have a young housekeeper because it would complicate matters. A man who didn't wish to marry at all would never want to marry *her*.

"Don't worry, Mr. Hopkins. You can just take me to the train and I'll head back somewhere. Maybe there's work I can do in Chicago," she reassured him. "I was hysterical the day I arrived. I didn't think about what I was asking of you or your family."

Both men turned to stare at her as if just remembering that she had been listening to the conversation.

"No, Miss Stewart. The blame lies at my door. I was the one who should have made other arrangements for your housing. Or maybe I could have looked for a companion for you. I sent for you and made the decision to bring you to my home. I will fix this somehow."

Pastor MacKinnon stepped in closer, speaking directly to Will. "I don't think you understand the seriousness of the accusation. If Miss Stewart refuses their option, the Scotts boys are ready to take this to the church elders and demand a vote on whether either of you can be allowed to stay in the church. Even if Miss Stewart were to leave the area, you would still be held responsible, Will."

"But, Colin, you know that's blackmail," Mr. Hopkins rasped.

"I know. And I'd like nothing better than to be able to give you a different answer, but I would hate to see you turned away from the gathering of the brethren and Miss Stewart turned out of a safe home. I know you will be a good provider. I know you love God and would provide a godly lifestyle, bringing her with your family to church on a regular basis and leading the family in Bible study. I can't say the same for either Elvin or Herbert." Having mentioned their names, the pastor glanced at the duo and shook his head.

Turning back to Mr. Hopkins, he hesitated

a moment before he started the conversation again. "As for Miss Stewart, you know her better than anyone else here. Is she a believer?"

"Yes, Colin. Her faith is real. I shared the letter she wrote about her conversion with you."

"Then on the basis of that, I would encourage you to consider this as God's opening a door for you. Your boys need a woman's touch in their lives. So do you." Pastor MacKinnon said the last part in a quiet voice, holding Mr. Hopkins's gaze.

"But we both know how that worked out last time," Mr. Hopkins muttered, his hand brushing though his already messy hair, standing the sandy-brown strands straight up in the back.

"You don't have to sacrifice your freedom for me, Mr. Hopkins. I have caused you enough discomfort and irritation as it is. If you could just find a way to get me to Twin Oaks —" she tried to appeal to him once again.

"That is out of the question, Ab . . . Miss Stewart," Mr. Hopkins interrupted, tripping over her name. For some reason, to hear her given name on his lips, even if unconsciously stated, made her feel a second of peace and belonging. "You don't know

160

anyone in Chicago."

"But I didn't know anyone here before I came. If God brought me here for a purpose, then why is it causing all this trouble? If it weren't for my insistence, you would have sent me back East as soon as I arrived and you wouldn't be having this problem now. If you won't take me, maybe Pastor MacKinnon could see his way to getting me to the train station. Surely he has a wagon, as well."

"Miss Stewart, I think you need to see there are other issues here. Can you tell me if there is a reason you cannot marry Will?"

"He doesn't want to marry me." Humbling as it was, it was the only reason.

She realized the first day she laid eyes on him how handsome a man he was. As each day passed she became more aware of his love for God and for his family and his dry humor. He was a good man, and she was sure he would be a good husband. But he didn't want her. What kind of a marriage would it be to force a man to marry, only to have to live out the rest of her days with him, loving him, but not being loved by him? Surely if she continued to live in close proximity to him, she would quickly grow to love him, while she held no hope that any man would ever love her.

"I think his opposition to my suggestion comes from his issues with marriage itself and what he went through in his first marriage, not with you personally. Is that right, Will?" he clarified, turning to Mr. Hopkins, who just glared at him and then mumbled something resembling a yes.

"Now, are you engaged or do you have an understanding with a beau?" Pastor Mac-Kinnon continued his questioning.

"No, sir," Abby answered, humbled all the more to have to admit it before both men.

"Is there anything we should know about your character that would impede you in being a godly wife and mother?"

"I don't think so. . . ."

"Did your church excommunicate you for unrepented sins?"

"No, sir. Of course not!" She felt her cheeks glow red with embarrassment under their scrutiny.

"I have it on good authority you make a great chicken soup with dumplings and pot roast. You also don't burn the oatmeal for breakfast and you made the boys very comfortable even when they had 'the pox thingys.' Even Jake is coming out of his shell. I have a hunch God put you in their home so you can bring them happiness and complete this family. This day was designed by our Lord because God knew it would be the only way Will would marry again." Pastor McKinnon patted Mr. Hopkins on the shoulder and actually chuckled at the angry look Mr. Hopkins shot him.

"Why don't I let you two talk it over for a few minutes?" he suggested as he headed toward the Scotts, who were looking a little less smug than they had been before.

The pastor guided the men out of the chapel, leaving Abby alone with her employer. Mr. Hopkins began pacing the aisle next to her. The man took one more pass, huffing like the big bad wolf about to blow the little pig's house down. The poor man was in this mess because of her. Would it be better to marry one of the Scotts boys and let Mr. Hopkins off the hook?

She had come to care deeply for Tommy and Willy. The idea of leaving and not seeing them again . . . it broke her heart. It was different than the pain she had felt when she left her nieces and nephews. They had been staying in a home where all their physical needs were met and where others in the community were on hand to look out for their spiritual and emotional care. But Mr. Hopkins didn't seem to be able to even cook a filling meal, much less see to the care and education of his sons *and* make a go of the farm at the same time. What would he do with the garden she had just planted and the lessons the boys had begun? It was too much for him and Jake to take care of on their own.

"Ahem . . ." He broke into her thoughts. She hadn't noticed that Mr. Hopkins had stopped pacing and was standing next to her, watching her face. "Could we discuss this for a minute?" he asked, his humility surprising her.

"Of course. Do you have any other suggestions?" She looked up hopefully. His look was a mix of frustration and tenderness. It took her off guard after his anger a few minutes before.

"I'm sorry. I didn't handle any of this very well. Colin is right." He sighed and ran his hand through his hair once again. "If I were looking to marry anyone, I would be looking for a woman like you. Colin's also right that the boys already see you as part of the family and I don't know what I would do if you had to leave. You have been a blessing to my family and I'm grateful. I just wish keeping you with our family didn't have to involve marriage. For me, the covenant of marriage isn't something to be taken lightly — it's a commitment for a lifetime. And my first go-around wasn't pleasant. In fact, you should know . . ." He looked away for a minute and then gazed into her eyes, swallowing as if he were swallowing his pride. "You deserve to know that my first marriage . . ."

He gripped the end of the pew and she instinctively shifted over on the bench so he could take a seat. Whatever he had to say, it was obviously hard for him. Without thinking about what she was doing, she covered his clenched fists with her own small hands.

"My first marriage had a lot of problems." He said it so softly that she wasn't sure she heard him correctly. What should she answer to that? Who was she to judge? She looked down at her hand atop his and bent her fingers around his fist, wishing she could make everything better. He loosened his fingers, turning his palm up to let her hand rest in his. She looked up to find his eyes on their intertwined fingers. Hers were so much smaller and lighter than his, which were so strong and sun-bronzed.

"Caroline didn't like the prairie. She wanted to go back to Philadelphia — but I couldn't leave. Not when I had just started to see my dream and Mathew's become a reality. I worked as hard as I could to give her everything she wanted, but . . . I don't even know what it was. It was as if she were a plant that just shriveled up in a drought. I tried to be a better husband, father . . . I did everything I could think of. Everything except go back East. But in the end, she just couldn't survive out here." As he explained, his grip tightened. Abby flexed her fingers and he let her hand go.

"I'm sorry. Did I hurt you?" His concern was sweet, as he rubbed his thumbs over the backs of her hands. She remembered the night he took out all of her splinters. How could hands so strong and callused caress her with such tenderness?

"No, you squeezed a little but I think they're still attached." She smiled and wiggled her fingers in the air to prove her point. The gesture brought a half smile from Mr. Hopkins.

"My mother would have boxed my ears for squeezing a girl's hand that tight." He ducked his head and studied his hands, flexing his fingers out and curling them up.

"Then it's a good thing she wasn't here to see you," Abby quipped.

"That's for sure." They both sat in silence for a moment, both occupied with their own thoughts. Abby's were spinning in her head so fast that she couldn't make sense of anything. Could she really be contemplating marrying a man whom she barely knew?

166

And one who didn't want to marry her or anyone else? Could she pass up this opportunity to marry a Christian man who would do right by her?

All she wanted was a home where she belonged — a family that she could call her own. Was this her chance to finally claim her dream . . . or would this contrived marriage keep her from ever finding what she sought?

CHAPTER SEVEN

How could the day have gotten off to such a beautiful start and end up a disaster? Will sat in the pew next to Abby wondering what must be running through her head. She hadn't dropped his hand when he had confessed his failure as a husband, but maybe she still was too shocked to process it all.

She was bright and pretty. He realized the morning he found her sleeping between the boys' beds just how much he had come to expect a smile and a soft greeting with the cup of coffee when he entered the house each morning. To think that she wouldn't be there anymore . . .

The boys would be devastated and it would be his fault. His fateful ad had started this whole mess. He had paid her train fare; picked her up — well after they finally realized the mistakes that had brought them together — and brought her out to the homestead. It was his fault she was in this position and there was no way he was going to let either one of the Scotts brothers have her. She deserved better. Even when they were in church, they eyed her like a dog salivating over a T-bone.

If he had never been married before, never seen what it was like to watch a woman fade away in front of his eyes without any way to stop it, he would have jumped at the opportunity to marry a woman so caring and capable. Her cooking was excellent and the house had never been as clean. Even when she was tired, she kept a cheerful disposition and was always willing to do one more task. She was responsible and quickwitted. The boys adored her and she already had Tommy writing his alphabet. Both boys insisted she tuck them into bed each night, craving her kind words and warm affection. He would be a fool if he let her walk away from his family now, but would he be able to give her what she needed?

What would she do once she saw there were no fancy balls to go to on the holidays or stores where she could get the latest fashions? How would she handle the brutal challenges of a prairie winter, or the daily struggles of a farmer's wife living far from civilization? How could he ask her to promise her life to him when she didn't yet know all the shortcomings that life entailed?

Marrying her was the only way to protect her at the moment, but he realized he would have to keep things the same as now — just marry her in name only and continue sleeping in the barn. When the time came that she had her fill of the prairie and the life out on the frontier, then she could ask Colin to annul the marriage. She could go back East and find a place to work. Maybe he could write his mother and ask her to find suitable employment for Abby for the fall.

"Listen, Abby. If we're contemplating marriage, I think we should use our given names. Please call me Will." Wide-eyed, Abby nodded, so he continued. "I know most women dream of their wedding day and being courted and all that, but the situation isn't going to give us a chance. I want to do the right thing, and protect you. In order to do that, I think what we need is a marriage of convenience, in name only. It would protect your reputation and give you a place to stay where you'd be safe — at least until you have a chance to find a different employment back East. Then we could annul the marriage."

Words flowed one over the other, and he wondered if what he had said made any sense. He lifted his gaze to see disappointment for a fraction of a second before she dropped her gaze to the floor, effectively closing him out of her feelings.

Unable to resist contact with her, he lifted her chin with his fingertip. He reasoned to himself it was to get her to respond and let him know if she was even open to the idea or if she was offended by the whole mess. Her eyes shimmered and a tear hung suspended by two eyelashes, slowly losing the battle against gravity. It slipped down her porcelain pink cheek and slid to a stop next to her rosy lip. Will couldn't tear his eyes away from her face, so perfectly combined by God to make an adorable picture. But the picture was contorted in pain and he had the sinking feeling he had caused it. As if it had a life of its own, the finger that had lifted her chin gently traced a path to the tear and swiped it away. If only he could wipe the pain from her heart with the same ease.

"I think what I was trying to say is that I would be honored to marry you, Abby. I'm sorry I made such a mess of all of this." He felt suddenly anxious. He waited, holding his breath without realizing it, for her to answer.

"I'm sorry. I could still go to Chicago. . . ."

Will fought a wave of disappointment. "Is that what you really want? You want to leave the boys and the farm and all this work you've done and go to a place where you'll be alone?"

"I might be alone here even if I stay," she murmured.

"What do you mean?" he asked, confused. Did she understand he was offering a way for her to stay with him and his family for as long as she wanted?

"Um . . ." Colin's voice interrupted their silent stare. Will dropped his hand from Abby's cheek as if it had been burned. She straightened her spine as if she had been poked with a cattle prod. "Are you about ready to give us your decision?"

Why couldn't he have just waited for a few more minutes? Will barely kept from growling at him, knowing that Colin was just trying to keep this from getting ugly. Will didn't envy him the task. Abby turned her big blue-green eyes on him as if to ask him to make the decision for her.

"I have just asked this fine young lady for her hand in holy matrimony, but I believe she is still thinking through her options." He called to Colin without taking his eyes off Abby. When this discussion had started, he had not wanted to even consider marriage, but now he was sure that he would be crushed if Abby didn't accept his suit, feeble as it was.

"Are you sure?" she asked, clearly confused.

"Yes. I want you to stay with us. You belong at the farm. We need you to stay." As he said the words he realized how true they really were. They did need her at the homestead and he didn't want her to walk away, especially if she would be walking away as the new Mrs. Scotts. He clutched her hands, and his heart turned in his chest when he felt how cold they were.

"You won't hate me later?" she whispered. He leaned closer to hear her and caught the aroma of her clean hair and the rose-scented soap she used. It made his nose quiver, and his stomach clenched at the idea of having a woman once again at the house for a prolonged time. This time she would be his wife to protect and provide for but not to touch. Could he do it?

He squeezed her hand once more, gently this time, and tried to flash her his most reassuring smile. "I doubt I could ever hate you," he answered honestly. It wasn't her fault they were in this mess. If anyone needed to shoulder the blame, it was him. "Let's go," he encouraged her. "We've got a wedding to get to."

"So, has she given you an answer or is she holding out for someone better looking?" Colin teased, the tension from a while ago still lingering in lines around his eyes.

"She can't get much better than what she's got here in front of her. But she still has me on pins and needles," he volleyed back, hoping to help Abby relax. If only she would smile, even just a little bit, he knew that they would be able to get through the rest of the afternoon. Her wan look did little to reassure him, but he figured that she hadn't run the other way yet and her fingers still clutched his.

As if she could read his thoughts, she looked down at their hands together and then searched his eyes as if she could find some sort of answer there. "Are you sure you want to saddle yourself with me? I could still go."

"I'm not saddling myself with anyone, Abby." Will turned his full attention on her face once again.

If only she knew she would be such a blessing. If only she would be staying forever. She was already becoming a good friend. She took away some of the loneliness he had felt since Matt and MaryAnn died. But he was sure that one day she would grow tired of the hard life in the prairie and choose to go back East.

When that day came, she would leave yet another gaping hole in their lives. He had tried to avoid all this by bringing out someone older. If he wasn't careful he was going to be back to asking the "why" questions again. The questions God chose not to answer last time. Questions he and Colin prayed over and grappled with for the better part of a year after Caroline's death.

"You are a lovely young lady and I would be pleased to have you for my wife. I don't want you to feel pressured, but I don't really see any other way around this. At least God is supplying you with a safe place and a better option than Elvin or Herbert." After he said the words, he realized how arrogant that sounded. "Not that I —"

"No. You don't need to explain. I do thank the Lord that you're offering, but I know you don't want . . ." She turned her face away and he saw the tears pool against the edge of her eyelids.

"It'll all work out. You'll see."

"Would you do me a favor?" she asked tentatively without looking directly at him.

"What would you like?" He would consider doing just about anything to help fix this for her.

"Would you pray with me about this? Would you pray for God to give us both peace with this decision?"

It humbled him that she had asked for prayer. He should have been the one leading in prayer without being prompted. It was one more reminder why he didn't deserve a godly wife.

"Dear God." It was easy to start, but what was he supposed to say? God knew what was going on in his heart and mind and just how little peace he felt at the moment. Well, he could pray for his future wife. "Guide us and bless this day. Give Abby peace and comfort her."

Colin slid up closer to the pew they were sitting in and rested a hand on Will's shoulder. Will was glad for a good friend to stand with him. When Will ran out of words, Colin took over. "God, we give You honor today, and take solace in the knowledge that You've brought all this together for the best for both Will and Miss Stewart. You have a plan for them and for the family You will form with them today. I pray You will be always the center of their marriage and their home. May Your name be blessed by the way they live and serve You together for the years You give them.

"Be with us as a congregation and teach

us to live in a way that is above reproach and a testament to Your faithfulness. We pray for Your peace in our midst today and especially with Miss Stewart. May Your Spirit comfort her and guide her in her new roles as wife and mother. In Jesus's name, Amen."

Colin clapped Will on the shoulder and grinned. "Well, I sure didn't foresee you marrying this morning when I woke and greeted the Lord. I guess you can never tell what the good Lord has in store for a body from one minute to the next. I'll go let the people know there's to be a wedding today. Maybe Mrs. Ryerson and Mrs. Phelps can come and help Abby get herself arranged. We'll have a short ceremony and then let everyone go home since there were no plans for a picnic." He chuckled and Will was torn between punching the man of God in the middle of the church and begging him to stay a moment longer and forestall the inevitable.

Colin must have sensed Will's mood because he moved away but held out his hand in a handshake. "Let me be the first to congratulate the groom. God's seen fit to give you a lovely bride even though you're the ugliest thing He's placed this side of the Mississippi. Congrats."

"Thanks," Will croaked out. He stood and shook Colin's hand, then turned back and offered a hand up for Abby. She stood and he waited for a moment more to see if she had anything else she wanted.

"Are you going to be okay? Do you need anything?" His mother's lessons about how to be a gentleman were rusty, but he determined to put them to use, starting that instant. How he wished his mother were there. She would know how to help. She would have hugged Abby and reassured her that everything was going to work out.

Abby shook her head without looking up at him. What he wouldn't give to know what was going through her head at that moment. But then again, it might be better he not know what she thought of him. There was nothing either of them could do about the situation now.

Before he could say anything else, the door at the back of the chapel opened. Mrs. Ryerson and Mrs. Phelps entered, gushing about how they were going to help Abby fix her hair and get ready for the wedding. They cackled and pecked at him like a couple of hens and he was quick to obey their orders to "get out until his bride had been made ready."

Abby was beautiful just as she was, so he

wasn't too concerned about them taking too long with the hair and such . . . but he did wonder if they knew a way to get both the bride and groom "ready" for a wedding that they had not anticipated or wanted. Getting "made ready" might take a bit longer than they had anticipated. He doubted if they would have been as excited if they knew what had caused all the last-minute plans.

Stepping out into the bright sunlight, he stood still for a minute while his eyes adjusted. Clapping erupted and he looked around to see they were all looking at him. Neighbors, old and new, congratulated him, some men calling out encouragement. Obviously Colin had already announced the ceremony about to take place.

"Pa, Pa!" Tommy's excited voice caught his attention as he started down the stairs. "Is it true? Are you making Auntie Abby my new ma? I told you she'd make a good one. She's nice and smells good and even —"

"Yes, Tommy. I'm marring Auntie Abby, but she's . . ." He glanced up to see the Scotts brothers standing to the side of the church, not nearly as smug as before. It gave him a sense of satisfaction that he had thwarted their plans. He shuddered at the idea of Abby marrying one of them.

"I just knew it! Yeeppie! I get a new ma!"

Tommy went running off to tell Willy. Will searched around the yard and spotted Jake standing next to their wagon, a goofy grin on the teen's face. From the nod he gave Will, he radiated pleasure. Before Will could walk over to talk to him, Mr. Phelps stepped forward to shake his hand.

"It's about time you found yourself a new wife. A young man like you needs a helpmate to keep the farm going and someone to give you a passel of kids. I'll bet you're as pleased as punch."

Will tried to be polite and pay attention, but his mind drifted off to worries about the boys and how they would react when Abby left in the fall. How would *he* react in the fall? Was there anything he could do to convince her to stay for good? If only their marriage could be for real and not for show. If only he could find some kind of faith that a woman could adapt to the life of the prairie farmer and enjoy it. . . .

If only he could make himself believe that he could ever make a wife of his truly happy.

Abby stood at the foot of the church steps for the second time in one day, listening to the church bells ringing. This time, however, the bells were heralding her wedding. How could it be? She hadn't imagined anything like this would ever happen to her. As a child she had dreamed of marrying some handsome man who would sweep her off her feet with his declaration of love and devotion. Mr. Hopkins fit the handsome part. But where was the rest of her dream — the fairytale romance with a man who brought her flowers and proposed on bended knee?

In spite of his promises to not hate her, Abby felt certain that instead of building a marriage or even a friendship, this coerced wedding would create resentment on his part after a time. If only she were more like Emma, it wouldn't be so scary. Emma had married for money and station. It didn't seem to bother her that her husband held her in disdain, as long as he continued to provide their lavish lifestyle. But Abby craved love, affection. Even if Mr. Hopkins — Will — treated her with the same kindness and respect he'd showed thus far, he wouldn't give her what her heart truly desired.

"It's time, child." A soft voice to her right broke into her thoughts, even as Mrs. Phelps handed her the bouquet of wildflowers hastily collected and wrapped with a hair ribbon from someone's reticule. "He's a fine young man and so handsome," the older

181

woman continued, pulling her by the arm up the stairs. "He's a gentle man, so you have no reason to be frightened. He'll be a good husband —"

Before she could continue, the door opened and Mrs. Reyerson smiled at her. "You look lovely, dear."

Through the open door, Abby could see that most of the congregation had stayed to witness her wedding. Or maybe they were just here to see Mr. Hopkins married against his will. No matter their reason, as she stepped through the portal, they all stood and watched her. On shaky legs, she started forward, unsure where she was even headed until she lifted her eyes and caught sight of her groom standing at the front of the church watching her. He was so handsome. His gaze locked with hers and pulled her toward him. He looked sure of himself. He looked safe.

Unaware as to how she got there, she was suddenly standing in front of him as he extended his hands to cup hers. It felt right — her smaller hand nestled inside his larger, rougher ones. Everyone else in the place disappeared and for a moment, she stepped out of time and felt safe. "It'll be all right, Abby," he whispered just before Pastor McKinnon started to speak.

"We are gathered here today to join the lives and hearts of F. William Hopkins and . . . Is it Abigail or Abby, Miss Stewart?" he asked, stopping the service mid-sentence.

"Abigail," she answered, not daring to look away from her groom.

"Yes, and Abigail Stewart in holy matrimony," Pastor MacKinnon continued. Abby felt as if she were an observer on the peripheral, watching a drama play out around her. "Do you, F. William Hopkins, take her to be your . . ." Pastor McKinnon's voice droned on, but Abby couldn't concentrate. What was she doing?

"I do." Will's voice was steady and sure. He gazed into her eyes and she wondered if he knew how scared she was.

"And, Abigail, do you take William Hopkins to be your lawfully wedded husband, to honor, respect and obey from this day forward?"

Mr. Hopkins squeezed her hands gently and she shook off her fears. It was her turn to speak. "I . . . I do." Her voice caught, not because she didn't want to be tied to this man, nor because she didn't trust her life in his hands. She did. But in the middle of all of this, she realized it wasn't until death do them part, it was until he could get her off

183

his land and send her back East. It was only until the harvest was in. How could it be that she already wanted to weep for the home she was losing before she ever really had it?

"I now declare you husband and wife." The pastor's voice broke into her confused thoughts once again. "You may kiss your bride."

She had forgotten about this part. No one had ever kissed her before. What if he chose not to kiss her? The marriage was in name only. Will was already standing so close, but he stepped even closer. Letting her hand go, he raised her chin with his finger, forcing her eyes to his. His gaze held her place as his lips descended on hers, or *almost* on hers. His touch was soft and warm, more of a whisper than a touch on the corner of her lips, her cheek. She felt herself tremble as he pulled away. But instead of releasing her as she expected him to, his fingers inched up her cheek and his lips descended once again, this time directly on hers, and the kiss felt like a seal on her heart.

Someone started clapping and Will opened his eyes, lifted his head, squeezed the hand he still held and smiled into her eyes before looking out to the people seated in the pews.

"Ladies and gentlemen, may I introduce

Mr. and Mrs. Hopkins," Pastor McKinnon announced to the congregation. Cheers and whistles filled the air.

CHAPTER EIGHT

As soon as Will lifted her from the wagon and set her on her feet by the kitchen door, Abby headed inside, her mind on putting dinner on the table for the men. How strange to enter the house she had left only hours before as just the housekeeper and return as Mrs. Hopkins. It felt more like a strange dream. Would she wake at some point and realize none of it was real — not the blackmail threat, or the ceremony . . . or the way he had kissed her with a gentle passion after they were declared man and wife?

After all, she could still remember the stories her mother had told her about her parents' courting and wedding. Her father had carried his new bride across the threshold of their home after the wedding. . . . Here Abby was entering with her new stepsons. She didn't even know what Will wanted from her or even how long he had planned to keep her there before he annulled the marriage and sent her packing.

Not that she could blame him, really. He hadn't wanted the trouble of having a wife. Surely he was still in love with his first wife and didn't want anyone to take her place. But in all honesty, Abby knew that she would never take the first Mrs. Hopkins's place. From the color of the boys' eyes and hair, she imagined a beautiful woman who had charmed and enchanted Mr. Hopkins. It was obvious Will blamed himself for not being able to make her happy. He must have loved her very much. Why else would he still keep her things in his room and refuse to consider looking for a second wife to ease his burdens of raising his boys?

She pushed a wisp of hair away from her cheek, and her fingers came away wet. Stunned that she had given into self-pity, she stood just inside the doorway of the kitchen and gave herself a good shaking. If she gave in to her tears right now, she wouldn't get anything done for the rest of the afternoon. She needed to get to work. More than ever she needed to earn her keep while she was here.

Maybe with a little bit of work, she could ingrain herself into the family and workings of the farm to the point she'd earn a permanent position — maybe not as the loved mother and wife, but as the caretaker and homemaker who kept everyone well fed and comfortable. That would be her way to ensure her permanence with the Hopkinses.

Taking her emotions firmly under control, she stepped to the sink and started to get dinner on the table. The boys followed her in and she almost didn't register their chatter as she worried about the chicken that had to be overbaked and burned to a crisp by now. What a way to impress her new husband and the preacher by offering them inedible chicken!

"Something smells good!" Tommy exclaimed. "I'm sooo hungry I could eat a horse."

"Oh. I didn't know that you had a hankering for horse today. I just made plain old chicken!" She forced herself to tease Tommy. Even though her mind was a scramble of different emotions, she didn't want the boys to feel left out. What would today's events change for the boys? For the farm?

"You're silly," giggled Tommy. Even Willy grinned at her joke.

"Why don't you boys go up and change out of your Sunday clothes?" she suggested.

"Yes, ma'am," Willy answered, ushering

his little brother up the stairs ahead of him.

Abby knew she should stop to change, too, but the men would only take a few minutes to see to the afternoon chores, and then they'd be ready to eat. She just hoped she had something to offer them. She tugged an apron over her favorite dress, glad that she had worn it today.

Who would have thought that today would be her wedding day? And yet she didn't feel any more married now than she had felt before the ceremony. Shocked and disappointed better described her state of mind. She figured with the expectation of annulment in the near future, she might never feel married. She wasn't the kind of woman a man would want to be married to forever. The sooner she accepted the truth, the sooner she would be able to resume her chores and life would go back to normal.

Pushing her unruly thoughts aside again, she pulled the large pot out of the oven. She said a silent prayer and held her breath to see what was left of the chicken she had set in the oven hours ago. The impromptu wedding meant that they had been away much longer than she had planned, and almost all the water had dried out, leaving a mush of potatoes, onion and carrots. Still, maybe it would be edible after all. It did smell good. She scraped out the vegetables and put them all in a big serving bowl. Minutes later, she stared at her concoction. Instead of white mashed potatoes, they were orange, but she added butter, milk and salt and tried a taste. It was actually pretty good.

The boys appeared back at the door as she finished doctoring the "mush" as she dubbed it in her mind. They stood just a pace away from the table and watched with fascination every move she made. The chicken fell apart when she lifted it onto the serving platter. What little juice remained she drained off to make gravy.

"Auntie Abby, can we eat now?" Tommy looked longingly at the platter as if he wanted to eat the whole chicken by himself.

"Not yet. Your pa, Jake and the pastor haven't come in from the barn yet. As soon as they come in, then we'll eat." She made a face at him. Giggling, he made one in return.

Turning back to the stove, she could hear Willy and Tommy whispering. They often discussed things like they were little old men. Tommy came up with all sorts of ideas and Willy, always claiming to know it all, explaining the whys and hows of life.

"But she is, too," Tommy argued, louder this time. "Aren't you, Auntie Abby?" he asked, his voice belying how much he wanted to be right.

"What are you talking about, Tommy?" she asked pleasantly, remembering the times she intervened between her nephews. She just hoped it was something that she knew the answer to. Her nephew Peter would come up with questions about why the sky was blue or why the geese flew away from the pond in the town square every winter and where they went to.

"I told Willy that you're our new ma. Pa said he was marring you at church and Jill said if you married our pa, that made you our ma. Can we call you Ma? I'd like you to be our ma since our old one is dead." Tommy's matter-of-fact statement caught Abby completely off guard. How could she answer the boy when she didn't know the answers herself? She had so many questions and she was afraid that even if she and Will were to sit and discuss things, they still wouldn't be completely settled for a time.

Abby searched for words, ideas, anything to be able to reassure the boys, but came up with nothing.

"I told you she didn't want to be our ma. Our real ma didn't even want to be our ma, so why would a stranger?" Willy's words only tore at Abby's heart and confused her.

What had Mrs. Hopkins been like? Why did Willy say that she hadn't wanted to be his mother? Had she been sickly or more uninterested in children, like Emma? Either way, it helped her to understand his belligerence and why he held himself away from others.

Abby slid the pan off the stove and set it aside. The gravy could wait. The boys were more important. Kneeling before them, a hand on each boy's shoulder, she gazed into Willy's eyes and then Tommy's.

"It would be the biggest honor in the world for me to be your ma. But that's a question you need to ask your pa. I know that things are hard to understand. . . ." She paused to organize her thoughts and beg God silently for the right words. "I will always love both of you and I will be here as long as God gives me the opportunity. Everything that happened today was a surprise and I'm still trying to figure out what to do. I don't know what your pa would think if you called me 'Ma.'"

She swallowed hard. She would love to be "Ma" to these precious boys. After all, her heart's desire had always been to be a mother. In many ways, she had been a second mother to her nieces and nephews, but she'd had to leave them behind. Even if she would never have children of her own, she had already come to care for these boys deeply. But was it fair to let them get attached if Will was planning to end their marriage and send her away in a few months? Would he think she was trying to usurp his first wife's place in the house and with the boys?

In spite of all her questions and doubts, she couldn't resist pulling the boys closer to her and hugging them tight.

Willy was less receptive, but having nursed them through the chicken pox, she had gotten used to the facade he showed at her attempts of affection. The first day the boys had been sick, she had tried to give him more space and not baby him as much, but then she saw the look of longing on his face when she held Tommy. She slowly began to touch his shoulder, forehead or finger his hair out of his eyes since then.

"I want you to be our ma," Tommy said with a pout, but before she was able to correct his attitude, they heard the men clomping up the back steps.

"How about we talk about this later?" she offered, not wanting to have this discussion with everyone else in the room. Maybe later in the afternoon, she would be able to approach Will about the changes that were happening on the farm and what he wanted from her. In the meantime, she had dinner to put on the table.

"Something sure smells good in here!" exclaimed Colin as soon as the door opened. "I can tell that you've been hard at work, Mrs. Hopkins."

Will glared at his friend. He wasn't sure what to do in this new situation he found himself thrust into, but he knew that it didn't make him look good to have his friend beat him to the punch on complimenting the new bride. Colin was right about the food smelling good. It made his belly growl and he realized it had been hours since breakfast.

He waited while Colin and then Jake washed their hands and faces. When he had walked in, Abby had been kneeling in front of his boys, hugging them close. He noticed that she and the boys looked upset, but he wasn't sure what to do about it. Maybe once they had eaten, he could think a little more clearly.

After Colin had asked the blessing on the food and "the newly formed family," everyone dug in. Abby was hard put to get more than a few bites before someone needed something. As soon as the boys finished their food, they begged to leave the table.

Without giving it a second thought, Will waved them away and Jake followed them out into the barnyard. The door slapped shut behind them before he glanced at Abby and the strained look on her face.

"Pastor MacKinnon, would you like more?"

Her voice was as pleasant as always, but Will suspected that he had done something wrong and hadn't an idea what it was.

"There's plenty of mush. I'm sorry for the appearance . . ." She was repeating the same excuse for the third time.

"Don't worry about a thing, Mrs. Hopkins. I happen to be a confirmed bachelor, so it's a real treat to have such a good, home-cooked meal."

Colin was his usual congenial self, but this fact bothered Will today. His friend was more at home with Will's new wife than he was. It grated on his nerves that Colin insisted on calling Abby "Mrs. Hopkins," as well. The formality was just another reminder to everyone of the big changes that had happened that afternoon.

"Mr. Hopkins, did you want more?" Abby asked, starting to rise even though her own plate was still half-full.

"Not until you finish what's on your plate," Will answered gruffly. "And remember, we agreed that you'd call me Will from now on."

Humbly, she sat back down and began to eat without lifting her eyes from her plate. Guilt assaulted Will as he realized that she was acting afraid of him. Colin caught his eye — his look condemning.

"Listen, I'm sorry if I spoke harshly, but you didn't even sit down to eat!" His voice rose as he struggled to keep his temper. He hadn't wanted to be married ever again. Now that he was, he hadn't even gone for a full three hours without having to apologize to her. In the last three weeks, they had become friends and now he felt as if he didn't know what to say to her.

"I guess I'm not really that hungry," she mumbled, pushing back from the table and standing once again. She had reached out to collect his dishes when he stopped her by clasping her wrist. A jolt ran down his hand to his arm, stunning him, and he released her.

"Wait." His conscience got the best of him. It wasn't her fault he was in a bad mood. It wasn't even her fault that they had this problem to begin with, and now he had ruined her meal. "Listen, Abby." Will didn't know what to ask, but he didn't want her to leave the table, either. "How about if I help with the cleanup while you rest for a bit?" he offered.

"No, I can do it." She took his plate.

Standing, Colin started to stack the boys' plates in a pile and headed over to the sink. Abby followed with her dishes and Will's. She took a pot off the back of the stove and poured the warm water into the basin, added soap and set the dishes in to soak. Will placed the platter of chicken bones and the empty serving bowl next to the sink on the counter.

"Thank you, Mrs. Hopkins. Dinner was excellent."

"Thank you, Pastor MacKinnon. I'm glad you enjoyed it." She turned from the sink and took a platter and the sugar bowl out of the cabinet. "I have cookies. Would you like to sit and have a cup of coffee with dessert?"

"That's a tempting offer, ma'am, but I don't know how wise it would be. I think I'm about as stuffed as I can get before I burst one of my seams. I might be able to handle a little more coffee, though."

Will fought the jealousy rearing its ugly head. She hadn't offered any to him. But then again, he hadn't commented on her cooking. Instead, he almost bit her head off for trying to get him something more. If he told her now that he had enjoyed her cooking, it would look as if he was just trying not to lose face.

"W-Will, would you like some more coffee or some cookies?"

"Sounds good," he managed to mumble, feeling more miserable by the minute.

Abby held the kettle up and poured coffee into a big earthen mug instead of the fine china that she had used at the dinner table. Obviously, she had learned a few things about men's habits during her stay. She filled the second mug, set them both at the table. The sugar bowl and a small pitcher of cream came next, followed by the plate of sugar cookies. Once everything was on the table, she glanced hesitantly at Will and then the back door.

"I hid these from the boys so that they wouldn't ask for any until after they had finished their meal, but I hadn't expected them to be done so soon. Should I call them back in?"

"No, that's fine. We'll enjoy a little peace and quiet and then they can have some," Will answered, selfish enough to exclude his own sons from dessert in an effort to find some more solid footing with his house-keeper turned wife.

Nodding, Abby turned back to the sink

and started her washing again.

"Aren't you going to join us?" Colin asked, obviously uncomfortable.

"No, thank you. I need to finish this. Is there something else you need?" She lifted her hands from the sudsy water and started to wipe them on her apron.

"No. Everything is fine," Colin reassured her.

Will sipped his coffee, scalding his mouth in the process. Looking at Colin, he could see his friend was having a hard time trying to piece everything together. Within a few minutes, Abby left the kitchen spotless and excused herself to go outdoors. Will wondered if she was going to see the boys or just wanted away from him.

Colin asked about some of the families in the area and the farm in general and they sat talking and sipping the now-cooling coffee for a time. Even as Will answered questions about the neighbors, Abby's face came to mind. With her face came a list of questions that he had no answers for. For years, he had concentrated on getting through each day and then each season, providing for his family and caring for his boys. Now he was going to have to learn how to live comfortably with Abby and yet not let her tear his heart out the day she chose to leave.

"Hey, Will, you'd think I was boring you!" Colin's voice yanked him back to the present. "I think you've got a pretty little blonde on your mind and I imagine I don't quite compare." Colin's teasing grated on Will's raged nerves.

"Knock it off, Colin. It's not something to tease about," Will barked.

"Hey, easy there, my friend — she's young and pretty. No one would blame you for thinking about her instead of listening to an old, ugly preacher. I know this marriage wasn't what you expected, but God's hand of providence brought her out here to be your helpmate. You said yourself that God would have to all but put a gun to your head before you'd marry again. I'd say He did just that today." Colin's words were light-hearted, but his eyes were somber.

He had listened through the years while Will fought God about the turns his life had taken. Colin had arrived in Nebraska Territory just a month before Matt and Mary-Ann's accident. He'd officiated at the funeral. And afterward, he'd done what he could to try to counsel Caroline and Will through those last, hard years of their marriage. Will trusted him more than anyone else in the world, but the events of the day had left him out of sorts. It was probably a good thing Abby had gone out and given him some distance.

"Why don't you go out and look for your little lady?" Colin asked, a smirk in his eyes.

"Because she's *not* my little lady!" Will lashed out. He regretted the words as soon as they came out.

"What do you mean?" Colin's head snapped up, all teasing gone from his eyes.

"She's not going to last out here. No young, pretty woman wants to make her life out on the prairie," Will explained. "It's not settled enough for someone so delicate. She might make it through a summer, but she would never endure a winter. I won't watch another woman shrivel up and . . . and die like Caroline. I won't do that to her. She has her whole life in front of her." *Not to mention the fact that she's good, wholesome and beautiful,* his heart reminded him. There was no way he would be part of her destruction.

Silence answered his outburst and Colin sat staring at him as if he had grown another head. "So, why did you marry her today?" Colin finally asked.

"So she could be safe. So she wouldn't have to marry one of the Scotts boys. So she can stay the rest of the season until the harvest and find a good position before she goes back East."

"But she's your wife now. You can't just let her walk away." Colin looked incredulous.

"Wife in name only. I'll still be sleeping out in the barn with Jake."

"Does she understand this arrangement?" Colin's voice was deeper than normal. Sparks flew from his emerald-green eyes, reminding Will of the stories he'd heard about the Irish temper.

"Yes. We spoke of it before the ceremony," Will answered tersely. He had invited Colin out to the farm so he could be a character witness when the time came to annul the marriage. He hadn't expected Colin's opposition to his plan.

"So, then why did you kiss her like you did?" Colin's eyes were burning holes into his, and Will tore his gaze away and fiddled with his empty mug. He'd been asking himself the same question since the minute he pulled his head back, wishing he could keep kissing her forever and realizing that he had taken the intended gentle peck on the lips to a whole other level.

In all the confusion of the hurried wedding, he hadn't gotten a chance to ask Colin not to have the groom kiss his bride, so when the moment came, he had to make it look real. The Scotts brothers were standing by, waiting for proof that he wasn't going to send her packing on the next train. He'd intended to only touch his lips lightly on the corner of her mouth, but then she'd shivered with the small contact.

She had kept her eyes open, staring at him as if frightened, so he put a hand on her cheek and held her closer. He wondered if his had been her first kiss. The reality of her innocence had sent a current through him and he hadn't been able to pull away from her. Instead, he'd deepened the kiss and felt her relax at his touch as his hand caressed her cheek and his lips met hers. They were both strangely short of breath and blushing when they glanced around and found everyone's attention focused on them. It had been believable, all right. Even Will had believed that it was something more than a simple kiss.

"I don't know. I had . . ." The admission made him angry with himself, but he lashed out at Colin. "I was still in shock. You know I didn't want to marry ever again. I wouldn't have done it if it hadn't been for you and those troublemaking Scotts," he accused.

"Hey. I know this was sudden, but you'd be a fool to let that woman walk out of your life now. She has done wonders with this house. It's clean! And her cooking beats your burnt oatmeal any day. She's wonderful with the boys, and I saw the way you watched her today, at the table and even in the wagon. Don't let what happened to you and Caroline ruin your future."

Everything Colin said was true. Will knew it in his head, but that didn't mean he wanted to hear it. It wouldn't keep Abby from walking away from him and the boys someday. He'd see to it that she was provided for — that she had a good job waiting for her out East when she left, and that she had a comfortable home until then. But he wasn't about to let himself get caught up in caring about another woman. It was just a matter of time. He had already sent a letter for his mother to look for work for Abby.

"My future is fine. I've got a good homestead, the crops are in and the house is built. I was thinking about next year. I could put in twenty acres more to the east of the fields than I've got planted now."

"Your future is lonely. The boys will grow up someday and start families of their own. God didn't mean for a man to live out his days alone. He created a helpmate for Adam. I'm thinking the good Lord sent you one, as well."

"If you like her so much, you should have

married her yourself!"

As soon as the words were out of his mouth, Will felt sick. He didn't want anyone else to marry Abby. She was *his* wife, and the boys had become attached. If he had to give her up, it would be only to keep her from becoming another victim of the prairie. He would send her back East, but he didn't want her marrying anyone else, not even his best friend.

"Nah, I couldn't do that," Colin replied.

"Why not?"

" 'Cuz I value my life," Colin snapped, but his eyes held mischief in them. "I saw the way you stiffened as soon as people started to crowd around the wagon today. You flanked her with your boys during and after church. You might say you haven't got attached yet, but I have eyes in my head. And if I had doubted before, that kiss that you gave her at the end of the ceremony confirmed everything." Colin chuckled and Will once again fought the urge to hit his friend.

"She came at my request, to my farm, and I am responsible for her well-being," Will argued, more to himself than even to Colin.

"Well, then all the more reason to treat her right. She is your wife now and you need to see to all of her needs and comfort."

Colin's look reminded Will of his mother's when she was laying down an order. "And if you're still so intent on being the biggest fool this side of the Mississippi, then you'd better not trifle with her, either."

"I know what I've got to do! I'd appreciate if you'd keep your nose out of my business. You sound like her father," Will growled.

"It became my business when I performed the ceremony. I'm not sure I would have done it if I had known that you don't plan on trying for a real marriage. As of today, Abby happens to be one of my parishioners and therefore my business. Since she doesn't have family in the area, I have to assume the role of older brother in Christ. You need to watch the way you treat that woman. She's a godsend and if you can't see it, well, then, my friend, you've got about as much sense as a fence post." Colin shook his head in disgust and scraped back his chair.

Will didn't take being called a fool easily. He regretted having invited Colin to stay with them for a few days. When Colin set his mug in the sink and then left the room without a word, Will sat back and breathed deeply. His hands were shaking and his breath came fast.

Of course he would see to Abby's needs.

Colin's implication that he would do anything else offended him. Colin knew Will well enough to know that he was a responsible man. Abby would be fed, clothed, protected and provided for while she was here. He would make sure her reputation was still intact and that she found a good home to work in when she was ready to leave.

His needs were what worried him. How was he going to face his kitchen alone, morning after morning, once she was gone? Colin was right; his boys would grow up and start lives of their own. In just the three weeks she had been on the farm, he had gotten used to her coffee first thing in the morning and a cup of tea on the back porch after the boys were in bed. A lifetime of loneliness was close to forever, but he wouldn't ask her to give up her happiness to keep him from a little loneliness. What kind of man would ask a woman to give up her life for his dreams? He had done it once and because of it his first wife now lay in a grave at the top of a knoll overlooking the farm. He wasn't going to ask that kind of sacrifice from another woman.

He stood from the table, picked up his mug and left it in the sink. He was almost out the door before he realized what he had done — expecting Abby to clean up after him. He retraced his steps and made quick work of washing the two mugs.

Wanting to be alone with his thoughts, he went out to the barn, saddled his horse and headed out to the fields. Abby was nowhere to be seen. Maybe she needed some time to herself, as well. Now, if only the memory of her face would stop filling his mind, maybe he could find a little peace.

"Thank you, God, for my pa and for my new ma. Thank you for giving me a family like Jill's. Bless Bess and Buttercup and help them to give us more milk and help my new ma to have lots of babies so that I can have little brothers an' maybe even a sister. Bless Jake and Willy and help him not to win again at horseshoes next time. Amen."

Abby sat at the side of Tommy's bed and listened to his prayers. Many times Tommy's ideas made her want to giggle in the midst of prayer time, but tonight's prayer had the opposite effect. He staunchly refused to call her anything other than "Ma" and since Pastor MacKinnon was here, there was no time to talk with Will and make sure that that was all right. She hadn't wanted to talk to him anyway. She needed some space and time to adjust. But even with space and time, she wasn't sure she would ever adjust. If things went the way Will planned, she would be out of the house before the first snowfall.

She turned her thoughts back on Willy's prayers even as her own heart cried out to God about her loneliness and need to find a place where she was loved and wanted. As soon as the boys were tucked in and she had placed a kiss on their smooth, cool foreheads, she turned and fled down the stairs, leaving Will behind.

She rushed to her room, shut the door and leaned her back against it. She felt foolish, acting like a small child who had been chased by the fear of a monster down the hallway. Her breathing was heavy and she tried to concentrate on slowing it down so that no one would hear her. She didn't even light the lamp on her nightstand or have her routine cup of tea. She wasn't about to risk coming face-to-face with Will in the kitchen now that everyone else was bedded down. They would have to talk things out but not tonight. Not with his words bouncing around in her head — "If you like her so much, you should have married her yourself!"

She hadn't meant to eavesdrop and she hadn't stayed to hear much more. What she had heard was enough. Still puzzled about what made her unlovable, she poured out her heart to God.

Her most secret dream lay within reach and yet had never seemed further away. A wonderful man had shared his name with her and promised to protect her, held her hand during the challenges of the day and kissed her lips as sweetly. . . . The dream she pushed into a closed corner of her heart, too extravagant to contemplate for a girl who had never once been courted, felt in some moments as if it had come true. Will personified the man she dreamed of — but he admitted to his friend he regretted having married her even before the ink had dried on the parchment. When she heard Mr. Hopkins suggesting Pastor MacKinnon should have offered to marry her so he wouldn't have had to, she'd known he would never come to love her. They were bound by a vow and all the witnesses from the ceremony, but she was more alone than ever.

As if her thoughts could conjure him up, his steps sounded on the stairs above her and then drew closer. Her heart pounded against her ribs faster with each footfall.

Tonight was her wedding night! Most new brides would be looking forward to being alone with their new husbands. Instead she was cowering in her room. They had already agreed that nothing would happen tonight or any other night. What did she have to fear — other than the loneliness that had been her constant companion for so many years?

"Why, God? Why is it that no man can love me?" she cried quietly, wishing that Will would just go away even as she tensed, aware he stood silently outside her door. Was he angry that he was stuck in this situation? He and Pastor MacKinnon appeared to be good friends and yet he had yelled at him.

The floorboards creaked under his feet as he shifted, standing just on the other side of her door. Would he knock? Would he send her away? Maybe it would be better for everyone if she just left once and for all. Her hand was on the handle, gripping it so hard her fingers had turned white, and she couldn't feel the tips anymore but she couldn't find the strength to turn the knob.

The flooring creaked once more, making her jump and hold her breath as she heard him move away from the door. His footsteps echoed back to her as he left the house, the back door closing almost soundlessly behind him. Relief and grief mixed together and suddenly the weight of everything was more than her knees could bear. As if her bones had turned into wet sand, she collapsed on the floor, a puddle of grief, hot tears streaking down her face. She hugged her legs to her middle and cried out her longings for a home, a family, for someone to love her.

Morning came too early. Or maybe it was the lack of sleep. Abby had sat on the floor crying for what seemed like an eternity the night before. When she finally did get up, she changed clothes and hid under blankets that she pulled over her head even though the night was too warm for them. She tossed and tuned but didn't sleep until very late. When she awoke, she was aware of dreaming about looking for something lost and never finding it.

The rooster crowed once again and Abby realized the sky was already tinged with pink. She was late getting up and starting the fire in the stove. This was not a good start if she wanted to prove what an asset she was to Will. Rushing, she pulled her hair out of the braids she hadn't even undone the night before and brushed out the kinks as best she could. She rebraided her hair but didn't even bother coiling it into a bun again. She would deal with it later.

Donning her tattered housedress, she splashed her face with tepid water and rinsed out her mouth. Without looking at the mirror she rushed out to the kitchen. Her face felt stiff and her nose was stuffy, but she couldn't worry about that when there were hungry men to feed. As she fed the embers of the fire she was starting, she gave a wry laugh. She had never thought herself vain, but what else could you call it when she was concerned about how she looked even when the two men that were coming to the table for breakfast had both clearly indicated their lack of romantic interest in her?

The coffee had barely started to heat when the door opened and Will stepped into the kitchen. His face was pale and his hair still stood on end on one side. His eyes had fine lines around them and he looked as if he hadn't slept all night. Before she could say anything, Pastor MacKinnon followed through the door.

Abby felt relieved and disappointed at the same time. This morning would have been almost like all the others if it hadn't been for the pastor's presence and the *minor change* of marriage. If the pastor hadn't been there, would Will have acted more like his usual self or would there still be the stilted formality between them?

"Good morning, Mrs. Hopkins!" Pastor MacKinnon greeted her jovially. He looked well rested with a glint of mischief in his eyes. Was there a reason that he insisted on calling her by her new title? Did he do it to goad Will? She had assumed the pastor was just being formal with his parishioners earlier, but now she wondered.

"Good morning, Pastor MacKinnon, Will. I'll have your coffee in just a minute." She turned back to the stove and wished that she could make the coffee boil faster.

"She's Abby. We don't go by titles here, Colin." Will's voice was deep and husky.

"That's fine by me, as long as it's fine by her." Both men had come to wash hands in the sink and Abby stepped away, pretending not to hear the conversation as she reached for the mugs. Pulling ingredients for pancakes out of the pantry, she returned to find both men studying her face.

"Are you feeling all right?" Will asked, concern etched in deep lines on his brow.

"I'm fine. I'll get you the coffee in just a minute." She offered what she hoped looked like a smile even though her face felt tight and dry.

"No need. We just brought in the eggs and milk." He indicated to the items that sat in their usual places on the counter.

"Thank you. I'll —"

"Don't worry about us." Will stood blocking her path to the stove where the coffee now boiled. "But are you sure you're all right? Your face is . . . well . . . it's all blotchy. And your nose is red. Are you getting sick?"

Heat burned her face as she realized why her face was blotchy. She'd cried herself to sleep. Her eyes must be all puffy and red rimmed. She should have soaked her face with cool water last night before bed or at least looked at a mirror this morning.

"I'm fine." Even as she spoke, she realized that her voice sounded deeper and a little raspy.

"Then why —"

"I think she's had a long night pondering her current state, isn't that right, Abby?" Colin jumped in and saved Abby from having to explain herself but at the same time, proved that her worst fear was true. Everyone would know that she had been crying last night.

"Abby, is that true? Were you up all night crying about what the Scotts said about you?"

She didn't raise her eyes to meet Will's but focused on his hands clenched into fists at his sides.

"I wasn't up all night," she denied, unsure what else to say. There was no way she was going to admit that she had been crying about what *he* had said, not the Scotts' behavior. "If you'll excuse me." Stepping past him, she lifted the kettle from the stove and poured coffee into the mugs. Scooping a spoonful and a half of sugar into the first one, she stuck the spoon in and gave it a good stir before handing it to Will. She poured milk into the other and handed it to the pastor.

"I didn't notice you take any sugar yesterday, Pastor McKinnon."

"No, this is just how I like it, thank you."

"Breakfast will take a few more minutes, so if you would like to take a seat . . ." She motioned to the kitchen table, but both men shook their heads.

"There are stalls to muck out and horses to check on," Will answered, glaring at the pastor.

Silence reigned over the kitchen as Abby turned back to the stove. Soon the smell of ham frying and pancakes browning in a pat of butter filled the kitchen. The only sounds were the occasional sip of coffee from one of the men and the sizzle from the stove.

Pastor Colin finally set his cup down next

to the sink. "Thank you, Abby. That hit the spot. You make mighty good coffee. I think just the smell of breakfast is gonna make us work twice as fast today." He smiled good-naturedly and headed out toward the barn.

"He's right. Your coffee's always good," Will said begrudgingly.

"I'm glad you're pleased, Mr. Hopkins." She didn't turn around but kept her eyes on the stove, embarrassed that she'd used his formal title after he'd asked her to call him Will. It was easy enough to think of him by his first name in the privacy of her own thoughts, but when she was nervous while speaking to him, she'd accidentally slipped up. Would he scold her for forgetting his request?

"I'd be more pleased if you'd just call me Will," he said, his voice soft and gentle — almost wistful. Then he headed out without looking back. If he had looked he would have seen surprise and confusion written on her face.

Why did that woman have him all tied up in knots? Will knew he wasn't handling things well, but why did she have to look as if she was about to burst into tears? It broke his heart and made him sick to think he had brought all this about. If only he had been more careful. She was far from home and in a marriage that was nothing more than a sham. The least he could have done was to be a friend for her. But all he had managed to do was trip all over his own tongue.

Judging from the look on Colin's face, he was going to hear all about how much he had to change to be worthy of that lovely young lady cooking his breakfast back in his kitchen. Hoping not to have to listen to any more accusations than what were already flying around his own head, he gave wide berth to Colin mucking out the first stall.

Will couldn't ask for a better friend. In fact, Colin had been his closest friend since he had lost his brother. But even Colin had skated on thin ice yesterday, telling him to hold on to Abby and not let her go. Didn't Colin realize Will was trying to do the right thing?

Seeming to sense the tension, Jake worked silently instead of jabbering on about a lot of nothing as he normally did. Not that Will minded most of the time. He'd become more of a son than a nephew to Will. They had worked side by side since the day Matt and MaryAnn had died. It worried Will that in private, Jake wouldn't stop talking, but he wouldn't utter a word around most people. Abby was changing that, slowly earning his trust and then openly chatting with him about topics she was sure he would be knowledgeable in. Will had noticed that yesterday at church, Jake had seemed much more comfortable chatting with others, bringing up things Will had overheard him discussing with Abby.

The silence from both his best friend and his nephew pricked his conscience. If only his own thoughts would leave him alone. They were making up for the silence of the other men. Finally the chores were done and the smell of breakfast was pulling them all like a lasso looped around their middles.

"Why don't you go on in, Jake?" Colin suggested. "I have something I need to say to your uncle." Will looked up and found a solemn gaze pinning his.

"Don't waste your breath. I know I didn't handle that well back there," he admitted with a long sigh.

"Last night I thought you had the sense of a fence post. You proved me right this morning. Of course she was going to have a rough night! She's a newlywed who spent her first night as a married woman all alone. Not only that, her new husband is snorting like a bull that got into loco weed. If I were a betting man, I'd wager she didn't cry over what the Scotts said. Did it cross your mind that maybe she feels you've rejected her?"

Will stared at his friend. Abby knew the marriage was just to save her from either marrying one of the Scotts or putting up with their disgusting accusations. It provided a way for her to stay at the farm until other arrangements were made. It would take some time, but she would be leaving.

And how do you know that she won't want to stay come wintertime? The question crossed his mind for the first time. He bit his lip to avoid answering out loud. The answer *Because it's happened before* bounced around in his head.

She was a better person than Caroline — braver, kinder, more honest and honorable — but in the end, she wasn't that different from his first wife or her aunt. Caroline and Shelia had both made it clear to him that they deserved better than the rough prairie life he had to offer. If it was true of them, then it was definitely true of Abby. She deserved to be coddled, to have parties and nice, fancy dresses with lace trim and the ease of living in a town. He wouldn't make Abby give up a life she would enjoy to be stuck on a farm with only hard work and worries as her daily companions.

"What do you think I should do? Make her my wife and let her shrivel up and die like Caroline? There's no way I'll let that happen to Abby. I have already sent a letter to my mother to see if she can arrange some sort of work for Abby where she'll be safe and happy. Somewhere she can go to dances and get all dressed up. Ma knows many people in Philadelphia."

Colin's hand gripped Will's shoulder. Will expected anger or even contempt in Colin's eyes, but the sympathy he saw caught him in the gut like a sucker punch.

"She's not Caroline. Don't sell her short. She's got *grit*. I only met Abby yesterday, but I see a lovely woman who would be a good mother to your boys. And since they're already calling her 'Ma' you're gonna have the fight of your life to convince them she doesn't belong to your family."

"She's not Caroline but she still deserves better than this life, just like Caroline always said."

"Don't let the past ruin the future, Will," Colin stated seriously. "You'd have to be blind not to notice how lovely your wife is. Don't let her get away or you'll regret *that* for the rest of your life."

Colin released his hold of Will's shoulder and headed toward the house. Will stood still contemplating his friend's words.

"I don't know about you," Colin called

back without breaking stride, "but your wife's cooking has my mouth watering. If you don't hurry, I'm gonna eat my share and yours, too."

CHAPTER NINE

Almost a full month had passed since the fateful day that Abby went to the chapel and came home married. More than three weeks of slow adjustments to a strange loneliness even as Abby found things to occupy her hands and her mind. Life on the farm had started to fall into a routine. The cooler mornings were for chores and then she and the boys would stay inside in the shade and focus on schoolwork until suppertime. She faithfully watered and weeded the garden. Any day now she would have lettuce, celery, cucumbers and tomatoes to add to her meals. The potatoes and pumpkins would take a while longer.

Each day was an adventure with the boys, who were now baked brown by the sun. On Mondays she washed the laundry and then they made a game of hanging all the clothes on the line. Tuesdays and Thursdays she took the boys down to the creek to fish for dinner while she read to them.

One morning they got so involved in the adventures of their hero that Willy lost his fishing pole to a large catfish. He jumped in the water after his pole and barely caught it. Abby hesitated for an instant, but as soon as Willy's head went under a second time, she splashed in herself. She might not know how to swim, but she wasn't going to let Willy struggle alone.

She found the water was only up to her waist and the current wasn't strong enough to knock her off her feet. Relief made her giggle. Even with her sodden skirts, she had no trouble catching hold of Willy, who was still battling with the catfish. She held him tight around the waist as he reeled in the fish. Tommy extended the net as they brought in the fish together. Having scored victory over the catfish, Abby and Willy climbed the bank of the creek and lay out in the dappled sunlight filtering through the tree branches overhead, letting the warm breeze dry them.

"Thanks, Ma. I was scared till you caught me! I can't wait to show Pa and Jake I got the big one."

Abby lay there in the warm afternoon and breathed deeply to keep the tears scratching her throat from cursing down her face. It was the first time Willy called her Ma. If only she could be assured she would always be here to catch the boys. . . .

She and Jake became friends, too. After dinner and the boys' bedtime stories, Jake would find Abby on the porch out back. They took advantage of the twilight hours for her to teach him math and science. His mother had taught him to read when he was small, but he only read when forced to, until Abby lent him some of her books. As Abby encouraged him, he started to tell her more and more about his life and his memories of his parents. They realized that they had been about the same age when they had each lost their parents. The common ground helped them both to understand each other.

Her husband was the only person on the farm who held her at arm's length. While she had grown accustomed to calling him by his given name, an uncomfortable civility could be felt in their everyday encounters that hadn't been there before. Often, she would barely lay eyes on him from sunup to sundown.

Foolishly, she waited for the minute she saw him walking toward the house and felt something akin to relief at the sight of him each night. Just to see his face made her heart beat a little faster. She never gave in to the desire to fling the kitchen door open and embrace him, but she would silently cherish his arrival.

Often he would spare her only a few words although he listened to the boys chatter happily about what they had done during the day. He looked over the slates they showed him with a critical eye. Was he happy with the progress she had made with them or was he just resigned with her presence here until she left? He would often sit on the stairs of the porch and listen to Jake read or Abby explain something from the text but rarely added to the conversations. Unsure if he stayed for the company or the mug of tea Abby always had ready for him, she cherished even the encumbered moments, stealing glances at her husband when she believed he wasn't looking at her.

She tried to do all she could to ease his life and make him comfortable. She learned which foods were his favorites and how he liked his clothes cleaned and pressed. She made more clothes for the boys and two men. This Sunday, when the Hopkins family walked into the chapel, each of the men would be wearing a new shirt and matching pants.

While he didn't outwardly show much interest in Abby, she began to note little things he did for her to make her life easier. At least she hoped they were to make her life easier. He always made sure there was a huge supply of buffalo chips for burning stacked against the wall on the porch. The smell took some getting used to, but with wood so scarce, it was an easier fuel to come by.

Most nights, he would stay and dry the dishes while she washed. He'd send the boys up to get ready for bed, but he'd have Jake sweep the kitchen floor, as if not wanting to be alone with her. Every evening, before he went out to the barn, he checked that the door was latched and that she had everything she needed.

As the days passed, she wondered how long before they would get a letter back from his family with job prospects for her after the harvest. She prayed that none came. If she were honest with herself, she'd have to admit she didn't want to leave . . . ever. She wanted to somehow win the affection of her husband even if it seemed impossible.

The third Sunday of the month approached and Abby once again felt apprehensive. Colin had arrived on Thursday afternoon, entering the kitchen with Will at dinnertime.

"Hello, Abby. How are you doing?" His eyes searched hers, as if he would be able to tell if she was being truthful or not.

"Just fine, Pastor Colin. How have you been?" she asked, taking another plate out of the cabinet and setting a place for him at the dinner table. *So this is what is feels to have an older brother,* she thought to herself. She hoped that this visit would be better than the last. Will looked pleased to have his friend back.

"I've been just fine. But I must be getting old. I wrote back to the seminary where I studied and asked if they would send more preachers out this way. I'd like to buy up some of this good-for-nothing sod and try my hand at settling down." He shot a quick glance at Will and then washed his hands. "I was even thinking that this area is as good a place as any to settle. You have any suggestions about where I might want to stake a claim, Will?"

Will mentioned some land to the west of theirs. He shot a strange look at Colin and then Abby but kept talking about streams and land formations as the men took their places at the table. After dinner, the boys played in the front room with their blocks while Abby cleaned up the kitchen. The men sat around nursing their second cup of coffee. Their talk ranged from land and farming matters to families in the area to the last chapter that they had been studying in the Bible.

It was nice to see Will relax around the table again. Sadly she learned more about her husband's thoughts and current concerns from watching him interact with his friend than from their own stilted conversations in all the time they had been married. The realization made her long to know him better. Maybe if she could learn more about him, she could make him more comfortable with her staying for good. Maybe someday she would fit here as part of the family, not just some hired hand.

Saturday nights were the nights that everyone got a bath, whether they needed one or not. Abby let Will take care of bathing the boys and then she had the kitchen all to herself for her own bath. Back in her room, she brushed out her hair. It was still too damp to braid, so she took a walk. Feeling restless, she headed down toward the creek where the boys loved to fish. The sun was about to set and she didn't plan on being away too long. Tomorrow was church Sunday and she would see all the people who had witnessed her marriage just a month before.

Colin planned a picnic with some of the women of the congregation for after the service tomorrow. It would serve as both a welcoming celebration for Abby and a belated wedding reception. During the week she had made cookies and other sweets as well as baked bread and prepared a large hunk of ham from the smokehouse. Will tried to reassure her that the other women would see to everything, but Abby wanted to do her part.

As Abby stood next to the creek meandering slowly through the flat prairie, she watched the sun sinking to the west with a beautiful display of God's creativity in burnt reds, auburns, oranges and plums. If God could do that for the sunset that had no real significance except to mark the end of another day, couldn't He make her lovely enough to inspire something in the heart of a man who needed a helpmate? "Sorry, Lord," she whispered, struggling again to be content with His unknown plan.

The rippling water and the gentle breeze soothed her spirit even as the mosquitoes started to buzz around her. Noise from behind her caught her attention, and for an instant, she panicked, realizing just how vulnerable she was alone out on the prairie without a gun. Grabbing the closest stone that fit into the palm of her hand, she spun around. Laughter spilled out from sheer relief when she saw the form lumbering toward her was only Colin.

"Good evening," he called out in greeting, eyeing her strangely as she released her rock and tried to control her giggles.

"Good evening," she answered, her laughter bubbling out in spite of herself.

"Something out here amuses you?" Colin stood a few paces from her, staring out at the sunset as well.

"I wasn't sure you weren't a coyote or something else interested in carrying me off for its dinner. I was glad to see it was just you."

"It's reassuring you consider me better than a coyote," chuckled Colin, his green eyes glancing her way and then holding her stare.

For a preacher, he looked very human out by the creek at sundown with his strawberry-blond hair and freckles. His eyes registered concern. "Are you all right, Abby?"

"It's just been so long since . . ."

"Since you were able to laugh with an adult?" He finished the thought that she

231

didn't dare express. She didn't want to be unfair to Will. It almost felt as if she was betraying him for laughing with someone else, even if it was his best friend and their pastor.

Colin sighed deeply and turned his gaze back to the sunset. "How have you two been getting along?" he asked quietly, and she sensed he was asking as much as her friend as her pastor.

"I don't know. I . . ." She bit her lip and waited. She had longed to confide in someone since the day she had become Mrs. Hopkins. She wished her mother were still alive so she could ask her how a woman went about making a man fall in love with her. But to confide in Colin just didn't feel right. It wasn't the kind of subject she would have been able to speak with Pastor Gibbons about, either, and he was old enough to be her father. She also felt as if she was somehow betraying Will's privacy.

"Just give it time. He'll come around. He's not going to admit he needs a woman in his life just yet, but I know God sent you here to be his helpmate. I've been praying for you to come for a long time. He needs to see that not all women are like his first wife. I don't know if he explained anything about her, and I won't say anything more, but you should know that she left him very disheartened and convinced he never wanted to love, much less marry again."

"She must have been very beautiful. He doesn't seem to notice me at all," Abby said wistfully. She was lost in her own thoughts and didn't realize that she had said the last part out loud.

"On the outside, yes, she was lovely. But bitterness cripples both the heart and the spirit. God's word says He sees the heart and judges man by what He views on the inside. I know God finds you very lovely and I suspect Will does, too, whether he'll own up to it or not. Just don't give up. I know this wasn't what you expected when you answered his ad, but the boys need you and so does Will. He is just too stubborn to admit it yet."

"He still is waiting to hear back from his mother about another job for me," Abby blurted out.

"God has a way of working things out. Just keep trusting." There was a moment of silence and then Colin broke it with a question. "You've come to care for him, haven't you?" He had lowered his voice, watching her again.

She had not admitted to herself how much Will and the boys had come to mean to her,

233

but now, with Colin's green eyes drilling into hers and seeing past her facade, she knew she needed to be honest with him and herself. She nodded, closed her eyes and prayed that God would protect them all.

"Good. God put that love in your heart. You're a very special woman. You're a wonderful mother to the boys, and I know you'll make Will very happy, once he lets you. If he starts to get too grumpy you just let me know. I'll knock him upside that big, hard head with a two-by-four."

Before she could respond, she heard a rustling sound from the direction of the house. Abby and Colin spun around at the same time, Colin stepping closer to her as if to shield her from whatever was coming at them. They both relaxed when they saw Will. At first, the relief that no wild animal or Indian was heading straight for them caused Abby to smile, but her smile faded just as quickly as it had spread when she saw the fury in Will's eyes.

"What are *you* doing *here*?" His glare pinned her to the spot.

"I . . ." She swallowed, trying to figure out what had happened. He never told her she couldn't take a walk. "Is everything all right? Did the boys wake?" She suddenly realized how far from the house she was. She wouldn't have heard them if they had called for her.

"The boys are asleep. They have nothing to do with this. Why are you here with *him*?" His voice was pitched low and shook with anger. He glared at her as if she had just committed some grievous crime.

He had never reacted like this before and for the life of her, she couldn't understand what had happened. If the boys were fine, then why was he so agitated? Colin bristled at her side. She'd forgotten he was even there.

"I saw her come to the creek and decided that it would be smart to keep an eye on her," Colin answered before she could form a coherent reply. "She and I were just discussing how the last few weeks have been. As her pastor, and *your friend,* I wanted to make sure she was adjusting and all was well." Colin moved closer yet, as if still wanting to protect her. "As for her being here with *me,* I think she needs a friend from time to time."

As Abby watched, Will stood rigid, his face darkened like the powerful storm clouds she had seen unleash torrents of water on the open prairie. She skirted around Colin, unwilling to hear any more of their argument. Words from their last visit still replayed in her mind. *"If you like her so much . . ."* She forced herself to stop the thought and headed toward the path back to the house. They could work out whatever they needed to without her. With her growing feelings for Will, she didn't think she could stand hearing him declare his apathy toward her or their marriage.

As she tried to pass Will, his hand snaked out and caught her upper arm. His grasp was firm but not painful. His sudden movement stunned her and an energy zinged up her arm and left her short of breath.

"I'll walk you up. You shouldn't be out here alone at this time of night." His voice was gruff but his hand gentle as he released her and then tucked her arm around his elbow as if they were out for a walk in the city. It made Abby feel protected. She would have been almost pleased if he hadn't glanced over his shoulder and glowered at Colin.

"I'll see you in the barn." His voice promised that they still had unfinished business.

"I'll be there," Colin promised without heat in his voice or his eyes. "Good night, Abby. Get a good night's sleep so that you can stay awake tomorrow. I hear the preacher can sometimes get a little long-winded." His lips twitched and she tried not to smile at his teasing. Surely Will would take her laughing with Colin all wrong.

Once they were out of hearing distance, Will glanced at her, his scowl telling her all she needed to know. He was still upset.

"What were you thinking?" he questioned as if he were sure that she had gone completely crazy.

"I only wanted to take a walk. I wanted some air," Abby argued, hurt that he would treat her like a small child. Tears threatened to spill over, frustrating her. In the last few months she had cried more than she had in years back in Ohio.

"You've been here long enough to know better. There are animals that hunt at night, coyotes and wolves, and there is still the possibility of Indian unrest. I don't want you out at night. I don't want . . ." The anger in his voice diminished as he talked.

"You never said I couldn't take a stroll after dinner." She dropped her voice and slowed her pace, forcing Will to slow with her. Suddenly she felt forlorn. Whom was she trying to fool? She had only managed to bother Will again. Sighing deeply, she trudged on.

"It gets dark fast. You should be in the house, safe and sound." His voice carried on the still air of the evening and she wondered if Jake could hear them from the barn as they came into view of the barnyard. She had left the boys' window open and didn't want them waking at the sound of grown-ups arguing, either.

"Are you feeling all right?" His voice dropped and he slowed to a stop, turning her to face him in the shadows near the front of the house.

"I'm fine." It wasn't really a lie. She was healthy and uninjured — well enough to do all of her duties. If her heart was troubled . . . Well, he didn't need to know that, did he?

"No, you just shivered. Did you get a chill down by the creek?" His voice spoke of his concern and it warmed her somewhere close to her heart.

"No. I'm fine," she asserted more convincingly.

She wanted to tell him that she was shivering because he was upset with her and the fact broke her heart. That she cared about him, and hated the distance that had sprung up between them. But he didn't want to hear any of that, so she mumbled an excuse and fled into the house. Once again, she curled up into a ball in her bed, hidden under her sheets, and cried her heart out to God.

Why did loving Will hurt so much? And now she knew that she did love Will. She longed to see him smile, wished he would hold her close and kiss her again, as he had done the day of their wedding. She missed him when he was out in the fields, away from her and the boys, and she missed him when he sat across the porch from her, within a stone's throw and a million miles away. If only he could love her in return.

CHAPTER TEN

"So, my brothers, God is telling us here in Psalm 90 verse 12 that the true measure of wisdom is to 'number our days' so we can live in a way that serves God and his children. Now, you may say to me, 'But, Colin, how am I supposed to count my days if only God knows how many days or years I have left?'

"And I would answer you that you are correct. It's the very point Moses is trying to get us to understand. Just a few verses before, Moses writes that the days of man are fleeting and a thousand years for the Lord is like a day. He depicts our life like the grass that spouts in the morning and withers by the afternoon. We may have the next fifty years at our disposal or we may be standing in God's presence later on this very day. Since we don't know what the number is, then prudence would dictate we live every day as if it were to be our last — as if

240

what we do with the next ten minutes may be the only legacy we leave behind."

Colin looked out and caught Will's eye. The church was crowded and Will wished there were more windows to open. It was stuffy inside and he felt grumpy and fidgety — though those feelings probably had less to do with the airless room and more to do with the way he had mishandled everything last night. Like a snorting bull, he had seen red when he finally found Abby contentedly conversing with Colin by the creek.

Colin's words about treating each day as your last gave him a guilty shiver. Thank goodness the previous day hadn't been his last one, because he sure would like to have done better. After dinner, he'd had the urge to stay and talk with his wife, but she had needed to bathe and get ready for the Lord's Day. Finally settling on the pretext of checking to see if she was ready for the picnic the following morning, he'd gone back to the house. When he didn't find her in the kitchen or in the boys' room, he dared go toward her room only to find the door was still standing open. Assuming that she was in the outhouse he headed out the back door. His heart plummeted to his toes and his hands felt like ice when his search gave no clue as to where his wife had gone.

Searching the barn and the yard around the house, he started to suspect she had gone somewhere with Colin. For a minute that reassured him, until he began to wonder if they were even then whispering sweet nothings. Colin had already admitted he admired her cooking and her mothering skills. Now he was talking about settling down. Didn't he understand that Will wanted to save Abby from the hardships of being a farmer's wife? If she was going to stay in Nebraska, then it should be by *Will's* side — he was the one whose sons needed her. He was the one who knew and appreciated all her wonderful abilities. He was the one who cared for her . . . more deeply every day, for all that he tried to avoid her.

But because he cared for her, Will was the one who was going to do the right thing. He was going to find a job for Abby in some comfortable city far from the prairie. She'd be happy there, which was what mattered most. And he wasn't going to let Colin convince her otherwise.

As the trail to the creek twisted around and he could see the two of them standing a few paces apart, relief made his heart leap because she was safe! Then his anger returned because she was out for an evening stroll with his best friend.

When Colin came back to the barn, he had not so much as said a word about their exchange by the creek except to chuckle about how quickly Abby had gotten under Will's skin. It was the final straw as far as Will was concerned. He'd told Colin to keep his nose out of other people's business and not follow Abby around in the evening without staying within view of the house. Colin had just laughed and offered to pray before they hit the hay. Now he stood calmly preaching to his congregation and Will wondered, with a sinking sense of dread, if Colin's sermon was personally motivated. Had Colin decided that the best way for him, personally, to live life to the fullest would be to settle down on a claim in Nebraska . . . with Abby as his wife? He'd have to talk Colin out of it and make his friend see that Abby didn't belong in Nebraska — and certainly not as any farmer's wife. Not even Will's.

"Here in this very community, we have had our share of heartbreaks and funerals." Colin continued his sermon, his eyes roaming the congregation and once again settling on Will. "None of the brothers and sisters who have gone before us woke on the morning they were to meet their Savior knowing it was their last day. They went about, living their lives as they always did and then, without God asking them leave, He collected them to Himself.

"While we may have mourned them for a time, and still miss them, I doubt any of us who truly understands where our departed loved ones are today would ask to have them returned from Paradise to the suffering in this fallen world. I have to confess there are days when I grow weary of the drudgery and suffering here and plead with God to take me to my eternal rest, but most mornings I rise with the desire to see another sunset and another sunrise. I hope to someday settle down and find some near-sighted girl who will take pity on my sorry hide and decide to make a family man out of me. There are mornings when I beg God to hurry that day and others I resign myself to the life God has chosen for me to serve Him, even if it means living the rest of my life like a Gypsy, not having a home to call my own or a family waiting for me around the hearth at the end of the day. But while I can't know what God has planned for me, I *can* make the choice to embrace His blessings to the fullest of my ability, enjoying every day I'm given and never holding back from all the happiness life offers. No matter how many days the Lord grants every one of us, we need to spend each day full of joy for the wonders of His gifts, and praise for His name."

Soon Colin brought the service to a close with a prayer of blessing and protection for the families of their church. "Don't forget, we have a picnic planned for after service. I have been informed by a very reliable source that there's enough food out there to feed an army. Since we're all part of the army of the Lord, I hope that's true. Once the ladies have the food set out, we'll ask the good Lord to bless the food and our fellowship. This is a special day when we get to welcome Mrs. Hopkins to our community. As you all know she and Mr. Hopkins were married just last month in a ceremony after the service. Today we'll have the reception."

In a matter of minutes, the women assembled all manner of tempting dishes on the two long tables made out of sawhorses with flat boards laid across that the men had set up earlier. Once Colin said grace for the food, the serving began. Mothers collected their children and filled their plates before withdrawing to the blankets that had been laid out in the shadow of the church. Then the men surged around the tables like a swarm of bees. Will saw to Willy and Tommy and then stood to the side and watched as Abby graciously greeted everyone and helped serve.

He was just about to get into line when Abby's eyes found his and she smiled shyly. His pulse tripled and he could hear his heart pounding in his ears. A hurt look crossed her face and her smile slipped away as she busied herself with the plates of two more farmers while he edged closer. Had she expected him to smile back? Of course, he reasoned with himself. She was the stranger here and she deserved to know that he was so proud of how well she was getting along with everyone. What a dunce he was to squash what little joy she was getting from the potluck.

Stepping up in line, he stopped in front of her and found that she had already served a heaping plate of all his favorites. "You look like you're enjoying yourself," he stated, hoping to make up for his coolness just seconds before.

"Everyone is so nice and welcoming," she answered without looking up at him. It bothered him that he had hurt her again.

"Thank you for the food, Abby."

"You're welcome." She started to prepare another plate of food — presumably hers since everyone else had their plates — so he waited until she finished. "Did you need something else?" she asked, clearly surprised to find him still waiting on the other side of the table when she reached for a slice of bread.

"I thought it only proper I escort my lovely wife to our blanket with the boys," he explained, proud that he had managed to compliment her. Her eyes found his for a second and then she nodded.

"Oh, we need to appear to be together for the Scotts," she whispered as he led her across the thick grass he and Colin had cut down the day before in preparation for the picnic.

"In part, but I also wanted to say you look lovely and did a wonderful job with the meal. Everything looks delicious." Her surprise looked turned to pleasure and a slight blush graced her cheeks, but before he could say any more, they arrived at the blanket the boys occupied and the opportunity to talk privately was gone.

He held her plate for her while she twisted and settled all her skirts so she could sit on the blanket and then she held both plates as he flopped down next to her. The boys, their food half gone, crowed around and kept a constant chatter as he and Abby started to eat. Will watched Abby as she patiently answered all of Tommy's questions and told funny stories to him and Willy. To everyone around them at the picnic they must have appeared to be a real family — especially with both boys calling her Ma.

"Pa!" Tommy plopped down next to Will, his hazel eyes bright and happy. "Did you hear me, Pa?" Tommy's little hand nudged his arm, pulling his focus back on his little boy.

"Sorry, what did you say, son?"

"I said Ma taught me to count all the way to thirty. Wanna hear? She showed me a cal . . . can . . . calendar — it has boxes and numbers. Just like Pastor Colin said today. Ma taught me to be wise 'cuz she taught me to number the days."

Will cast a questioning look at Abby. The knowing grin she sent him told him that not only had she followed Tommy's strange logic but she also knew Will didn't have a clue. She had come to understand his boys better in a few months than he had done in all the years he raised them. If only she could stay.

"Tommy, Pastor Colin was talking about something a little different today, sweetheart. I taught you how to number a calendar to tell us what day of the week it is or what month of the year. But what Pastor Colin was talking about was that if we really want to be wise, we will learn to live every day for God as if there might not be any more days here for us. I hope you grow up to be very old and have children and grandchildren. . . ."

"Yeah, and you'll get all wrinkly and your hair'll fall out like ol' Mr. Patterson," Willy added.

Abby took control back of the conversation. Grinning at Willy, she fingered his hair out of his face as she continued. "Sometimes God wants us in heaven before we get to be all old and wrinkly. The Bible says no man knows when he will be called to stand before God and give an account for his life. We can't wait till we're old like Mr. Patterson to start living the life God wants us to live."

"What's that mean?" Tommy asked.

Will took a deep breath, praying for wisdom and answers, but Abby already started to explain. Nodding his encouragement, he started praying that God would give her the right words to share the message of salvation with Tommy.

"God's got plans for all of us," she began.

"Like when you make plans for our lessons?" Tommy asked.

Abby laughed. "Well, a little like that, I guess. God's plans tell us where we're supposed to go, and what we're supposed to do to be good people, and find happiness."

"Did God tell you to come out here to us?" Willy questioned, leaning against Abby's side. She wrapped an arm around him in a hug.

"He certainly did." The words hit Will like a pleasant shock. She still believed that — that God had brought her out here, that their humble home in Nebraska was where she was supposed to be? He pushed down the sense of hope that that gave him, reminding himself that she still didn't understand just how grim prairie life would be. She'd come to hate it, just as Caroline had. And she'd come to resent him if he tried to keep her there. He needed to remember that.

Will listened as Abby explained God's ultimate plan — to save mankind with the gift of His son. As she talked about sins and the forgiveness God offered through Jesus's sacrifice, Will was reminded of his own shortcomings. If he'd been more careful, if he'd paid more attention, then he wouldn't have led Caroline on, leading to their disastrous marriage. If he'd been more considerate, more aware of her needs, maybe she wouldn't have wasted away. If he'd been more diligent getting information from Abby before hiring her as his house-keeper, maybe they could have avoided the misunderstandings and complications that led to —

That led to this: sitting on a picnic blanket, surrounded by a happy, healthy, well-fed and well-dressed family while a kind, beautiful woman gently spoke of God's message to his youngest son. How could he regret this? How could he repent his actions when they led to the gifts Abby had brought to his family?

Was there any chance that his marriage to Abby was truly part of God's plan? Was this really the life that God wanted him to lead?

"Someday," Abby concluded, "each one of us will reach the end of God's plan for us, and it'll be time to go home to Him in Heaven. If you want to be able to go to Heaven, you have to tell Jesus that you know you are a sinner and you accept the gift of His forgiveness. He promises in the Bible that He will forgive anyone who asks Him to. Would you like to ask Jesus to forgive your sins today?"

Tommy nodded his little head and Abby took him into her arms, snuggling him close. She told him to close his eyes and she led him in a prayer to open his heart to the forgiveness Jesus promises to all who ask.

"I bet Pastor Colin would very much like to hear that you just asked Jesus to be your Savior, Tommy," Abby suggested. "Would you like me to go with you so you can tell him or do you want to take your pa?"

"I want you both to go with me," Tommy answered.

"Sure thing, son," Will managed to choke out. "I'm so glad you let Jesus be your Savior."

"Did you ask Him to forgive you, too?" Tommy asked innocently.

"I did. I wasn't much bigger than you are now. I remember my grandpa took me to go fishing and while we were waiting for the first fish to bite, he started to talk to me about how life is too short to wait until we get big to make the most important decision in our lives. He said that I needed to get my life right with God before I could be a good man."

Tommy stood and threw himself into Will's arms. The force almost knocked him onto his back, but he managed to keep upright. "I love you, Pa. I'm glad you could be a good man 'cuz then you could be my pa."

"I love you too," Will whispered as he hugged Tommy tight. He hooked his other arm around Willy and pulled him into the hug, as well. Seeing Abby watching them, he smiled and mouthed, "Thank you" to her. She smiled back and he felt the force of it all the way to his toes. She had a lovely — powerful — smile.

Both boys pulled away and cuddled with Abby for just a moment before they were ready to run off and tell Colin. Will stood and extended his hand to Abby to help her stand. Her fingers slid into his palm, and their eyes caught for just a second before she looked away. The same burning question from before filled his head. Was she the one God wanted for him — part of a life that followed God's plan? He wanted to believe it, but he couldn't be sure. He'd been selfish with his first marriage, forcing his choices onto Caroline, believing he knew what was best for them both. Was he letting his own selfish wishes get in the way again? Until he was certain, he couldn't open his heart to Abby with all of his feelings for her. But there was still one thing he had to say.

"Thank you. I . . . I'll always be beholden to you for taking the time to get to know my boys and being sensitive to the Holy Spirit working in my son's heart. Today his eternity was determined and I have you to thank for that."

"No. You have the Lord to thank for that.

The time was right and God just chose to use me to explain to him. I'm sure you would have said the same things, or maybe Jake or Colin. But I am glad I was here for it. No matter what happens, I'll always remember this day." Her voice cracked at the end and she turned away, following the boys.

CHAPTER ELEVEN

"Good morning, Jake. How are you today?" Abby greeted the young man she'd truly come to see as her nephew. In the last five months since she had arrived to Nebraska, they had become as close as she had been with Emma's boys.

"Great, Abby. Uncle Will is thinking we'll be done harvesting in a few more days. He thinks maybe I could go into the town with him when he goes to sell the wheat and extra vegetables."

The news shouldn't have been surprising, but it still shook her. Will hadn't said anything to her about it. Despite the rocky beginning, they had managed to return to friendship during their four months of "marriage." Friendship — but nothing more. Will and Jake continued to sleep out in the barn and even though Jake didn't ask questions, Abby felt his curiosity at times. Will treated her no differently than he had when she was just his housekeeper. It was a relief to have the odd distance between them from their first month of marriage gone, but she still wished their relationship could be something more. Sometimes she wondered if Will felt the same way. There were times . . . times when she felt him watching her moving around the kitchen or when she was on the porch and he would sit in the quiet and just wait. It felt as if he were being pulled toward her but was holding himself back.

"That sounds exciting. How long has it been since you've gone to town?" Abby asked, forcing herself to sound interested instead of panicked. Would Will expect to take her to the train station then or would he leave her back at the farm with the boys? She would rather stay on the farm for the next ten years and never see the town again if it meant staying with her family.

"We went every fall with my parents. It's been a few years. Not since they passed," Jake answered with a shrug, but by now Abby knew the young man too well to be fooled by his pretended nonchalance.

"That was almost seven years ago! Why haven't you gone back?"

"Well . . . someone had to stay with the livestock." Jake explained it away but Abby saw something else in his eyes.

"Didn't you want to go this last time, when the others came to meet me at the train? I'm sure Will could have gotten someone from another farm to come out and check on the livestock or even take them over to someone else's spread until you got back," Abby argued.

"I was fine staying here. See, I'm not . . ." His face turned a bright red and he ducked his head as he tended to when she had first arrived.

"You're what?" Abby prompted in a quiet voice, waiting for him to raise his eyes and answer.

"I'm not very cultured or educated. I'm just a country bumpkin and I, well, I'm not really fit to go to town."

"Since when? You are a very well-mannered young man. If you weren't, I would have let you know by now. You were terribly shy when I first came, but you do really well now, talking with everyone at church."

"But I don't have any schooling," Jake disputed.

"You've been taught the basics of reading and writing and I've helped you with some of the more advanced math. You're very smart."

"No, she said . . ." Jake turned away and seemed about ready to head back out the kitchen door without breakfast.

"Wait, Jake. Who said what?" Abby pressed, grabbing his hand to keep him from leaving.

"It doesn't matter. She was right. I'm just a simpleton. I don't know how to treat a lady or how to act in public."

"Who said that to you, Jake? Was it someone from church?"

He shook his head and Abby tightened her grip.

"I want to know who lied to you, Jake. You're a wonderful person. It's been a pleasure to get to know you. Your own parents and then your uncle raised you very well. I'd be proud to introduce you to my nieces if they were here. You have nothing to be ashamed of. You might find some things in town confusing because you didn't grow up there, but that doesn't mean that you're worth any less than any city boy. You just need to learn." He stopped fidgeting and listened but he didn't look her in the eye.

"Jake, I want you to believe that God made you special. You're young yet, but you're so handsome we're going to have to beat the girls back with a broom one of these days." Abby grinned, but he didn't even smile.

"Who said those horrible things to you, Jake?" Abby entreated.

"My aunt," Jake stated flatly, in a voice just above a whisper.

"Do you mean your aunt Caroline?" Jake didn't answer, but Abby didn't really need the confirmation. Caroline was the only aunt Jake had known, growing up in Nebraska.

"She lied. I'm so sorry that she said those horrible things to you, but they were lies. You can't possibly believe her." Abby moved to stand directly in front of Jake. "You have to understand — I never met her and don't want to speak ill of the dead, but she lied to you. Don't let the words she said dictate who you are or who you become. When I see you, I see a wonderful young man who is very smart and capable. Someday you can have your own farm just like this, or breed hoses or cattle or anything else you want."

"No. I'll always just be a stupid farmhand. Uncle Will needs me and he has given me everything I've ever needed. It's an okay life. I don't mind."

"Have you ever thought about what you'll do for yourself?"

"No. I can't run my own farm. I'm too

stupid. I can't read enough and someone would just swindle me out of everything."

"Is that what you know or what your aunt told you?" Abby pressed; her gaze was steady as she waited for Jake's answer.

"That's a good question, Jake. I'd like to hear the answer to that myself," Will said, startling both Jake and Abby.

"I heard what Abby was saying through the window," Will informed Jake.

After a pause, Will took a seat and motioned Jake to take the one next to him. "I'm sorry I didn't realize what Caroline had said to you, or how it's hurt you all these years."

Jake flopped down in the chair at the foot of the table. Abby turned back to the stove, caught between the urge to leave to give the men some privacy for their conversation and to stay so that she could be of help. Will looked like a fish out of water, trying to deal with the fragile ego of his nephew. Emotions didn't seem to be his area of expertise.

"You were always so busy trying to keep everything together. She was always saying stuff about you being . . ." Jake stopped and looked down at his lap.

"I don't care what she said about me," Will answered, his voice soft. "I know she was angry with me. That's nothing new. But

I didn't know she'd hurt you, as well."

Will reached out across the empty chair between the two and briefly squeezed Jake's shoulder. "Listen, Jake, you're your father's son and I knew Mathew better than anyone. So I know, for certain, that he'd have been very proud of you. You are very smart. You have a special way with horses, and I wouldn't be able to get nearly as much done without your help. I can't believe you didn't tell me about these doubts you've got about yourself. All this time I just thought you didn't want to go to town because it brought memories of when your parents went and didn't return."

Silence filled the kitchen. Both men sat staring at their hands, resting on the table in much the same loose fold. If Abby hadn't known that Will was Jake's uncle and not his father, she wouldn't have been able to tell by looking at them. She knew that Will loved Jake as much as he loved Tommy and Willy.

"Jake, I need to ask you to forgive me. I was struggling so much with all that was going on that I didn't pay enough attention to you and how you must've been feeling." Will looked Jake in his eyes and Abby held her breath, waiting for Jake to acknowledge his uncle.

"It's no big deal. You had your hands full with everything else. I was just glad that you didn't send me back East to live with Grandma or in some orphanage." Jake ducked his head and didn't make eye contact.

"Jake . . ." Will stood and cleared his throat. Squatting down next to his nephew, his hand on the teen's shoulder, he looked him straight in the eye. "Your pa and I had a covenant, kind of like David did with Jonathan in the book of Samuel. I promised to see to you, your ma and any other of his kids if anything ever happened to him. He promised to do the same thing if the tables were turned. Half of this homestead is yours when you come of age. You've worked by my side like a man and deserve it. This was his dream before it was mine. If, when the time comes, you want to concentrate on breeding horses or raising cattle or anything else God puts in your heart, you have my blessing and my help if I can."

Will stood and Jake unfolded from his chair, as well. Both men stood face-to-face, Will only a few inches taller than the boy. Soon Jake would be as tall as his uncle. Neither one seemed to know what to do or what to say.

"Come on, now, give each other a hug. If

you don't, I'm not gonna feed you for a week." It slipped out so easily she was turning back to the stove to give the men some privacy when she realized what she had said and felt her face turn the shades of sunset. While she was Will's wife in name, she was just his housekeeper in truth, and wanted to keep that position as long as possible. Threatening to not comply with her work was not exactly the way to ensure her stay.

Jake was the first one to laugh. "Well, now, Auntie Abby, you sure know how to threaten a man. You've got us so spoiled we'd probably starve to death the first day."

"So don't make me do it," Abby threatened playfully, pleased that Jake was teasing her.

"You heard the woman," Will mock-growled at his nephew. "I guess we've been given our orders."

A moment later, they both shook hands and then Will pulled Jake into his arms. The hug resembled a wrestling match between bear cubs as Abby watched it in her peripheral vision. She swallowed back the lump in her throat and sniffed to keep from crying, forcing a smile instead.

Ever since Pastor Colin had preached about "numbering one's days," she had tried to do just that — live each day as if it would be her last day to interact with Will and the boys. She looked for ways to encourage them or to teach them so that when she left, they would have a host of memories that would keep her alive in their hearts.

She also prayed for them and their daily growth. Even as she sewed seam after seam into their new winter clothes, she prayed God would sew His Word in their hearts so they would carry it with them always. Abby thanked God with tears streaming down her face the night of the picnic when she had the privilege to help Tommy accept Jesus as his Savior. Now she added to her precious memories the privilege of seeing Jake and Will draw closer and Jake overcome hurtful lies his aunt had told him years ago. Lies that had kept him from enjoying social activities with his peers and other adults.

She placed a cup of coffee before each man and returned to her work. Listening to Will and Jake take their seats again in the kitchen and just sit in silence, a peaceful silence that no one wanted to spoil with words, she felt as though this had been part of the reason God had brought her all the way out to Nebraska. He had a divine plan to use her in the boys' lives and in Jake's. Even as she resigned herself to the truth that she might not have many more days with the Hopkins, her heart cried out to God. If she had been able to bless them in little ways, it would only stand to reason that staying for a lifetime would bring a lifetime of blessings.

But the words *Teach me to number my days* rang in her mind. Hers were but a few days on earth. She would have to find a way to survive when the allotted number had been spent here and then she'd have to accept when it was time to move on.

Later that night, the boys already tucked in bed and the kitchen set to rights, Abby slipped out onto the porch with a cup of tea and a light shawl draped around her shoulders. Now the evenings cooled quickly once the sun began to set. The nice part was the bugs didn't bother nearly so much as they had done in the heat of the summer. She settled into the swing with her knitting on her lap. There was a lantern on in the barn and she could hear the frogs still singing in chorus down by the creek.

She had often been tempted to take a stroll down by the creek at this time of night, just to get away from the house and enjoy God's peace and quiet. No wonder He had chosen this time of day to meet with Adam and Eve in the Garden. But she had never ventured away from the house again.

She had sensed Will's deep concern for her the night he had found her and Colin talking by the creek, and she hadn't wanted to worry him again.

As if just thinking about him conjured him up, he emerged from the barn and headed toward the house. "Good evening," she called out from the shadows of the porch. "Everything all right?"

"Good evening," he called back. His eyes searched her out in the shadows and then, when he spotted her, a smile lit his eyes and his lips curled at the edges. It was a warm, friendly smile. She reminded herself not to read anything more into it than that. "Everything's fine."

"Want a cup of coffee or tea?" Abby offered, setting her knitting to the side and starting to stand. In a blink, Will was up the stairs and held out a hand to steady her on her feet.

"A cup of tea sounds good tonight. But stay put. I can get my own," he reassured her, motioning her back toward her chair.

"No, sir. I just washed up in there and I'd rather make a little mess than have to deal with the bigger mess you'll make," she teased, rewarded by his boyish grin in return.

He held the door for her, then waited as

she prepared the tea. By mutual accord, they returned to the porch with their mugs. She settled on the swing and he sat next to her, leaving as much space between them as possible.

"I wanted to say thank you for your help talking to Jake earlier today. You've done wonders pulling him out of his shell. You've done wonders for all of us, really. I don't know what I would have done without your help this summer," he started, his gaze holding hers.

Abby bit her lip and tried to calm her racing heart. What was he saying? Was this the opening of a discussion about how she'd done enough for them, and now it was time for her to leave? Until now, he hadn't heard back from the East. At least he hadn't told her about anything from his family in the post. In fact, just a few days before he'd commented how strange it was that his mother hadn't sent her regular letters.

In the same span of time, her nieces, Megan and Hanna, had both written letters to her, telling her how much they missed her. Her breath caught in her throat when she dreamed about having her family around her. If only her marriage had been a real marriage, maybe her husband would have let her bring out the girls for a visit.

The second letter had arrived just before meal time last month. Colin had brought it for her. She waited to read it until right after they had finished the meal. She had sat at the table and drunk in the information from her nieces. Their words had her missing them so much that they sent her rushing to her room for a good cry, leaving behind three confused and uncomfortable men. A few minutes later, the boys knocked on her door and then came in and curled up on the bed on each side of her and offered her a handkerchief until she had calmed down. Tommy asked if he could kiss her "owie" and make it better, but she had explained that it was an "owie" inside her heart that was sad without her nieces and nephews.

She cringed at the thought of how sad her heart would be missing Willy, Tommy, Jake and Will if the time had finally come for her to leave.

Sitting out on the porch, Abby felt at home. It felt so natural to enjoy the calm of twilight by Will's side. For a moment, she let herself indulge in the dream that this would be her life. Working hard and laughing at life, hand in hand with a godly man, was all she could ask from God.

"I . . ." He shifted, then stood and paced to the railing, leaning on it with his forearms, his gaze taking in the barnyard, his back to her so she couldn't read his expressions.

"We're almost done with the threshing and I'll need to be taking the wheat to Twin Oaks so I can get it to the miller and then get our winter supplies. I had expected to have heard from my mother by now."

Abby held her breath and waited as Will kept his back to her. "I don't have any place to send you to. I'm sorry. I bet you're champing at the bit to get out of here. Do you have a family or somewhere . . ."

"No. I don't have anywhere to go. But I don't mind it here. In fact, I've become quite attached to the boys." Abby swallowed hard, not willing to expose all of her feelings. For all their warm, friendly conversations over the past few months, this was something they had never discussed. The topic of what would happen when she left had been studiously ignored. Now that they were finally talking about it, she had no idea what to say. What words would convince him to let her stay? "I feel safe here."

She watched Will's shoulders relax and it almost seemed as if he had let out a sigh. Did he truly think that she wanted to leave? "I don't know how you can say that. There's always the threat of bad weather, insufferable heat in the summer and harsh cold that penetrates the bones in the winter. Then again, the Indians could pillage the farm or we could get a swarm of locusts like there was three years ago. Or a draught could kill off the plants. . . ."

"If life is so hard here, why do you stay?" Abby blurted out, shocked at Will's pessimistic outburst.

"Now, don't you start! I've put too much work into making this dream happen. I've lost Matt and MaryAnn and even Caroline to this place. I'm not leaving."

"If you're staying, then shouldn't I stay, too? You need someone to take care of the boys. And someone to see after your needs, as well. You can't even cook. What'll happen to the boys once I go?" Abby's question was more a whisper but carried on the still night.

"They'll be brokenhearted. It was what I wanted to avoid. I didn't want them hurt."

Abby stared through the gathering darkness and tried to understand this man. "Would it have been better for them to not have had someone to feed them and take care of them all summer than to have heartbreak and know someone out there loves them even across the miles? My life will forever be richer for having known your family, for having loved your boys." She bit her tongue before she could add "for loving you."

Will shifted his weight against the banister and breathed deeply but didn't reply. The silence stretched out. Finally, Will turned toward her but didn't make eye contact. "I don't know. I . . ." He swallowed and shook his head. "Good night, Abby. Thank you for the tea."

He strode away to the barn as if someone were chasing after him. Abby didn't move until he was inside the barn and the door had shut. Collecting her mug, her knitting and the mug Will left behind, she went into the house, still pondering the abrupt end to their conversation. Could Will possibly consider it better to never experience love than to love and have to say goodbye?

Chapter Twelve

Will watched the horses plodding along and smiled to himself. He and Jake had left early and were making good time with their heavy load. His wheat had gotten a good price and now he had barrels of flour to get him and the boys through the winter. He'd purchased sugar, spices, limes, apples and raisins, too. All the ingredients Abby had on her list and a few extras.

The vegetable garden Abby had painstakingly cared for all summer had yielded an overabundance of tomatoes, onions, carrots, beans, lettuce and a number of herbs. She'd spent the better part of the last three weeks canning the produce and had sent some with him to sell, as well. The pumpkins vines slowly twining around the border of the garden all summer promised some large pumpkins for pies in the next month. This growing season had been a success and he admitted it was in large part due to the woman who would be waiting back at the house with dinner ready for them. He fought the urge to hurry the horses.

"So, you miss her?" Jake asked from the wagon bench next to him, bringing Will's focus back to the road and the here and now.

"The farm?" he responded, ignoring the jab in his conscience. He knew exactly whom Jake was referring to.

"Uncle Will — you taught me never to lie," Jake tsked.

"I think I liked you better when you weren't quite so mouthy," Will quipped, but even as he said it, he knew that the changes in Jake were due to Abby's attempt to bring out his shy nephew. She'd coaxed Jake into trusting her and then taught him a few social graces. If Will didn't keep a close eye on the young man, he was going to start thinking about things like courting and noticing the girls. . . . Not that there were many to notice in the area.

Abby was the youngest over the age of thirteen in the whole area.

"Come on, Uncle Will. You've got to admit you miss her just a little bit," Jake insisted.

"Yeah, she cooks a lot better than either of us. I can't wait to get back and see how she fared with the boys and the farm while we were gone."

"She had Colin there," Jake reminded him innocently.

"I know. I'm sure that everything is fine." Will said it as much to himself as to his nephew. It had been the best solution to have Colin stay in the barn so he could see to the livestock and chores while Will and Jake were away. His friend's presence should have served to reassure Will, but he also felt jealous. He was worried that Colin had been a better companion for Abby than he had been.

The men continued traveling in silence, Jake still smirking and Will fighting a battle with his emotions. Truthfully, he missed Abby something fierce. He even contemplated asking her to stay . . . to make their marriage a true marriage, not just a business arrangement. But he knew it wasn't fair to her to ask her to make her life with him in the middle of the harsh, wonderful prairie.

"Uncle Will, are we gonna keep sleeping out in the barn?" Jake interrupted his thoughts again.

"I . . . I don't know." It was another topic he had been debating.

The weather wasn't going to let him put off the decision much longer. The last three mornings he'd woken to frost on the ground. Soon the snow would come and then he and Jake would need to be sleeping indoors. Maybe he should rebuild the soddy where they had first lived. But was he being foolish to ignore the warm, sturdy house he'd built just because he'd have to share it with Abby? They were married, her reputation was secure — and of course, they'd continue to sleep not just in separate rooms but on separate floors. There'd be no harm in that, surely . . . except for the way it would make it feel as though they were all one, united family that would be staying together all winter. And that was something he knew couldn't be true.

Abby had been listening for the sound of a wagon since the day before, or more honestly, since the minute Will and Jake pulled out of the barnyard a few days before, but when it finally came, she almost missed it. She was canning some of the late tomatoes from her garden, her face matching their color from the heat of the stove. Will had promised to bring more canning jars for the squash and pumpkin, as well.

"They're here! They're here!" Tommy came bursting into the kitchen and swept past Abby, out the door and into the yard before Abby could even react. Willy was only two steps behind his brother, leaving the door wide open in his haste to see his father and cousin.

"Willy!" she called after him. He rushed back long enough to slam the door behind him. She had to fight the urge to hike up her skirts, dash out after the boys and throw herself into Will's arms just as his boys were doing now. Instead, she turned back to the stove before she gave in to the impulse. She tried to rein in her thoughts; she had never before wanted anyone to hold her, save her father when she was small. She gave herself a sharp rebuke about wayward daydreams and forced her attention on the tomatoes.

But even her eyes wouldn't obey and they kept straying to the window where she could see the men hugging and laughing with the boys. The sound of the boys' happy chatter mixed with the deeper notes of praise and questions from Will and Jake. All the voices floated on the wind and comforted her in the lonely kitchen. Colin met the group at the door of the barn.

By the time they had all trooped back to the house, Abby managed to set the table and have the roast, mashed potatoes and salad served and ready. Glasses of chilled milk were poured and standing at attention

as the door opened. She had wanted everything to be perfect, not that the men would
ever really notice little details.

The minute Will entered the room, Abby
felt her breath catch in her throat and her
heart speed up. The noise of the boys and
men talking seemed to fade into silence,
and for an instant, her eyes connected with
Will's. His face lit with happiness and he
stepped closer. She thought maybe he
would pull her close and hug her as a
normal husband would, but then the light
in his expression dimmed to something
more controlled and polite. Friendly, but
nothing more.

"Looks like a meal fit for a king, Abby,"
Will commented, taking his place at the
head of the table, not having come close
enough to shake hands, much less hug her.
Her disappointment choked her and she just
nodded.

"How were things here while we were
gone?" he asked as she settled in the chair
next to his.

"Fine, everything went just fine. And how
did your trip go? It's good to have you
back," she blurted out.

"It's good to be back!" Jake answered
from down the table. "Uncle Will's cooking
hasn't gotten any better since you've been

here, that's for sure. I'd like to have starved if it weren't for the thought we'd be coming home to your fine meals. Ain't that right, Uncle Will?" Jake tossed his uncle a knowing grin and ruffled Tommy's hair.

Colin said grace and thanked God for His protection on the men who had traveled and the family left behind. Once "Amen" was uttered the silence was broken only by the scrape of a fork on the plates and the boys chewing with their mouths open. The boys seemed to be in a race to see who could finish first and then they waited impatiently while the others finished, peppering their father and cousin with questions and squealing with delight when Will promised if they helped unloading supplies, he just might be able to find the stash of peppermint sticks he'd bought.

Soon, Abby was alone again with the dirty dishes. As she worked in the kitchen, she smiled to herself and hummed a hymn. At least for the night, her family was all home, safe and sound. Tomorrow would bring enough worry. As the men started filling her pantry with the sacks of flour and sugar, spices and dried fruits, Abby thanked God for the provisions for the winter months. It looked to her as if Will had purchased enough to hibernate for two winters.

She put some water on the back of the stove to heat for tea for the men as Will went up to tuck the boys into bed. They had missed their father the last few nights he was away and she wanted to give them time together.

"Ma," Tommy called down the stairs almost as soon as he had dressed in his nightshirt. "You need to come up and hear me say my prayers."

"Why don't you let your pa listen to them tonight?" Abby called back up, standing at the foot of the stairs.

Not only did she want to give Will some time alone with his boys, but she was also afraid of what would show on her face if she were in the room with just him and the boys when her heart was so full of happiness to have them all together again. If only Will shared her joy at their togetherness! But it was his right to want her out of his house and life, as much as it hurt to think that after almost six months, he hadn't grown to care for her the way her heart had become attached to him.

"No, Ma, we want you to tuck us in. You need to give us hugs and kisses and all that," Tommy argued.

"I'll be up in a moment." Abby sighed, looked around the room for something else to straighten up. Wouldn't you know that everything was in its place? She ducked into her room to search for her knitting but couldn't find it.

"Ma?" Willy stood at her door, his eyes following her search.

"Yes, Willy?" Abby answered absentmindedly.

"Are you coming up now?"

"I was going to, but I can't find my knitting."

"It's up on the chair next to our beds. Don't you remember? You started to knit there last night when Tommy was scared."

"You're right. Thank you, Willy. Let's go on up."

Willy took her hand and they ascended the stairs together. He let her go only to climb between the sheets and then patted the bed so she would sit down next to him. Once prayers were said and the boys had been given their good-night hugs and kisses, Will escorted her back downstairs. It was the first time they had been alone in more than a week and she found herself suddenly shy. Her nerves weren't helped by the worry that a letter had come from his mother that he'd collected while in town. Would this be the conversation where they made the plans for her to leave?

"So." Will sounded as uncomfortable as she felt. "Did the boys behave for you?"

"Yes. You should be proud," she answered, glad he had chosen a safe topic.

"Most of their good behavior comes from what they've learned from you these last few months."

"It's been my pleasure to be here with them, but you laid the foundation." Her mother had always encouraged her to say something nice and true at the same time. If ever a statement were true, it was that. Abby had so enjoyed getting to know and love the boys. How could she possibly walk away from them now? She bit her lower lip and tried not to give in to the urge to cry at the thought.

"I really appreciate all you've done out here. I know the conditions aren't what most women would expect and we're certainly a little rough around the edges. . . ." By now they had entered the kitchen and Abby started to prepare two mugs for tea without even asking.

"I don't mind. I've come to value all your hard work and sacrifices to make this place work. And look what a harvest God's blessed you with. Out here, it's easy to be mindful of our Creator. After all, if He doesn't send the rain, you don't have a harvest. If He sends too much rain, you won't get a harvest, either. I can see why Jesus asks God for our daily bread. In the city, we can forget our food and livelihoods don't come from the market but from God. The silence and the richness of this land, the flowers, the plants, the sky. . . ."

"It sounds like you have gotten used to this place. But you haven't seen a winter here. That might change your mind a bit."

"Hmm . . . I don't think so." She bit her lip and wondered if he would give her the chance to make up her mind for herself or if he was even now holding the tickets for her to return to the East.

He swiped his hand through his hair, standing it on end. Abby recognized his tic, hinting at his frustration. Maybe it was a good sign. Maybe he was at least a little bothered to have to send her off.

She handed him his mug of tea and instead of leading her to the table, he motioned to the door. "It's still light out. How about sitting out on the porch awhile?" he offered.

"Sure, let me go get my shawl." She was gone and back in a few seconds.

Seated on the rocking chair, she waited for whatever news Will wanted to share with her. He seemed suddenly nervous as he settled on the swing. He sipped his tea, looked over his land, put the swing in motion and then tried to sip more of his tea, succeeding only in spilling some down his shirtfront. Abby had to bite the inner part of her lip to keep from chuckling. He set the mug down on the windowsill behind him and continued swinging.

"Listen, Abby, I don't know what to tell you. I was hoping that by the time I got to Twin Oaks I would find a letter from Ma. Not that I want to get rid of you. Just the opposite. I see how much the boys have come to depend on you. They love you. Jake wasn't joking about my cooking. It hasn't gotten any better over these last months. If anything, it's gotten worse or maybe it's just that we've gotten spoiled by your expertise. And you have to know how good you've been for Jake, how you've helped him believe in himself. While I . . . I can't tell you how grateful I am for all that you've done.

"But it's not fair of us to think only about us and not about you. You need a family of your own. You need to be in the city where you'll have everything you want and someone who can give you more than just a load of dirty laundry and backbreaking work from sunup to sundown."

He stopped the swing and stared straight into her eyes. "I have to admit that I don't want to see you go. You lighten our day and make me smile. You should've seen Jake in town. I was afraid I wouldn't be able to get him to come back home. He had so much fun talking with all the young ladies. And I happen to notice the shirts and pants you made for us were as nice as the ones that Mayor Hoffman was wearing. Somebody, I think it was the waitress at the restaurant, made a comment about how nice Jake's hair looked."

"So, why are you so set on sending me back?" Abby whispered, her heart breaking with each word.

"Caroline always said, 'No woman on the face of the earth would want to be stuck out here, in the middle of nowhere.' She said she 'didn't want to spend her dying days out here,' but that's just what happened. This land is inhospitable for most, especially women.'"

Caroline had really said all of that? Abby knew Will's first wife hadn't liked the prairie — he'd told her as much on their wedding day — but she hadn't known the woman's opinion of the place had been that low. It went a long way toward explaining why Will was so convinced she'd be better off somewhere else.

But why wouldn't he believe her when she tried to tell him otherwise? Maybe Caroline hadn't wanted to spend her dying days out on the prairie, but Abby did. She wanted to spend every day she had left cooking and cleaning in this house, laughing and playing with the boys, being part of the family that Will had made. Maybe it would have to be enough for her to see his family was well cared for. Maybe they would never truly be her family, but it would be the closest she would ever come to having one of her own. After this summer, she would never be the same. She was sure because she would be leaving the biggest part of her heart behind with Will and the boys. Maybe there was still time to convince him. She could be happy as long as they were happy.

"Ma didn't write back," Will said, breaking the silence. "At least, I haven't gotten a letter from her yet. I'm of half a mind to send you on back to stay with her until she can get you established with someone from town. I don't know what's taking her so long, but if you stay too long, you're liable to get snowed in and then you won't be able to get out for a few more months."

"Please don't send me away yet," Abby urged. "I'm not ready to leave. There's still so much to do. . . ." She thought franticly of all the chores she still had before she felt ready for winter. "I haven't gotten the entire garden in yet. And the pumpkins are just about to ripen. You can't possibly tell me you know what to do with pumpkins or how to make pumpkin pie if you can't even make oatmeal! There's still the sweaters I'm knitting for the boys. That's why I asked you to bring me more yarn. I need to still take a look at all of your winter wear and patch anything that's gotten threadbare. I —"

"Abby, there's nowhere I can send you just now, so don't get yourself all worked up. I don't want a repeat of the first day." His eyes, full of compassion and something else, held hers for a moment before she remembered what he was referring to.

"There's something else we need to talk about," Will stated, and once again Abby held her breath. "It's gonna get too cold at night to have Jake and me sleeping out in the barn. I was wondering if it would be okay with you if we started sleeping upstairs, in our old rooms." He hesitated a moment and then continued, "You could still keep the parlor and of course we'd respect your privacy like always. If there were some other way I'd do it, but the snow is going to come soon and I don't want Jake getting sick."

"Of course!" Abby exclaimed, laughing out loud. The silliness of the owner of the house, asking her to let him sleep under his roof, tickled her funny bone. Or maybe it was the relief that Will wasn't set on sending her away quite yet. "I'll make up the beds right away."

"No, not tonight, Abby. Tomorrow will be soon enough," Will reassured her. "In fact, it will be sometime next week since Colin will be staying for a few more days."

Abby watched as Will looked out toward the barn. He looked distracted, probably thinking of all the things that needed to be done around the farm now that the harvest was in. The chill of the night stole into her bones, making her tremble with the reminder that summer was truly over, and her remaining days in Nebraska would soon be coming to an end. "I think I should be going in now," she said in a quiet voice.

She stood and picked up her mug. Will stood just as she tried to pass him and she tripped while trying to avoid a collision. His hands caught her upper arms and kept her from falling. Instead of letting her go once she was steady, though, he waited, seeming to force her eyes to meet his. When she did, she wondered at the emotions there. She saw fear, kindness, endearment and something more. Something that made her confused and excited all at once.

With a start, she realized that this was the first time in months that Will had touched her for more than the bare moment necessary as he handed her up and down on the wagon when they went to church. Maybe it was his warmth that pulled her like a magnet or maybe he really did pull gently on her arms, but suddenly she was taking a step closer and found herself engulfed in his arms, buried in the strength of his chest. She closed her eyes and pretended she would never have to leave the shelter of his arms.

"Oh, Abby. I . . ." He swallowed but didn't continue.

This was what he had kept himself from doing earlier in the afternoon. This was what she had seen in his eyes — the need to hold her close. His hand slid in a circular motion on the center of her back and she felt safe, protected and cared for. She let her arms wrap around his waist and felt as if she had finally come home. Was this what it felt like to be loved by a man? There was no doubt now, *she* loved *him.*

Almost as if he could hear her thoughts, he pulled away from her, holding her at arm's length. "I'm sorry, Abby. I guess I'm just tired tonight. I'm not thinking straight. You'd better get inside and stay warm."

The trembling started again, as the cold rushed in to embrace her much as Will had. Only this time, the cold started from inside. It had been too good to be real; Will hadn't held her close because he had feelings for her but because he was tired and lonely.

Without saying anything more, Abby rushed into the house and straight to her room. She heard Will enter a few minutes later, put the dishes in the sink, walk halfway to her door, then retrace his steps and leave out the back. Once again, she found herself weeping on her bed, wondering if she wouldn't be better off leaving. Living here, near a man she loved, and yet never having him return her feelings, would be harder than living miles away from him with just the memories to keep her company. Memories of being held and a fleeting kiss on her wedding day. Those two precious memories might be all she'd ever keep from her marriage to Will, but she cherished them and would remember them always.

"God, only You know the plans You have for me. . . . But I'm not happy about them right now. It hurts to not belong to Will while he holds my heart in his hands."

"I know the thoughts that I think toward

you . . ." The verse from Jeremiah echoed in her heart. *"Thoughts of peace and not of evil, to give you an expected end."*

"But, God, if they're supposed to give me peace, why do they hurt so much? Why did You bring me here to fall in love with a man who can never love me? Why did You bring me here to be part of a family that will never be mine?"

Chapter Thirteen

Will kicked a rock as he made his way out to the barn. He probably looked like Tommy having a temper tantrum, but he didn't much care. How could he have lost his head so easily? He had almost kissed her! He had taken her in his arms and held her close and she had fit perfectly in his embrace.

Not only had she fit, but she had melted against him so innocently, without knowing what that was doing to him. He would never forget the feel of her in his arms. Until the day he died, he would remember how he held her and she'd come willingly. But he couldn't let himself forget that he had her interests to consider. Whether she realized it yet or not, the prairie wasn't where she belonged. He was going to stay away from her as much as he could until she left, and then . . . then he'd have the rest of his life to miss her smile and laughter. He'd have the rest of his life to know that he had done the right thing by her. At least he could be proud that she would be able to go on and find a true love who would give her everything she needed.

"You don't have to come and sleep out here on my account," a voice called out to him from the doorway of the barn. "I'm sure it's much nicer in the house."

"Night, Colin." Will acknowledged his friend, even though all he wanted to do was turn and stomp away. He didn't want another lecture from his friend about how he was making the wrong decision. Right or wrong, it was his decision to make — and he was going to do what he knew was best for Abby.

"Why don't you just go back in there and tell that woman of yours that you love her?" Colin pried.

" 'Cuz you know if I do, she wouldn't go back East when my ma sends for her." A second too late Will knew his answer confirmed Colin's suspicions.

"Well, I'm glad you're not denying that you love her. And we want her to go back because . . . ?" Colin left the sentence hanging as if to prompt Will to admit to his own folly. Sometimes Colin was like a dog with a bone; he just wouldn't let it go.

"Just leave me alone, Colin," Will answered grumpily.

"No, not until you explain this to me. I saw how she wore a hole in the floor by the window, watching for you to come home. She took pains with that meal tonight and you know it's because you were back. Don't you see the gift God has given you? A beautiful woman who loves your boys and has fit into your life as if she had always belonged? How many other men in this territory would give their right arm to find a jewel like her? And here God just dumps her in your lap and you want to send His precious gift back East as soon as possible. Can't you see she wants to stay here with you?"

"She's young and doesn't know any better."

"She's older than you were when you first came out here. Have you ever asked her what she wants? You and the boys aren't going to know what to do if she goes. Most men would have made sure she didn't have a reason to leave here long ago."

"I'm not most men. I wouldn't leave for Caroline and look what happened. I don't want to be responsible for another woman shriveling up and dying out here."

"When she first arrived, I admit, there were a number of people who doubted she'd last more than a month or two. But no one doubts her anymore. She's shown herself to be a true farmer's wife."

The decisions Will made were for Abby's sake. He might be sacrificing the greatest gift short of salvation to let her go, but it was for her own good. His heart wanted him to go back to the house and let Abby know how he really felt. As much as he wanted to deny it, Colin was right about one thing. He loved Abby. If he didn't love her this much, he might be more tempted to try and convince her to stay.

Poor thing, she was probably all confused and upset. Just the thought that he might have caused her distress was tearing him up inside, but it was better this way. It would be better for her and for him in the long run if she believed that he didn't harbor any feelings for her. Not that he believed it was all that likely he could convince her he had *no* feelings for her. If she hadn't figured it out from the kiss on their wedding day, tonight must have proven his folly. But as long as she didn't realize how deep his love ran, she wouldn't feel obligated to stay out with him on the prairie where he was sure she could never be truly happy.

Will shouldered his way past Colin and climbed up the ladder to the loft. Jake was already bedded down. He shot a pitying look at his uncle.

"Colin, you might as well come on up and get some sleep. Trying to talk to my uncle now is like talking to a brick wall," Jake called out, then turned on his side and pretended to doze off.

Before the rooster even could crow his "good-morning" to everyone, Will headed down below, mucking stalls and milking the cows. By the time most of the chores were done, Jake and Colin still hadn't bothered to come down. It was probably better they leave him to work in peace, but now he had to face Abby. He'd planned to send the milk in with Jake, hoping to avoid her unless others were around, but Abby had had the fire started for a while and she would need the milk soon. She'd already been out to the outhouse and then the henhouse. Feeling every bit the coward, he watched her from the shadows of the barn as she had stood on the back porch for a minute, studying the barn as if pondering what to do about life or maybe just what to do about him.

Well, there was nothing more to do than go bring her the milk. He gritted his teeth as if he were about to face the firing squad. He trudged across the yard and up the stairs, tempted to just leave the pail inside the door, but the smell of coffee called to his grumbling stomach. As soon as he opened the door, he saw her square her shoulders and take a deep breath. Not a good sign.

"Good morning, Abby." He hadn't wanted to sound so pleased to see her, but his voice betrayed him. What he really wanted was to cross the room and take her back into his arms as he had done the night before.

"Morning," she answered, not turning to look at him. That was definitely a very bad sign. It was the same thing his mother would do when she was upset with his father.

"Here's the milk." He stated the obvious, wanting to find some neutral ground.

"Thank you." She half turned and he could see her profile. Her eyes were puffy and her cheeks and nose were red. Stray wisps of her hair were pulling free from her bun, making her seem more vulnerable. He fisted his hands and stuffed them in his pockets before he gave in to the urge to hold her close again.

Before he could think of some excuse to leave, she was handing him his mug of coffee, their fingers brushing accidently. The contact burned a trail of fire all the way to his soul. "Thanks," he murmured. He'd planned to leave it at that, but the look of pain in her eyes undid all his best intentions, breaking his heart.

"You're welcome," she whispered, and spun away, back to the stove to care for what looked like the beginnings of French toast. He involuntarily took two steps closer.

"Listen, Abby. I don't want you all upset and all." His hand reached out on its own accord, ignoring his common sense. He pushed a wisp of hair away from her face, hooking it behind her delicate ear. His index finger tracing a path from her ear to her jaw, but warning alarms in his head finally broke through his fog and shook him. He dropped his hands to his sides.

"You know that this is better this way. You need to be in a place that's safe. This is the prairie. There's always the threat of an Indian uprising, of bad weather, of the harvest not giving us enough to get through the winter. . . . I can name a hundred other ways that a body can become just one more victim of this barren place. It's the place that I love and I won't leave, but it's not right for you."

"What gives you the right to decide that for me?" Abby turned and glared at him. He had never seen her look angry, not even when the boys were fighting. "I don't think I've said anything about the prairie being wrong for me. In fact, if you had been listening to anything I have been saying in the last few weeks, you would have heard how much I've come to love this farm, this family, the land. This place isn't just the land you dream about. It's become my dream, as well. But you're too busy playing God to listen to anyone else."

"I'm not playing God!" Will gritted out. He was a God-fearing man. He would never —

"Of course you are. 'I'll not be responsible for another woman dying out here. . . .' " she parroted him. "As if you appointed the time for Caroline to die! As if there are not any dangers in the city. What if I go where you send me and I die of influenza? Would that also be your fault? What if someone attacks me in the city or I get trampled by a runaway carriage? Or is danger only here in the horrible wilderness?" Her sarcasm surprised him. She had never once been sarcastic before.

"All Caroline wanted was to go back to the city and I wouldn't go. She . . ."

"She what?" Abby exclaimed, but then she dropped her voice and a look of compassion filled her eyes. "I know you still love her. You must miss her something fierce, but you've got to realize God appoints each of us a time. He called her home, just like He called my parents home before I felt ready to let them go. But no one can tell God how or when to work His will. He does as He sees fit and He loves us. It's for our good."

"But I didn't love her!" Will exploded, but stopped in shock as his words echoed in the now-silent kitchen. He dropped his eyes to the floor, wanting to leave and never return to see condemnation that must be in Abby's eyes at that moment.

"I don't understand. You married her. . . . Had children with her. You still have her things in your room." Abby swung away from him and scraped the now-burnt French toast from the skillet. She pushed the fry pan onto the back of the stove.

"I married Caroline because *she tricked me.* I didn't want a wife since I was already planning to come out here with Matt and MaryAnn that spring. I think Caroline believed she could talk me out of my plans once she forced the engagement, but I held firm. She got the husband she wanted and I got the journey I wanted, but neither one of us was happy. Once we were married — especially once the boys came along — I tried to be a good husband, tried to tell myself that I loved her, but, well . . ."

Had he really not loved Caroline? Even now it hurt to admit it. It made him feel like even more of a failure as a husband.

"I made a lot of mistakes," he admitted. "Did a lot of things that I now regret. I'm not sorry I came out to Nebraska, or that I helped build this farm along with Mathew, but I am sorry that I made Caroline so unhappy."

"I think there's a part of you that felt you should have left and seen to her comforts and yet another part that feels you were justified in staying since she was the one who forced the marriage," Abby said. "You need to forgive her. You need to let God be God and control life. You aren't going to be able to protect all those you love. You aren't going to be able to change God's will. If He calls me to Him today, you won't be able to keep me here no matter what you do. But if He sees fit to let me spend the next fifty years here on this earth, I'd rather spend them with you and the boys than going to the city, no matter the conditions." Abby swung around and faced him, squaring her shoulders once again. She bit her lower lip and it was all Will could to not to reach out and wipe away a stray tear.

"I guess what I'm trying to tell you is I'm not Caroline. She and I might both have forced you into marriages you didn't want, but we had very different reasons. I don't expect you to love me or find me appealing like you must have found her, but I want a chance to prove I can be a good mother to your children. Maybe even a good wife to you."

"But you'll be missing out on your own life," Will countered. It was all he could come up with. He was not going to give in now. Not when he had kept his emotions in check for so long. He would not be responsible for another woman dying on the prairie.

Even as the thought crossed his mind, he recognized it as the very thing Abby said was sin. But it was what had kept him from getting too close. And if he got close, when she did finally get tried of the prairie life, he would be truly heartbroken because unlike with Caroline, he really did love Abby. She was right; she would be a great mother for his children and a very good wife. If only he could claim her as his without endangering her life or her happiness.

Knowing he was too close to giving in and letting her win the argument, he did what any self-respecting man would do. He turned on his heel and left. Stalked out the door and let it slam behind him. Even as the smell of coffee and French toast enticed him to return, he kept on walking. He'd survive on water and whatever bread Jake could smuggle out to him later. At least that's what he told his rumbling stomach. He had lots of work to do — work that wouldn't get done unless he saw to it himself.

Work that would distract him from the woman he loved, and wanted to beg to stay by his side forever.

CHAPTER FOURTEEN

The Monday after their return from town, Will, Jake and Colin left as soon as morning chores were done and spent the day building the foundation for Colin's cabin. He'd filed on a homestead a half hour's ride from theirs. It was close enough to church that anyone could find him if they needed the preacher in a hurry.

The next morning, the three men did their morning chores and then left for Colin's cabin, returning at afternoon chore time and eating the evening meal with Abby and the boys. The pattern continued until Friday morning.

"Well, Abby, I am forever indebted to you for feeding me so well." Colin thanked her after breakfast on Friday morning. "I reluctantly have to bid you and the boys goodbye until Sunday. My cabin's finished enough for me to sleep in it and not have to worry about unwelcomed visitors or water dripping on my head. I imagine that being such close neighbors, you and Will can invite this poor preacher over from time to time to enjoy your good cooking."

He stood and hugged her close as a big brother would. Stepping back just a space, he whispered, "I'll be praying for you both. Don't give up. Even though he denies it, he loves you. It'll just take time. Trust the Lord. You're the best blessing the Lord has ever lavished on that old hardhead."

Colin winked and it made Abby giggle. It felt good to smile. As the three men saddled up, Abby stood on the porch and waited for them to wave goodbye. Will circled back and kept his horse prancing at the foot of the steps. It put him eye level with Abby. She liked not having to look up to him while they spoke.

"Listen, if you get a chance, could you make up my room, and Jake's? I guess there's no need for us to be sleeping in the barn when there are two perfectly good beds inside to use."

Abby nodded.

"Well, I'll see you tonight." And before she was able to come up with a fitting reply, he reined his horse around and trotted off after the others.

That night, Abby noticed that she felt

safer somehow, knowing Will slept just upstairs instead of out in the barn. It made the house seem smaller, cozy. She liked having everyone under one roof. If only Will would admit that this was the way things should be. But he remained stubbornly insistent that she would never be happy out on the prairie. At times she wondered if it wouldn't just be better to move back East somewhere and bury herself in mundane work, far from the reminders that she was married to a man who didn't want her. A man who refused to even entertain the idea of making her his.

But no matter where she went, she knew she would always be able to close her eyes and picture his face, his blue eyes sparkling as he laughed with Tommy or his forehead wrinkled in thought as he tried to answer the boy's questions. And when she closed her eyes, she could still almost feel the gentleness of his lips on hers on their wedding day or smell his scent as he hugged her close the day he returned from his trip to town. She'd cherish the time she had with Tommy, Willy and Jake, too. But her heart had become attached to Will more than any other.

Abby hesitated at the door of the church.

She felt tired and discouraged. Will barely took the time to spare her a word much less take a cup of tea with her on Friday or Saturday nights. She had hoped that now that Colin was in his own home and Will and Jake were staying indoors, they'd have more opportunities to talk, but it hadn't worked out that way at all.

Mrs. Scotts and Mrs. Becker both greeted her as she entered the church building, but what she longed for was a true friend. Someone like Mrs. Gibbons, the pastor's wife back in Ohio, or even her own nieces. A woman whom she could confide in and who would understand her. Instead, Colin greeted her as she followed Will and the boys to their pew. He was kind and a good friend, but he didn't make up for a woman who could understand her heart.

"Before you leave, I need to speak to you," Colin whispered. Abby nodded just before sitting down next to Tommy.

During the service, Abby had the strangest sensation that Colin's message was somehow directed toward her and she tried to drink in every word. He spoke about how God's plans and timing are not always ours. He pointed out that God made promises He fulfilled years later, sometimes even centuries later. Colin read from Genesis and from Hebrews about how God used faithful men and women to do His work, many of whom never saw a reward for their labor this side of heaven. As Colin spoke, Abby felt torn. She knew that Colin was using these passages to encourage everyone to keep serving the Lord, letting God use their lives for His purpose. But she also understood that Colin's message meant that sometimes God answered prayers only after the faithful souls reached heaven. Was that His plan for her prayer for a home and family of her own?

By the end of the service, Abby dreaded speaking with Colin because she suspected he held news from the East.

"Good morning, Abby, Will," Colin greeted them as they exited, Will right behind her. "Before you go . . ." He reached out, stopping her, and didn't let go of her hand. "I just wanted to tell you I will continue to pray for . . . for what we talked about last time. I'm sure God has a plan and it's just His timing, but . . . keep in touch." He finally looked up into her eyes and she knew he was saying goodbye.

She didn't trust her voice. She swung away and fled down the steps to the wagon. The boys were playing with their friends and ignored her. She was almost to the sanctuary of the wagon when Mrs. Scotts called out to her.

"Hello, Mrs. Hopkins. How are you doing, my dear?"

The older woman had always been pleasant with Abby even though Abby had chosen to marry Will instead of one of her sons. Abby swallowed the lump in her throat and tried to force a smile, as if her life weren't falling apart once again.

"Hello, Mrs. Scotts."

"How have you been?" The older woman's eyes were sharp and she looked Abby over from head to toes. "Do you need me to help you into the shade?"

"No, thank you. I'm fine. I've been busy. This is the first year I've been on a farm. It's a little different than what I'm used to." Abby found herself blurting out anything that came to mind.

"Have you been feeling all right? You look a little pale." Mrs. Scotts eyes looked more merry than concerned. "You aren't nauseated in the mornings or lightheaded? Do you get extra tired?"

For a moment, Abby wondered what Mrs. Scotts meant. Then realization hit. She felt her face turn crimson and swallowed back the taste of tears. If only she could be concerned about being in the family way.

"There you are, Abby." Will's deep voice called out from behind her, making her heart speed up and her stomach flip. He came to stand beside her, resting a hand on her shoulder. It was odd that he should do that now, after weeks of avoiding her, especially when he must now hold in his hands the letter that would send her away.

"Good afternoon, Mrs. Scotts," he greeted the other woman. "You'll have to excuse us. We need to get home to the chores. We'll see you next week." He didn't even wait for a reply before he was leading Abby toward their wagon, calling out to Jake and the boys to say goodbye to their friends and come along.

He lifted her up by the waist. Though he released her as soon as she was seated, she could still feel the heat of his hands halfway home. Why did the letter have to come now? Her heart and mind raged at God even as she sat silently on the wagon bench, mindlessly gazing out at the prairie. She couldn't help noticing its changes since she had arrived all those months before.

Now everything was dry and brittle. The plants that were light green spouts when Will brought her home from Twin Oaks in May had already grown, flowered, given their fruits and seeds and were now dying.

The breeze that would have brought cool relief from the scorching sun just a few months ago now tore through her like a sheet of ice, numbing her face and fingers. She pulled her woolen shawl tighter around her shoulders.

Strange how her life mirrored the plants. She had been here just for a while, growing to love Tommy, Willy, Jake and especially Will, but that love seemed only to have planted seeds to what would never be. The plants, though, were fortunate enough to be staying in Nebraska. Next spring they would once again burst out of the seemingly dead ground, but Abby would be miles away. It would be only a memory, the prairie and her instant family. . . . The one her heart claimed as its own even though Will never wanted her.

It had finally come. Will hadn't realized what Colin was handing him until he glanced down and saw his mother's flowing script on the envelope. Now it all made sense. All those looks that Colin sent Abby during the service this morning were because Colin knew that Ma had finally written back. It was a good thing the letter had come today. He wasn't sure if he could have made it through another week. Each day had been harder than the last to get through without seeking her out and confessing that his life was never going to be the same once she left.

Abby hadn't said a word since they'd left church. At first, Will thought she was just in a quiet mood, but when she didn't even answer the boys' constant chatter, it dawned on him that she must have realized he'd be receiving the letter, too. His glace at her confirmed his thoughts. She was looking out at the landscape, turning her face away from him, her shoulders slumped and her chin down. An urge to fix it, make things better almost loosened his tongue. Almost. But maybe it would be better this way.

He was going to get home and read the letter and then tell her that she could leave during the week . . . assuming his mother had found a place for her to work. It had better be a good place, where they would treat her right and pay her well. Abby worked hard and deserved much more than what he could offer.

His barn came into view, then the rest of the property, and without too much thought he pulled up by the house, tethered the brake and jumped down, ready to help Abby from the wagon. It was a habit formed from good training on his mother's part and had never meant much to him before. But as he stood next to the wagon, waiting for Abby to stand up, he found himself looking up into her eyes. They were red rimmed and her nose was also red as if she were getting sick.

"Do you feel okay, Abby?" Concern colored his voice and his words.

Instead of answering right away, she looked away, cleared her throat and nodded.

"Were you cold on the ride?" he tried again. "You should have said."

"No, I'm . . ." Her voice sounded husky and cracked before she could finish her sentence.

He reached up and caught her around the waist, stepping forward to examine her more closely. He studied her eyes carefully, sure something was wrong.

Her face was drawn, as if she was tired and hadn't been sleeping enough lately. Under her eyes were dark, purple smudges, reminding him of the time she had nursed the boys through the chicken pox and in the process, worn herself completely out. Seeing them made him want to send her to her room to rest, as he had done back then. Who would pay attention to her when she needed rest if she went back to Philly?

"I, um, need to get down." Her voice brought his wandering thoughts back to the present.

He lifted her down, yet even when she was planted on solid ground, he couldn't take his hands away. He held his wife, the one he had come to love, knowing that she would be going within the week. Something caught in his throat. His arms ached with the longing to pull her closer and hide her in his chest, letting her find comfort in his tenderness. He tried to remind himself that he was sending her away for her own good, but the reminder was no comfort now.

She pulled away and fled up the stairs, leaving him to wonder if she was fleeing from his touch. Just before the door shut, he heard her sniffle and then she was gone. What had just happened? She had looked so forlorn. Turning away, he found three pairs of eyes watching him with accusing looks.

He pulled the wagon around and put it away in the barn. Jake and the boys played horseshoes out in the yard, but Will puttered around the barn, looking for something to do with his hands. A part of him was tempted to read the letter from Ma once and for all. He had impatiently waited for it for so long, but now that it was finally in his hands, doubts filled his head.

What if the employment his mother arranged for Abby didn't meet his approval? Should he take her back to Philadelphia himself to make sure that she arrived safely? It would be almost impossible to leave the farm for that long unless Colin was willing to stay with Jake. In his mind he started to plan what needed to be done. Until that moment, he hadn't really considered that he was planning on sending a beautiful young woman on a train without anyone to see to her welfare. It was amazing that nothing had happened to her on her trip out.

"You're too busy playing God." Her words echoed in his ears again. He was forgetting that God would be with her. God would take care of her. But what if God had wanted Will to be the man to protect her and he let both God and Abby down? He had given his word. To honor, protect, provide . . . until death do them part. What if . . .

What if she wanted to stay, just as she had claimed a week ago? The thought snuck in and blindsided him, stealing his breath. What if she actually learned to live out on the prairie? Mrs. Scotts and Mrs. Phelps had. Would it be too much to hope for?

Sooner or later there would be other settlers closer to their farm. Now that Colin was going to be just a quick ride away, others would surely start to settle near the church and a town would spring up in no time. His heart quickened with the thought. Before, he had dreaded the idea of more neighbors, busybodies nosing around in his business, but more neighbors might mean a school for his boys someday, other women friends for Abby to chat with, to trade recipes with, to visit and hold sewing bees with. A town would mean a sheriff. Maybe she would be willing to . . .

He had to stop this silliness. He was daydreaming like some young schoolgirl with her first crush. He called himself every kind of fool for not thinking about this until now. What he should really do was read the letter, but he didn't want to now. He wanted to see Abby. He wanted to sit across the table from her and be able to let her know that he didn't want her to leave. That he wanted her to stay with him, on his farm, until they were both old and gray. A sudden image of Abby carrying his child came to mind and stole his breath away. Could it be possible?

Abby called from the back step for everyone to come in for dinner. He set his letter in the tack room and went into the house.

For at least one more meal he would act and think as if there were no changes coming.

Dearest Son,

It is so good to finally hear from you. I waited expectantly for word all summer. I pray and trust that you are all fine and healthy. I pray for you all each night.

I believe God has a hand in everything that has happened to you this year. I'm glad the woman who responded to the advertisement is truly a Christian, even if you do not find her acceptable for your wife or family. (I admit I hope God impeded your first letter from coming to me so you could come to care for your unexpected wife.)

I have found a family who is looking for additional help, but I would rather meet your Miss Stewart first. I want to make sure she is able to do the work you claim she can do and at the same time, determine if she will be comfortable with the Standish family. Please send her whenever it is convenient.

Ma's letter rambled on, asking about her grandsons and then telling all the latest news about his sisters and their families.

316

He had waited until he was alone in his room in the quiet of the evening before he had dared open it. Now that he had done that, he was surprised his mother wanted him to rethink sending Abby back. Could this be a sign that God was showing him? He already had a head full of doubts about pushing Abby away. But in the end, he kept coming back to the idea that he needed to protect and provide for her. What was the best for her? God couldn't possibly want her to waste away in the prairie when she had so much to give others. Joy, laughter, love, attention. . . . What a blessing she would be to any family and yet Will knew he selfishly didn't want to bless anyone else. He wanted her to stay with them, and if he were truly honest with himself, he was self-ish enough to want her to stay for *him.*

Daybreak came with little light peeking through dark, thick clouds the color of dirty wool. Will climbed out of bed, shivering with the cold, and quickly dressed, heading out to the barn and the cows before he could find himself face-to-face with Abby. He stirred the embers to flame and then tossed two logs on the fire in the kitchen on his way out. The air smelled of winter. The grasses were covered in frost. Would they get an early snowfall? That might force him into making a decision about Abby. One way or the other.

His stomach soured with dread at the thought of sharing his mother's letter with her. Would she be happy or disappointed with the news? He hadn't done anything to make her feel welcome for a long time. Maybe she had all her things packed already.

Will sent the milk in with Jake. By the time he actually returned to the house for breakfast, the boys were seated around the table and there wasn't another opportunity to talk with Abby alone throughout the day. It was only at night, when the boys were in bed, that Will worked up the courage to speak with her.

"Um, Abby?" he asked quietly as she poured her nightly cup of tea. "Could I talk with you for a bit?"

Instead of responding, she bit her lower lip and reached for another mug. As she turned to face him, Will saw tears already filling her eyes. The sight broke his heart and his resolve. She nodded and he debated a moment before leading her out to the front room. Taking a seat on the rocking chair, he motioned for her to sit on the davenport.

"Well, Abby. On Sunday . . ." He hesitated, unsure how he wanted to explain his mixed feelings.

"You received a letter from your mother." She finished his sentence in a quiet, sad voice when he didn't continue.

"Um . . . Yes." She'd known and yet she hadn't said a word. He studied her face, wondering what was going on behind those beautiful blue-green eyes. She didn't smile, nod or even flinch. She just sat there, staring at the floor. His heart lightened a little bit when she didn't jump for joy at the prospect of leaving.

"How is she?" Abby finally asked when the silence drew out too long.

"She's fine."

"And your father?" she asked after another pause.

"Pa's fine. She said she hadn't gotten any mail from me since last spring. I guess the first letter I sent got lost somewhere."

She straightened her shoulders and glanced at him but quickly let her gaze fall back to the floorboards. "So, when do I leave?" Her question sank heavily into the air and extinguished the small flicker of hope he had felt a minute before. If she had indicated even the slightest interest in staying, he would have been overjoyed, but she didn't even mention it. She must have changed her mind about wanting to stay.

He swallowed hard.

"The outbound train comes every Monday, early, roughly eight in the morning. You'd have to spend the night in the hotel the night before."

"Then we'll leave on Sunday?" she asked, still not meeting his eyes.

He clenched his hands in tight fists until they shook from the effort. His heart cried out to lift her chin, push her hair away from her forehead and ask her if she still wanted to stay or if she wanted to go . . . but he refrained. If she said she wanted to go, he'd be crushed. And if she said she wanted to stay . . . He didn't know if he'd be able to resist letting her, in spite of the regrets he was certain would follow.

"Um, well, no. I think we should leave on Saturday. That way we won't be traveling much on the Lord's Day. We could stay at the hotel where we met." He stopped talking as memories of that day flooded his head — her tears, how small and vulnerable she'd seemed to him then. He hadn't recognized her that day. But now her face, etched in his heart as if carved into stone, was more familiar to him than the backs of his hands. When he became old and gray, he might forget his own name but he wouldn't forget the shape of her eyes or the curve of her smile, the sound of her voice or the smell of her hair. . . .

"Then I'll be sure to pack. Is there anything else you wished to discuss with me?" she asked in a voice so soft and forlorn he inched closer to hear her. The smell of cinnamon wafted to him.

"Um . . ." He searched for anything that would keep her here with him in the quiet of the night a few minutes longer but came up empty. "No, that was it." His mouth obeyed his head even as his heart threatened mutiny.

She stood and left the room. For a very long time, Will sat in the living room, wondering if he had done the right thing.

"God, You know best. If You want her to stay, You're gonna have to do something between now and Friday. Not that I have any right to put any limitation on You or tell You what to do, but I can't do this. . . . I don't know if I can let her walk out of here. Give me strength to do the right thing."

For the first time since Abby's parents' death, she didn't feel like dragging herself out of bed the next morning. She wanted to hide under the covers and pretend Will hadn't said she needed to leave on Saturday. How could she possibly tear herself away from the boys? They had been calling her Ma for the better part of the summer. It would be like cutting off her arms. She couldn't believe she had come to love them so quickly, nor so completely.

Why couldn't Will just let her stay? She didn't have to be part of the family. He didn't have to claim his husbandly rights — she understood there was something lacking in her that kept him from loving her. But if he never planned to marry again, then would it be so bad to live with a wife whom he didn't find attractive as long as she fed his family and taught his boys?

The rooster crowed for the second time and Abby forced herself up. If not for herself, she would make these last days special for the boys. Hopefully they would always remember her just as she would keep them in her heart. They were the closest she would ever come to having a family of her own. From now on, she would guard her heart. She would work whatever job God provided for her, but she wouldn't let herself love anyone again.

"Ma! Ma! Look outside! It's snowing! It's snowing!" Tommy shouted right before lunchtime, running into the kitchen at full steam. "I wanna go out and play. We can go sledding! Come on, Willy!" Tommy jumped and wiggled like a happy puppy in his excitement.

"No, not yet. It's almost lunchtime. When your pa and Jake come in, then you can ask them." Abby didn't want to make promises. She knew what to expect for a November snowstorm in Ohio but not out here in Nebraska.

"But, Ma! We just gotta —"

"Did your ma just tell you no to something?" Will's voice caught them both up short. He stood just inside the kitchen door with an armload of wood for the wood box.

"Yes, sir," Tommy answered, his head down. This was not the first time they had had this discussion.

"Then I expect you not to argue. Understood?" Will's eyes glued his small son to the spot until Tommy nodded.

"I'm sorry, Ma," he mumbled, glancing up at her and then away.

"It's okay to be excited about the snow, Tommy. You just need to get your father's permission before I can let you go out," she reassured him, pulling the boy into her arms and squeezing him close.

"Your ma's right," Will said, surprising Abby with his use of the title. He usually referred to her as "Auntie Abby" even though the boys had long since adopted "Ma." "I'm going to go get the cattle in from the south pasture right after lunch. I don't want you boys out there until I get back. The wind feels right for a whiteout."

"Aww, Pa. But I want to go sledding," Tommy whined.

"I think we'll have more than enough snow and winter to get you out sledding at least once or twice before spring comes," Will reassured Tommy, finally glancing at Abby and sending her a wink.

She almost dropped the dishes she was carrying to the table. He hadn't winked at her since the first month she was there — before they had been forced to marry. Could his returning jovial attitude be attributed to her leaving come Saturday? The thought brought unexpected tears to her eyes and she turned back to the stove in order to disguise her distress. How could he look forward to her departure while she dreaded it worse than the hangman's noose?

Somehow, Abby managed to keep from rushing out of the room during lunch. She even pretended to pay attention to Tommy's detailed stories of sledding in years past. Willy interrupted more than once to correct his little brother. Will kept sending her puzzled looks, but as soon as they finished lunch he headed out with Jake to bring in the straggling herd.

With dinner already made, she cleaned and dusted all the rooms upstairs, including Will's. She normally didn't go in there since it made her feel as if she was trespassing on his private sanctuary, but today she had wanted to make sure that the house was perfect when she left. His clothes and room had his lingering scent and it calmed her nerves about the snow. She could barely see across the barnyard to the outline of the barn. Abby returned to the kitchen and began to pace. They had been out for more than three hours. Where were they? Wasn't it past time for them to have returned?

She had been watching the snow come down harder and the wind howling at the windows and the chimney. What little dim light there had been during the day was now fading to darkness, and her worry grew exponentially. Were Will and Jake still out in one of the fields or had they both gone into the barn? She wanted to believe they were snug and warm with the cows in the sturdy building, but her fears whispered that they were trapped out in the snow.

"I'm sorry, Lord. I just don't want anything to happen to him . . . I mean them," she amended for the hundredth time. "What would I do without Will? What would happen to the boys? God, You know what they've already suffered. Don't take their father, as well. Or their cousin."

"Why are you out here again, Ma?" Tommy stood watching her from the doorway.

"I'm . . . um . . . I was just checking on dinner."

"It smells just fine. I want you to read another story to me. The one about the little boys."

With one more look over her shoulder toward the back door, Abby forced her trembling legs to carry her back to the living room with the boys. She sat and read for the better part of an hour but couldn't remember any of it. Even as she read, her ears were cocked, listening for any sound that would alert her to Will or Jake coming into the kitchen. She set the book down and had read three pages of the next one when the back door opened.

She was off the couch, almost upending Tommy in the process, and was halfway into the kitchen, before either boy could react. "Hello?"

Jake stood just inside the kitchen door, his coat covered in a layer of snow and ice. He took his hat off and even his hair underneath was wet from the thick snow. "It's miserable out there. That wind could freeze a man solid!" he exclaimed as he pulled his boots off.

"Where is your uncle?" Abby rushed to the stove, pulling the hot water forward to boil once more.

"He went out to find the last cow. Foolish heifer. Gerty never comes when we call her. She'll freeze out there, but will she follow the others to the shelter of the barn? No, she needs a special invitation. Uncle Will said to get the others in and bedded down for the night while he went out looking for her." Jake stepped out of his snowy boots and handed her the bucket of fresh milk.

"Could he be lost? How long has he been out there? What if —"

"Abby, Uncle Will knows this land better than anyone. He saw Gerty up on the north side of the pasture but wanted to get the rest in so if he had to coax her, he wouldn't have to do the same for all the others. Cattle can be some of the dumbest animals, but when they want treats, it's amazing how they learn to beg." Jake hung his coat and hat in the cellar stairway, letting the water drip onto the earthen floor beneath instead of Abby's clean kitchen floor.

"Are you sure your uncle's all right out

there? Maybe we should go out and look for him." She handed Jake his mug of spiced tea and crossed over to the window, peering out into the fading day.

"He'll be in pretty soon. It's milking time for Gerty and she'll come along easily if he offers those sugar cubes he has. The rest of the chores are done. Don't worry, Abby. He'll be fine. I'm going up to change."

Abby stood in the kitchen waiting for what felt like an eternity, but Will still didn't come in. Too frantic to stay inside any longer, she pulled on her boots and long winter coat, hat and gloves. She trudged out, fighting the wind that whipped through her clothes as if she were dressed in her summer dress. How cold must Will be by now? He'd been out for hours. What if he had gotten hurt?

She would only check the barn, hoping he was there. She knew better than to stray too far from the house in this weather. Everything seemed to look the same with the snow and wind in her face. At the barn door, she had to shove with all her might to get the big wooden beam out of its place to open the door. Stepping inside, she realized that if the door was closed from the outside Will couldn't have possibly been inside. Logic told her she should turn around and go back to the house, but the peace and relative warmth of the barn drew her in. Pulling the big door closed behind her, she ventured in, never having been inside in all the time she had been on the farm. While Will and Jake slept out here, Abby felt as if it was their private domain and she had chosen not to trespass. Now that she was out there, she wondered what she might find, even in the muted light.

Honestly, large animals spooked her. She liked the horses Will owned, but even those she preferred to see from afar, up atop the wagon on the way to church. In the dusky light of the barn something moved toward her. As her eyes adjusted to the scarce light, she saw that the cows weren't in stalls but were all around her and one was behind her, about to bite her. It nibbled at her hat and its tongue, moist and rough like sandpaper, scratched her neck. Shrieking, she fled to the ladder in the middle of the aisle. Tripping over her skirt, she battled her way up the ladder as if she were being pursued by a band of warrior braves. Only once she was up in the hay loft did she turn to see the cow happily munching on her hat, the scamp.

Afraid to come down for fear of the large animals, she sat on the edge of the loft and wondered how she could get out of this mess she had made. She should have at least told the boys where she was going. What if Will came in before she was able to get back down? He'd have all the right in the world to say that she was not suited to be a farmer's wife, and send her back on the next train just as he wanted to.

Pushing back from the edge of the loft, she looked around. It was full of hay for the winter, but there was a pallet still set out in the far corner with a pillow and a blanket. She sat down and plumped up the pillow. The now familiar smells of livestock, hay and Will wafted up to tease her nose as well as a crinkling sound that puzzled her. She lifted the pillow up completely. There were letters under the pillow. Her letters, all addressed to F. W. Hopkins. They were creased and worn at the edges as if someone had read and reread them. Why would Will have them here? Had he been trying to find a reason in the letters to send her packing earlier?

Thud! Something hit the door of the barn, causing her to jump and scatter the letters. She collected them again and hid them back under the pillows. Determined not to let the bovines get the best of her, she prayed for courage and breathed deeply. If the boys could come and play in the barn with all the animals and show no fear, then so could she. Armed with a false sense of valor, she pulled her skirts up above her knees, glad no one was around to see her folly, and then she struggled down the ladder.

Thankfully, the cattle were happy to ignore her. They all seemed to be more interested in a trough of oats. Strange, it hadn't seemed to be that full before.

Abby sighed with relief as she made contact with the door, sure she would escape safely now, except the door wouldn't budge. It was as if she were pushing on a solid wall. Had the snow drifted against it so quickly? Panicking, she shoved harder, again and again, until her foot slipped on something slippery and smelly. Crying, she pushed off the floor and once again made her way to the ladder.

For the first time since entering into the barn, she heard the wind howling outside and shivered. It was much warmer in the barn than out in the weather, but it was still cold. The heat from the animals helped, but she couldn't start a fire or the whole barn might burn down. What if she had to stay the night out there? She crawled back to Will's pallet and wrapped his blanket around her shoulders. It would keep her a little warmer while she thought of another way to get out.

Will pushed the kitchen door closed with his boot and dropped the last load of wood into the wood box. He'd brought in enough to hopefully last for days if need be. If it were up to him, he wouldn't be going out into the wind again until chore time tomorrow. What he really wanted was a nice cup of Abby's hot tea and her sweet smile to warm him all the way to his frozen toes. He'd asked God to intervene and keep him from sending Abby away and it had snowed. Maybe God had a message here.

Strange, the kitchen remained quiet and Abby hadn't appeared as she normally did every time the door opened. Dinner was on the stove and the water was boiling, but there was no sign of his wife. . . . His wife. Could he really ask her to stay? Would she be willing? After the snowfall today, maybe she would see the dangers of the prairie and change her mind. But he had to at least try.

Footsteps sounded on the stairs and he peeled his gloves off quickly, shedding his coat and hanging it in the stairwell to the cellar as he crossed the kitchen to greet Abby, except it was Jake who descended the stairs.

"So you finally came out of the cold." Jake chuckled. "I bet Abby's glad to see you're safe."

"I haven't seen Abby yet. Is she upstairs?" From the doorway he could see the boys were playing blocks on the front-room floor, but Abby wasn't with them.

"No, she's not upstairs. She was in the kitchen when I came in. And she was powerful worried about you." Jake grinned, like the Cheshire cat.

"Well, maybe she's down in the cellar. I'll go look." Will had turned around and was headed back to the cellar when he remembered what he had wanted to talk to Jake about. "Jake, next time you go out to the barn, especially in this cold, remember to shut it up well."

"I did. I made sure the doors were secure before I came in."

"Then why did I find Gerty back in the yard while I was bringing in more firewood?"

"I don't know. I haven't gone back out since I came in an hour —" But Will didn't wait for Jake to finish.

"Boys, have either of you seen your mother?" His voice must have conveyed urgency because both boys popped up from the floor and looked at him strangely.

"She put on her coat and hat after Jake went upstairs. Then we heard the door open and close a whole bunch of times. I think she was bringing in firewood," Willy reported.

"Maybe she went to go sledding," Tommy volunteered, blissfully unaware of the dangers of being out too long in a storm.

"I brought in the firewood," Will said, "and I didn't see her at all. Jake, go check back upstairs. Boys, I want you to stay here. I'm going to go back out to the barn. Jake, did she say anything to you? Did you tell her where I was?"

"I told her you were looking for Gerty but not to worry because you'd be in in a little while. Do you want me to go out to the pasture?"

"No. I'll check the barn first. Then, if she's not there, we'll go looking. But look for her inside first. And pray, boys. Pray that she's safe and out of the storm."

His heart pounding as if it were going to explode at any time, he retraced his steps through the kitchen, not even bothering to button his coat correctly and pulling his new knitted cap, compliments of his missing wife, haphazardly over his head. His fingers were still numb from being out so long, but he shoved his wet gloves back on his hands as he rushed across the slippery barnyard.

Just as he had left it, the barn door was shut from the outside. He hefted the beam and set it on the ground. Pulling the door open, he peered into the darkness of the warm barn. Only the moos of the cows greeted him. He lit a lantern and hung it from its peg. "Abby! Abby, are you here?" he yelled out, knowing the panic in his voice betrayed his feelings more than anything else. Rustling above him over by his pallet drew his attention to the loft.

"Will!" Her voice floated down to him above the din of the animals. "Are you all right?"

He pulled the barn door closed behind him, latching it from the inside this time, and raced over to the ladder as if the barn were on fire. He wanted to shake her silly for scaring him so bad but then he wanted to kiss her silly in relief. He was halfway up the ladder when her face peered out over the edge.

"Are you all right?" they both asked at the same time. She giggled and then sat back as he reached the top rung, putting him eye level with her.

"What are you doing out here?" he demanded, out of breath from his climb.

"I . . . I was worried about you and wanted to make sure you were okay. I couldn't stay inside any longer and came out, hoping you were in here. Then one of the cows tried to eat my hat and I got scared and climbed up here. When I came back down, the door was stuck and I couldn't go back to the house. I'm sorry. You're probably cold and hungry and here I am — like such a fool — making you come back out in the cold and worrying you. . . ." He could see her shaking and wanted to hold her tight, to promise her she would never be frightened again.

"Shush, don't worry, Abby. I'm so glad you're all right. You are all right, aren't you?" He pulled off his glove and caressed her cheek. Even with numb fingers, he felt her warm, silky skin and the moisture of fresh tears. She nodded, looking down below them instead of into his eyes. He'd do anything for this woman. If she couldn't be happy on the prairie, he'd leave. They could find somewhere else to live, he didn't care where, as long as they could be together.

"Don't worry about anything. We'll move South, where there aren't any snowstorms to scare you. I can sell the land or maybe leave Colin to sell it and take what we have.

Texas is always warm, they say. We can start over. It won't be as nice right away and we'll have to work hard, but —"

"What are you talking about?" Abby stared at him as if he were out of his mind. He grinned. How foolish it must have sounded.

"When you weren't inside the house and I knew you could be out in the storm, I was so scared. I had promised to take care of you, protect you. You could have been hurt or worse. . . ." He couldn't force himself to even finish the thought. "I realized no piece of land is worth losing you, Abby. I want a real marriage, and I'll do whatever it takes to prove to you that we can make it work. If you want me to move back to Philly, I'll do it. I'm just sorry I held you at arm's length for so long." He drew a ragged breath, wondering if it was already too late for them.

"But I don't want to leave here! I don't know why you think I do. I love the prairie that goes on and on forever. I know it's a dangerous place, but God is just as able to keep me safe here as He is in Philly or in Texas."

"You don't want to leave here?" Will asked, afraid to hope.

"No, I don't want to leave you, or the boys or the farm. I have come to love you all.

This is my home, my family. I —"

"You still want to stay with us? Even now that you've seen how the winter storms can be? And this is just the start. There will be more storms."

"Yes. I want to stay." Abby nodded but turned away.

Joy exploded in Will's chest, squeezing the breath from his lungs. She wanted to stay. She wanted to stay! Had she really said she loved him? Or just his family? It didn't matter. He could be patient. He'd learn to court her. He'd bring her flowers and tell her how lovely she was to him. Why had he waited so long?

"I know that you didn't want a wife either time you married and I . . ." She swallowed and he saw her struggle with some hidden emotion. "I don't understand the way it is between a husband and his wife. I guess I was too young when I lost my own parents and my sister never took the time, not that her marriage was a good model. Anyway, I guess I never will be a woman to attract a man's attention in that way, but —"

"Abby, sweet, beautiful, darling Abby," he whispered, his finger having silenced her ramblings, relishing the feel of her sweet breath across his fingertips. "There is nothing lacking in you. You had my attention from the day you fell into my arms at the train station."

"I — I did? But I —"

"Shush. Yes, you did. I did everything I could to keep from showing you how I felt because I thought you needed to move back East. I thought . . . I was a fool. Jake and Colin both told me, but I didn't listen to them. I didn't believe you could come to love us enough to want to stay. I do love you, Abby. I've loved you for a long time. That's why I wanted you to go, so you would be safe, not because I didn't care for you or want to be married to you. It was tearing my heart out to even think about letting you go."

Her bright eyes turned up to meet his, glinting in the semidarkness of the barn, the lantern he had hung down below sparkling off the green-blue specks in her eyes. Eyes filled with wonder and tears. "You —" she swallowed hard, staring at him "— you said you love me?"

"Yes, ma'am, Mrs. Hopkins. I love you." His fingers smoothed over her cheek, tucking her hair back behind her ear. She shuddered, whether it was from his touch or the cold he wasn't sure. "I'm a fool for not telling you or showing you before. I'll try and make up for that."

He grinned, wondering at how the cold and wind seemed to be in another time and place. Even his throbbing fingers as they thawed out didn't bother him nearly as much as they normally did. He needed to get her back to the house, back into the warmth of the kitchen and to the rest of their family so they could stop worrying, but he didn't want to spoil the moment.

"I love you, too," she whispered softly, her eyes closed, her face turned away. "I want to be your wife." Her voice almost inaudible.

"Do you, Abby?" Will asked, hoping she knew what she was saying. His fingers pulled her face back toward him. "Do you really want to be my wife? To live your life here, with me? To let me love you like a man loves his wife?" He held his breath for her response.

Instead of words, she nodded. Unable to keep her at arm's length anymore, he surged up over the lip of the loft and unceremoniously sat on the floor next to her. Without warning, he slid his hands once again over the softness of her cheeks and into her silky hair. Then he guided her lips to his own. Gently at first; he didn't want to scare her. She was precious to him. So precious he wanted to treat her like fine china. He let his kiss confirm his declaration of love for her. She might not understand how much she moved him or how much he had come to love her yet, but he was bound and determined to show her. It might take years, but someday she would know.

Finally, his lungs burned for lack of air and he knew he needed to give her a chance to catch up, to tell him to back off if she wanted to. He pulled his head back slightly, his arms around her shoulders, holding her to his heart, right where she belonged. He breathed in the scent of her hair and felt her shudder as he buried his face in the curve of her neck.

"Abby, we need to get back to the house. You're gonna catch cold out here and the boys have got to be worried by now." He sat up slowly. "Now, how did you get up this ladder in those skirts?" he wondered out loud as he started back down.

Instead of answering, she blushed. He grinned at her sweet innocence. "Here, let me help you." He showed her how to sit on the edge and find her footing as she turned. He let his body serve to protect her as they backed down the ladder, her back to his chest, his arms around her. A foreshadowing of how he would protect her in any way he could from now on. Once on the floor, he stepped back and waited for her to turn away from the ladder, right into his arms.

"Oh, I'm sorry —"

He stopped her apology midsentence with a kiss. Good thing Gerty started nibbling at his hat or he might have kept Abby there for a long time. Placing a final kiss on her nose, he sighed as he turned her around. "Let's go see what your boys are up to, Mrs. Hopkins."

Tucking her under his arm, he led her out of the barn, stopping only to put out the lantern and to bar the door. As they entered the kitchen, both boys raced up and tugged on her, pulling off her gloves and peppering her with questions.

"Did you get lost?"

"Did you go sledding?"

"Are you all right?"

"When are we going to eat dinner? I'm hungry."

Laughing, she smiled down at them. "One thing at a time, boys. I went out to the barn and couldn't get back right away. We'll eat as soon as I can get the table set and the food out of the oven. Go wash up while I get out of my coat."

Jake stood by the table, grinning from ear to ear. When Will looked at his nephew, the boy had the audacity to wink and nod as if in approval. "Auntie Abby, is there anything

I can do to help?"

"You never call her 'auntie,' just Abby," Tommy corrected.

"Well, she's my uncle's wife now, so she's my auntie, as well, I figure." Jake smiled at her surprise and stared to set the table.

Abby's eyes shone with happiness as she rushed around getting dinner on the table. Will watched her from a corner of the kitchen, a cup of tea warming his hands, and felt his heart expand with love for this beautiful housekeeper who came to keep his house and ended up capturing his heart.

EPILOGUE

Six months later

As soon as Will walked into the kitchen, Abby snatched the telegram from his hand and tore into it. He inhaled the fresh scent of his wife as he circled her small waist with his big arms. Pillowing his chin on her head, he gazed out to the barnyard from the kitchen window. He had gone over to Colin's homestead early in the morning to help Colin clear a field, and Colin had given him the telegram that had come to the church the day before. It was almost dusk and there were chores to do, but for just a moment, he held his wife close. Spring was forcing its way into their beloved prairie. Snow was melting, leaving puddles of mud and slush everywhere. But there was a promise of new things as green shoots started to push out of the frozen ground.

Ma and Pa had sent word that they planned to come out for a visit later in the summer. His poor, sweet wife had been in a flutter for days after the letter arrived. Abby foolishly worried they wouldn't like her. If only she knew how much they already loved her.

"Um, Will?"

"Yes, sweetheart?" he answered absentmindedly, his thoughts still on her meeting his parents.

"Remember about how I talked with you about an addition?" she asked, her voice sounding pinched.

They had lain in bed one night last week, talking about how they could expand the house if they added to their family. It was Abby's desire to have more children and Will couldn't have been more pleased. He wondered if there would be time to put a full addition on before his folks arrived with all the work that it took to get the fields planted. But they hadn't come to any decisions, except one. He and Jake had finally opened the door to Mathew and MaryAnn's room after so many years. Abby had cleaned it and Will suspected she was sewing a quilt to put on the bed for when his parents arrived. If they already had a room for his parents, why would she be talking again of expansion so soon unless . . . ?

"Yesterday you said that you weren't . . ."

he started, spinning her in his arms, his hand going to her flat belly, expecting to see her eyes alight with joy. Instead she looked worried.

"It's not that. The telegram is from my niece, Megan. She said she'll be arriving April fifth with her sisters and brothers for a visit."

Will studied Abby and then pulled her closer to the table, sitting on the closest chair and tugging her on to his lap. "So why the worried look?" he whispered against her ear. She shivered and he sensed she needed his reassurance.

"It's just that your parents are coming in a couple of months and I wanted to have everything ready for them. Now, what are they going to think about your wife who comes and brings all her family along, as well?"

"They'll love her all the more when they see how good she has been to their son and grandsons. Don't worry about the space. We'll figure something out. How many kids are there anyway?"

"There's Megan, Hanna, Peter, Harold and Katie." She leaned back into his arms and he smoothed his thumb over her elbow.

"We can have the boys sleep together and the girls can share Jake's room. He can take the parlor. My folks can still have Mathew and MaryAnn's room. See, honey, it'll all work out." He brushed a kiss on her forehead.

"Will." She sat up a little straighter. "Today is the third."

"That means they'll arrive the day after tomorrow. I'll go get them," he promised, wishing he could do more to reassure Abby.

"Thank you, Will." She ran her fingers over his rough cheek, sending a shiver down his back. "I think God's blessed me so much more than He's blessed you. He gave me an instant prairie family." She punctuated her statement with a kiss, but before he could return the favor, small footsteps thundered into the room.

"Ma, I'm hungry. You ever gonna stop smooching with Pa and make dinner?" Tommy demanded, pulling at her arm.

"I think you're just jealous," she teased with a glint in her eyes. "Come here and I'll kiss you, too!" To which Tommy ran shrieking, only to collapse in a puddle of giggles when Abby caught him in the living room and peppered his face with butterfly kisses.

"Young man, you'd better be nice to my wife. You hear?" Will pretended to be stern, masking his smile behind his hand.

"You can have her. I don't like yuckie

slobbery kisses. Uck!" Tommy yelled just before he broke out in a gale of giggles again.

"I'm gonna go see about my chores, Abby," Will announced from the doorway to the front room, smiling at his wife and son playing so contentedly.

"Hurry back, dinner's almost ready." Abby came into the room and stole another kiss from him, one he forfeited gladly. "I love you, Mr. Hopkins."

How could he have possibly thought he could let her walk away? "I love you too, Mrs. Hopkins."

Dear Reader,

I'm so glad you chose to read *Instant Prairie Family*. As I first sat down to write about Abby's journey, I prayed God would use her story to touch others' hearts and lives. Hopefully, you smiled (if you didn't laugh out loud) with some of Tommy's antics or maybe Willy's I-know-everything attitude. As much as I wanted to entertain you, I also hoped you could identify with Abby and her need to be loved. I suspect all of us can relate to the fact that life never plays out as we expect.

Only by trusting God to have a bigger and better plan than the one we have for ourselves can we face the bumps along the way. Jeremiah 29:11 and 12 are some of my favorite verses and played in my head as Abby's mantra as her story took shape. " 'For I know the thoughts that I think toward you,' saith the Lord, 'thoughts of peace and not of evil, to give you an expected end. Then shall ye call upon me, and ye shall go and pray unto me, and I will hearken unto you.' "

My prayer for you, dear reader, is that you may know the peace and fulfillment of being loved by God. He loves you more than anyone else ever will. I hope His love is the refuge you seek, just like Abby did, when life doesn't give you what you expect. I pray God will use my humble, often inadequate words to minister to your life. If you have never taken the opportunity to accept Jesus as your Savior like little Tommy did, do it today. No matter where life may have led you, you are not alone. God is waiting to answer your prayers and be your comfort. Seek Him in the Bible. He longs to chat with you today.

May you be wise and number your days. May God bless you richly.

I look forward to meeting up again with you, sometime soon. Maybe when Abby's nieces and nephews arrive. Until then, you can contact me c/o Love Inspired Books at 233 Broadway, Suite 1001, New York, NY 10279. Or email me at bonnie12navarro@gmail.com.

In Christ,
Bonnie Navarro

QUESTIONS FOR DISCUSSION

1. Abby flees her sister's home thinking she is coming to live with a widow. When she learns of her misunderstanding, what does she do? What should she have done? What would you have done if you were in her place?

2. Will almost sends Abby back. Why didn't he want her to stay? What should he have done?

3. Have you ever had to face something unknown? Moved to a new place, changed jobs, tried something new? How did it help you grow? Did it strengthen or hurt your walk with God?

4. I love to read historical fiction but must confess I like my indoor plumbing, central heat and air, cell phones and computers. . . . What part of your life now (crea-

ture comforts) would you find the hardest to give up if you were to go back in time and live as the sodbusters did?

5. Caroline, Will's first wife, was obviously a bitter woman. Do you think she was always like that or did it happen over time? What kind of legacy did she leave her children and those around her?

6. Is there someone in your life who once said something to wound your spirit like Caroline did to both Will and Jake? Have you come to the point of forgiving them? Do you know that God sees you as His son or daughter, holy, precious and worthy of love? Have you ever been guilty of being a "Caroline," letting your bitterness poison those around you?

7. Why do you think Will was jealous of Colin? Did Colin purposefully do anything to provoke Will? Do you think Colin was interested in Abby? Why or why not?

8. Will debated sending his boys back to the East so his parents could raise them and give them a better education. Do you think it would have been better for the boys? What would they have gained? What

would they have lost? Why didn't he send them back? What was his true motivation?

9. Colin preached about numbering one's days. What did he mean by that? In our modern, chaotic world, is it possible to number our days? If you adopted that custom, how would it change the way you live? Would it have an impact on other people's lives around you? Why or why not?

10. Colin also preached on faith as being something we hope for but sometimes don't see in this lifetime. Can you relate to this? Have you ever had hopes crushed and realized you won't see the attainment of your dreams until you are face-to-face with your maker? How did that make you feel? Did it inspire you to press on or give up?

11. What was Will's biggest obstacle in letting Abby close? What was he trying to do by sending her away? What lies did Abby believe about herself? Why?

12. Do you think that Abby will make a good farm wife or will the harsh climate, hard conditions and loneliness break her

down after a few years? What other things could change her opinion of the prairie? Do you think Will really would have moved to the city if she had wanted him to? Do you think they should move?

ABOUT THE AUTHOR

Bonnie Navarro and her husband of nineteen years reside in Warrenville, Illinois. Their four children range in age from seventeen to eleven. She works as a medical interpreter at a hospital and a teacher's aide in a middle school. She and her family attend a Spanish-speaking church, and everyone in the household is at least bilingual — including the dog! Bonnie attended Moody Bible Institute. While attempting to earn a degree in Bible theology, she successfully earned her MRS. degree, followed a year later by her MOM degree, thus ending her formal studies. She is a member of Voices, part of MyBookTherapy. Bonnie's hobbies include reading, writing, knitting and hanging out with her family.

The employees of Thorndike Press hope you have enjoyed this Large Print book. All our Thorndike, Wheeler, and Kennebec Large Print titles are designed for easy reading, and all our books are made to last. Other Thorndike Press Large Print books are available at your library, through selected bookstores, or directly from us.

For information about titles, please call:
  (800) 223-1244

or visit our Web site at:
  http://gale.cengage.com/thorndike

To share your comments, please write:
  Publisher
  Thorndike Press
  10 Water St., Suite 310
  Waterville, ME 04901